The Caesars

Thomas De Quincey

1st WORLD
LIBRARY
Literary Society

The Caesars

THOMAS DE QUINCEY

© 1st World Library – Literary Society, 2004
PO Box 2211
Fairfield, IA 52556
www.1stworldlibrary.org
First Edition

LCCN: 2004091276

Softcover ISBN: 1-59540-694-8
eBook ISBN: 1-59540-794-4

Purchase *"The Caesars"*
as a traditional bound book at:
www.1stWorldLibrary.org/purchase.asp?ISBN=1-59540-694-8

1st World Library Literary Society is a nonprofit
organization dedicated to promoting literacy by:

- Creating a free internet library accessible from any
computer worldwide.
- Hosting writing competitions and offering book
publishing scholarships.

Readers interested in supporting literacy
through sponsorship, donations or
membership please contact:
literacy@1stworldlibrary.org
Check us out at: www.1stworldlibrary.org

The Caesars.
contributed by Ed, Tim & Rodney
in support of
1st World Library Literary Society

THE CÆSARS.

The condition of the Roman Emperors has never yet been fully appreciated; nor has it been sufficiently perceived in what respects it was absolutely unique. There was but one Rome: no other city, as we are satisfied by the collation of many facts, either of ancient or modern times, has ever rivalled this astonishing metropolis in the grandeur of magnitude; and not many - if we except the cities of Greece, none at all - in the grandeur of architectural display. Speaking even of London, we ought in all reason to say - the *Nation of London,* and not the City of London; but of Rome in her palmy days, nothing less could be said in the naked severity of logic. A million and a half of souls - that population, apart from any other distinctions, is *per se* for London a justifying ground for such a classification; *à fortiori*, then, will it belong to a city which counted from one horn to the other of its mighty suburbs not less than four millions of inhabitants [Footnote: Concerning this question - once so fervidly debated, yet so unprofitably for the final adjudication, and in some respects, we may add, so erroneously - on a future occasion.] at the very least, as we resolutely maintain after reviewing all that has been written on that much vexed theme, and very probably half as many more. Republican Rome had her *prerogative* tribe; the earth has its *prerogative* city; and that city was Rome.

As was the city, such was its prince - mysterious, solitary, unique. Each was to the other an adequate counterpart, each reciprocally that perfect mirror which reflected, as it were *in alia materia,* those incommunicable attributes of grandeur, that under the same shape and denomination never upon this earth were destined to be revived. Rome has not been repeated; neither has Cæsar. *Ubi Cæsar, ibi Roma* - was a maxim of Roman jurisprudence. And the same maxim may be translated into a wider meaning; in which it becomes true also for our historical experience. Cæsar and Rome have flourished and expired together. The illimitable attributes of the Roman prince, boundless and comprehensive as the universal air, - like that also bright and apprehensible to the most vagrant eye, yet in parts (and those not far removed) unfathomable as outer darkness, (for no chamber in a dungeon could shroud in more impenetrable concealment a deed of murder than the upper chambers of the air,) - these attributes, so impressive to the imagination, and which all the subtlety of the Roman [Footnote: Or even of modern wit; witness the vain attempt of so many eminent sort, and illustrious *Antecessors*, to explain in self-consistency the differing functions of the Roman Cæsar, and in what sense he was *legibus solutus*. The origin of this difficulty we shall soon understand.] wit could as little fathom as the fleets of Cæsar could traverse the Polar basin, or unlock the gates of the Pacific, are best symbolized, and find their most appropriate exponent, in the illimitable city itself - that Rome, whose centre, the Capitol, was immovable as Teneriffe or Atlas, but whose circumference was shadowy, uncertain, restless, and advancing as the frontiers of her all-conquering empire. It is false to say, that with Cæsar came the destruction of Roman greatness. Peace, hollow rhetoricians! Until Cæsar

6

came, Rome was a minor; by him, she attained her majority, and fulfilled her destiny. Caius Julius, you say, deflowered the virgin purity of her civil liberties. Doubtless, then, Rome had risen immaculate from the arms of Sylla and of Marius. But, if it were Caius Julius who deflowered Rome, if under him she forfeited her dowery of civic purity, if to him she first unloosed her maiden zone, then be it affirmed boldly - that she reserved her greatest favors for the noblest of her wooers, and we may plead the justification of Falconbridge for his mother's trangression with the lion-hearted king - such a sin was self-ennobled. Did Julius deflower Rome? Then, by that consummation, he caused her to fulfill the functions of her nature; he compelled her to exchange the imperfect and inchoate condition of a mere *fœmina* for the perfections of a *mulier*. And, metaphor apart, we maintain that Rome lost no liberties by the mighty Julius. That which in tendency, and by the spirit of her institutions - that which, by her very corruptions and abuses co-operating with her laws, Rome promised and involved in the germ - even that, and nothing less or different, did Rome unfold and accomplish under this Julian violence. The rape [if such it were] of Cæsar, her final Romulus, completed for Rome that which the rape under Romulus, her earliest Cæsar, had prosperously begun. And thus by one godlike man was a nation-city matured; and from the everlasting and nameless [Footnote: "*Nameless city.*" - The true name of Rome it was a point of religion to conceal; and, in fact, it was never revealed.] city was a man produced - capable of taming her indomitable nature, and of forcing her to immolate her wild virginity to the state best fitted for the destined "Mother of empires." Peace, then, rhetoricians, false threnodists of false liberty! hollow chanters over the ashes of a hollow republic! Without

Cæsar, we affirm a thousand times that there would have been no perfect Rome; and, but for Rome, there could have been no such man as Cæsar.

Both then were immortal; each worthy of each. And the *Cui viget nihil simile aut secundum* of the poet, was as true of one as of the other. For, if by comparison with Rome other cities were but villages, with even more propriety it may be asserted, that after the Roman Cæsars all modern kings, kesars, or emperors, are mere phantoms of royalty. The Cæsar of Western Rome - he only of all earthly potentates, past or to come, could be said to reign as a *monarch*, that is, as a solitary king. He was not the greatest of princes, simply because there was no other but himself. There were doubtless a few outlying rulers, of unknown names and titles upon the margins of his empire, there were tributary lieutenants and barbarous *reguli*, the obscure vassals of his sceptre, whose homage was offered on the lowest step of his throne, and scarcely known to him but as objects of disdain. But these feudatories could no more break the unity of his empire, which embraced the whole *oichomeni*; - the total habitable world as then known to geography, or recognised by the muse of History - than at this day the British empire on the sea can be brought into question or made conditional, because some chief of Owyhee or Tongataboo should proclaim a momentary independence of the British trident, or should even offer a transient outrage to her sovereign flag. Such a *tempestas in matulâ* might raise a brief uproar in his little native archipelago, but too feeble to reach the shores of Europe by an echo - or to ascend by so much as an infantine *susurrus* to the ears of the British Neptune. Parthia, it is true, might pretend to the dignity of an empire. But her sovereigns, though sitting in the seat of the great king, (*o basileus*,) were

Thomas de Quincey

no longer the rulers of a vast and polished nation. They were regarded as barbarians - potent only by their standing army, not upon the larger basis of civic strength; and, even under this limitation, they were supposed to owe more to the circumstances of their position - their climate, their remoteness, and their inaccessibility except through arid and sultry deserts - than to intrinsic resources, such as could be permanently relied on in a serious trial of strength between the two powers. The kings of Parthia, therefore, were far enough from being regarded in the light of antagonist forces to the majesty of Rome. And, these withdrawn from the comparison, who else was there - what prince, what king, what potentate of any denomination, to break the universal calm, that through centuries continued to lave, as with the quiet undulations of summer lakes, the sacred footsteps of the Cæsarean throne? The Byzantine court, which, merely as the inheritor of some fragments from that august throne, was drunk with excess of pride, surrounded itself with elaborate expressions of a grandeur beyond what mortal eyes were supposed able to sustain.

These fastidious, and sometimes fantastic ceremonies, originally devised as the very extremities of anti-barbarism, were often themselves but too nearly allied in spirit to the barbaresque in taste. In reality, some parts of the Byzantine court ritual were arranged in the same spirit as that of China or the Birman empire; or fashioned by anticipation, as one might think, on the practice of that Oriental Cham, who daily proclaims by sound of trumpet to the kings in the four corners of the earth - that they, having dutifully awaited the close of *his* dinner, may now with his royal license go to their own.

From such vestiges of *derivative* grandeur, propagated to ages so remote from itself, and sustained by manners so different from the spirit of her own, - we may faintly measure the strength of the original impulse given to the feelings of men by the *sacred* majesty of the Roman throne. How potent must that splendor have been, whose mere reflection shot rays upon a distant crown, under another heaven, and across the wilderness of fourteen centuries! Splendor, thus transmitted, thus sustained, and thus imperishable, argues a transcendent in the basis of radical power. Broad and deep must those foundations have been laid, which could support an "arch of empire" rising to that giddy altitude - an altitude which sufficed to bring it within the ken of posterity to the sixtieth generation.

Power is measured by resistance. Upon such a scale, if it were applied with skill, the *relations* of greatness in Rome to the greatest of all that has gone before her, and has yet come after her, would first be adequately revealed. The youngest reader will know that the grandest forms in which the *collective* might of the human race has manifested itself, are the four monarchies. Four times have the distributive forces of nations gathered themselves, under the strong compression of the sword, into mighty aggregates - denominated *Universal Empires*, or Monarchies. These are noticed in the Holy Scriptures; and it is upon *their* warrant that men have supposed no fifth monarchy or universal empire possible in an earthly sense; but that, whenever such an empire arises, it will have Christ for its head; in other words, that no fifth *monarchia* can take place until Christianity shall have swallowed up all other forms of religion, and shall have gathered the whole family of man into one fold under one all-conquering Shepherd. Hence [Footnote: This we

Thomas de Quincey

mention, because a great error has been sometimes committed in exposing *their* error, that consisted, not in supposing that for a fifth time men were to be gathered under one sceptre, and that sceptre wielded by Jesus Christ, but in supposing that this great era had then arrived, or that with no deeper moral revolution men could be fitted for that yoke.] the fanatics of 1650, who proclaimed Jesus for their king, and who did sincerely anticipate his near advent in great power, and under some personal manifestation, were usually styled *Fifth-Monarchists.*

However, waiving the question (interesting enough in itself) - Whether upon earthly principles a fifth universal empire could by possibility arise in the present condition of knowledge for man individually, and of organization for man in general - this question waived, and confining ourselves to the comparison of those four monarchies which actually have existed, - of the Assyrian or earliest, we may remark, that it found men in no state of cohesion. This cause, which came in aid of its first foundation, would probably continue; and would diminish the *intensity* of the power in the same proportion as it promoted its *extension*. This monarchy would be absolute only by the personal presence of the monarch; elsewhere, from mere defect of organization, it would and must betray the total imperfections of an elementary state, and of a first experiment. More by the weakness inherent in such a constitution, than by its own strength, did the Persian spear prevail against the Assyrian. Two centuries revolved, seven or eight generations, when Alexander found himself in the same position as Cyrus for building a third monarchy, and aided by the selfsame vices of luxurious effeminacy in his enemy, confronted with the self-same virtues of enterprise and hardihood in his compatriot soldiers. The native Persians, in the earliest and very limited import of that name, were a poor and hardy race of mountaineers. So were the men of Macedon; and neither one tribe nor the other found any adequate resistance in the luxurious occupants of Babylonia. We may add, with respect to these two earliest monarchies, that the Assyrian was undefined with regard to space, and the Persian fugitive with regard to time. But for the third - the Grecian or Macedonian - we know that the arts of civility, and of civil organization, had made great progress before the Roman strength was measured against it. In Macedon, in Achaia, in Syria, in Asia Minor, in Egypt, - every where the members of this empire had begun to knit; the cohesion was far closer, the development of their resources more complete; the resistance therefore by many hundred degrees more formidable: consequently, by the fairest inference, the power in that proportion greater which laid the foundations of this last great monarchy. It is probable, indeed, both *à priori*, and upon the evidence of various facts which have survived, that each of the four great empires successively triumphed over an antagonist, barbarous in comparison of itself, and each *by* and through that very superiority in the arts and policy of civilization.

Rome, therefore, which came last in the succession, and swallowed up the three great powers that had *seriatim* cast the human race into one mould, and had brought them under the unity of a single will, entered by inheritance upon all that its predecessors in that career had appropriated, but in a condition of far ampler development. Estimated merely by longitude and latitude, the territory of the Roman empire was the finest by much that has ever fallen under a single sceptre. Amongst modern empires, doubtless, the

Thomas de Quincey

Spanish of the sixteenth century, and the British of the present, cannot but be admired as prodigious growths out of so small a stem. In that view they will be endless monuments in attestation of the marvels which are lodged in civilization. But considered in and for itself, and with no reference to the proportion of the creating forces, each of these empires has the great defect of being disjointed, and even insusceptible of perfect union. It is in fact no *vinculum* of social organization which held them together, but the ideal *vinculum* of a common fealty, and of submission to the same sceptre. This is not like the tie of manners, operative even where it is not perceived, but like the distinctions of geography - existing to-day, forgotten to-morrow - and abolished by a stroke of the pen, or a trick of diplomacy. Russia, again, a mighty empire, as respects the simple grandeur of magnitude, builds her power upon sterility. She has it in her power to seduce an invading foe into vast circles of starvation, of which the radii measure a thousand leagues. Frost and snow are confederates of her strength. She is strong by her very weakness. But Rome laid a belt about the Mediterranean of a thousand miles in breadth; and within that zone she comprehended not only all the great cities of the ancient world, but so perfectly did she lay the garden of the world in every climate, and for every mode of natural wealth, within her own ring-fence, that since that era no land, no part and parcel of the Roman empire, has ever risen into strength and opulence, except where unusual artificial industry has availed to counteract the tendencies of nature. So entirely had Rome engrossed whatsoever was rich by the mere bounty of native endowment.

Vast, therefore, unexampled, immeasurable, was the basis of natural power upon which the Roman throne reposed. The military force which put Rome in possession of this inordinate power, was certainly in some respects artificial; but the power itself was natural, and not subject to the ebbs and flows which attend the commercial empires of our days, (for all are in part commercial.) The depression, the reverses, of Rome, were confined to one shape - famine; a terrific shape, doubtless, but one which levies its penalty of suffering, not by elaborate processes that do not exhaust their total cycle in less than long periods of years. Fortunately for those who survive, no arrears of misery are allowed by this scourge of ancient days; [Footnote: "*Of ancient days.*" - For it is remarkable, and it serves to mark an indubitable progress of mankind, that, before the Christian era, famines were of frequent occurrence in countries the most civilized; afterwards they became rare, and latterly have entirely altered their character into occasional dearths.] the total penalty is paid down at once. As respected the hand of man, Rome slept for ages in absolute security. She could suffer only by the wrath of Providence; and, so long as she continued to be Rome, for many a generation she only of all the monarchies has feared no mortal hand [Footnote: Unless that hand were her own armed against herself; upon which topic there is a burst of noble eloquence in one of the ancient Panegyrici, when haranguing the Emperor Theodosius: "Thou, Rome! that, having once suffered by the madness of Cinna, and of the cruel Marius raging from banishment, and of Sylla, that won his wreath of prosperity from thy disasters, and of Cæsar, compassionate to the dead, didst shudder at every blast of the trumpet filled by the breath of civil commotion, - thou, that, besides the wreck of thy soldiery perishing on either side, didst bewail, amongst thy spectacles of domestic woe, the luminaries of thy

Thomas de Quincey

senate extinguished, the heads of thy consuls fixed upon a halberd, weeping for ages over thy self-slaughtered Catos, thy headless Ciceros (*truncosque Cicerones*), and unburied Pompeys; - to whom the party madness of thy own children had wrought in every age heavier woe than the Carthaginian thundering at thy gates, or the Gaul admitted within thy walls; on whom OEmathia, more fatal than the day of Allia, - Collina, more dismal than Cannæ, - had inflicted such deep memorials of wounds, that, from bitter experience of thy own valor, no enemy was to thee so formidable as thyself; - thou, Rome! Didst now for the first time behold a civil war issuing in a hallowed prosperity, a soldiery appeased, recovered Italy, and for thyself liberty established. Now first in thy long annals thou didst rest from a civil war in such a peace, that righteously, and with maternal tenderness, thou mightst claim for it the honors of a civic triumph."]

- "God and his Son except,   Created thing nought valued she nor shunned."

That the possessor and wielder of such enormous power - power alike admirable for its extent, for its intensity, and for its consecration from all counter-forces which could restrain it, or endanger it - should be regarded as sharing in the attributes of supernatural beings, is no more than might naturally be expected. All other known power in human hands has either been extensive, but wanting in intensity - or intense, but wanting in extent - or, thirdly, liable to permanent control and hazard from some antagonist power commensurate with itself. But the Roman power, in its centuries of grandeur, involved every mode of strength, with absolute immunity from all kinds and degrees of weakness. It ought not, therefore, to surprise us that the emperor, as the depositary of this charmed power, should have been looked upon as a *sacred* person, and the imperial family considered a "*divina domus.*" It is an error to regard this as excess of adulation, or as built *originally* upon hypocrisy. Undoubtedly the expressions of this feeling are sometimes gross and overcharged, as we find them in the very greatest of the Roman poets: for example, it shocks us to find a fine writer in anticipating the future canonization of his patron, and his instalment amongst the heavenly hosts, begging him to keep his distance warily from this or that constellation, and to be cautious of throwing his weight into either hemisphere, until the scale of proportions were accurately adjusted. These doubtless are passages degrading alike to the poet and his subject. But why? Not because they ascribe to the emperor a sanctity which he had not in the minds of men universally, or which even to the writer's feeling was exaggerated, but because it was expressed coarsely, and as a *physical* power: now, every thing physical is measurable by weight, motion, and resistance; and is therefore definite. But the very essence of whatsoever is supernatural lies in the indefinite. That power, therefore, with which the minds of men invested the emperor, was vulgarized by this coarse translation into the region of physics. Else it is evident, that any power which, by standing above all human control, occupies the next relation to superhuman modes of authority, must be invested by all minds alike with some dim and undefined relation to the sanctities of the next world. Thus, for instance, the Pope, as the father of Catholic Christendom, could not *but* be viewed with awe by any Christian of deep feeling, as standing in some relation to the true and unseen Father of the spiritual body. Nay, considering

Thomas de Quincey

that even false religions, as those of Pagan mythology, have probably never been utterly stripped of all vestige of truth, but that every such mode of error has perhaps been designed as a process, and adapted by Providence to the case of those who were capable of admitting no more perfect shape of truth; even the heads of such superstitions (the Dalai Lama, for instance) may not unreasonably be presumed as within the cognizance and special protection of Heaven. Much more may this be supposed of him to whose care was confided the weightier part of the human race; who had it in his power to promote or to suspend the progress of human improvement; and of whom, and the motions of whose will, the very prophets of Judea took cognizance. No nation, and no king, was utterly divorced from the councils of God. Palestine, as a central chamber of God's administration, stood in some relation to all. It has been remarked, as a mysterious and significant fact, that the founders of the great empires all had some connection, more or less, with the temple of Jerusalem. Melancthon even observes it in his Sketch of Universal History, as worthy of notice - that Pompey died, as it were, within sight of that very temple which he had polluted. Let us not suppose that Paganism, or Pagan nations, were therefore excluded from the concern and tender interest of Heaven. They also had their place allowed. And we may be sure that, amongst them, the Roman emperor, as the great accountant for the happiness of more men, and men more cultivated, than ever before were intrusted to the motions of a single will, had a special, singular, and mysterious relation to the secret counsels of Heaven.

Even we, therefore, may lawfully attribute some sanctity to the Roman emperor. That the Romans did so with absolute sincerity is certain. The altars of the emperor had a twofold consecration; to violate them, was the double crime of treason and heresy, In his appearances of state and ceremony, the fire, the sacred fire *epompeue* was carried in ceremonial solemnity before him; and every other circumstance of divine worship attended the emperor in his lifetime. [Footnote: The fact is, that the emperor was more of a sacred and divine creature in his lifetime than after his death. His consecrated character as a living ruler was a truth; his canonization, a fiction of tenderness to his memory.]

To this view of the imperial character and relations must be added one single circumstance, which in some measure altered the whole for the individual who happened to fill the office. The emperor *de facto* might be viewed under two aspects: there was the man, and there was the office. In his office he was immortal and sacred: but as a question might still be raised, by means of a mercenary army, as to the claims of the particular individual who at any time filled the office, the very sanctity and privilege of the character with which he was clothed might actually be turned against himself; and here it is, at this point, that the character of Roman emperor became truly and mysteriously awful. Gibbon has taken notice of the extraordinary situation of a subject in the Roman empire who should attempt to fly from the wrath of the crown. Such was the ubiquity of the emperor that this was absolutely hopeless. Except amongst pathless deserts or barbarous nomads, it was impossible to find even a transient sanctuary from the imperial pursuit. If he went down to the sea, there he met the emperor: if he took the wings of the morning, and fled to the uttermost parts of the earth, there also was the emperor or his lieutenants. But the same omnipresence of imperial anger and

Thomas de Quincey

retribution which withered the hopes of the poor humble prisoner, met and confounded the emperor himself, when hurled from his giddy elevation by some fortunate rival. All the kingdoms of the earth, to one in that situation, became but so many wards of the same infinite prison. Flight, if it were even successful for the moment, did but a little retard his inevitable doom. And so evident was this, that hardly in one instance did the fallen prince *attempt* to fly; but passively met the death which was inevitable, in the very spot where ruin had overtaken him. Neither was it possible even for a merciful conqueror to show mercy; for, in the presence of an army so mercenary and factious, his own safety was but too deeply involved in the extermination of rival pretenders to the crown.

Such, amidst the sacred security and inviolability of the office, was the hazardous tenure of the individual. Nor did his dangers always arise from persons in the rank of competitors and rivals. Sometimes it menaced him in quarters which his eye had never penetrated, and from enemies too obscure to have reached his ear. By way of illustration we will cite a case from the life of the Emperor Commodus, which is wild enough to have furnished the plot of a romance - though as well authenticated as any other passage in that reign. The story is narrated by Herodian, and the circumstances are these: A slave of noble qualities, and of magnificent person, having liberated himself from the degradations of bondage, determined to avenge his own wrongs by inflicting continual terror upon the town and neighborhood which had witnessed his humiliation. For this purpose he resorted to the woody recesses of the province, (somewhere in the modern Transylvania,) and, attracting to his wild encampment as many fugitives as he could, by degrees he succeeded in forming and training a very formidable troop of freebooters. Partly from the energy of his own nature, and partly from the neglect and remissness of the provincial magistrates, the robber captain rose from less to more, until he had formed a little army, equal to the task of assaulting fortified cities. In this stage of his adventures, he encountered and defeated several of the imperial officers commanding large detachments of troops; and at length grew of consequence sufficient to draw upon himself the emperor's eye, and the honor of his personal displeasure. In high wrath and disdain at the insults offered to his eagles by this fugitive slave, Commodus fulminated against him such an edict as left him no hope of much longer escaping with impunity.

Public vengeance was now awakened; the imperial troops were marching from every quarter upon the same centre; and the slave became sensible that in a very short space of time he must be surrounded and destroyed. In this desperate situation he took a desperate resolution: he assembled his troops, laid before them his plan, concerted the various steps for carrying it into effect, and then dismissed them as independent wanderers. So ends the first chapter of the tale.

The next opens in the passes of the Alps, whither by various routes, of seven or eight hundred miles in extent, these men had threaded their way in manifold disguises through the very midst of the emperor's camps. According to this man's gigantic enterprise, in which the means were as audacious as the purpose, the conspirators were to rendezvous, and first to recognise each other at the gates of Rome. From the Danube to the Tiber did this band of robbers severally pursue

Thomas de Quincey

their perilous routes through all the difficulties of the road and the jealousies of the military stations, sustained by the mere thirst of vengeance - vengeance against that mighty foe whom they knew only by his proclamations against themselves. Every thing continued to prosper; the conspirators met under the walls of Rome; the final details were arranged; and those also would have prospered but for a trifling accident. The season was one of general carnival at Rome; and, by the help of those disguises which the license of this festal time allowed, the murderers were to have penetrated as maskers to the emperor's retirement, when a casual word or two awoke the suspicions of a sentinel. One of the conspirators was arrested; under the terror and uncertainty of the moment, he made much ampler discoveries than were expected of him; the other accomplices were secured: and Commodus was delivered from the uplifted daggers of those who had sought him by months of patient wanderings, pursued through all the depths of the Illyrian forests, and the difficulties of the Alpine passes. It is not easy to find words commensurate to the energetic hardihood of a slave - who, by way of answer and reprisal to an edict which consigned him to persecution and death, determines to cross Europe in quest of its author, though no less a person than the master of the world - to seek him out in the inner recesses of his capital city and his private palace - and there to lodge a dagger in his heart, as the adequate reply to the imperial sentence of proscription against himself.

Such, amidst his superhuman grandeur and consecrated powers of the Roman emperor's office, were the extraordinary perils which menaced the individual, and the peculiar frailties of his condition. Nor is it possible that these circumstances of violent opposition can be better illustrated than in this tale of Herodian. Whilst the emperor's mighty arms were stretched out to arrest some potentate in the heart of Asia, a poor slave is silently and stealthily creeping round the base of the Alps, with the purpose of winning his way as a murderer to the imperial bedchamber; Cæsar is watching some mighty rebel of the Orient, at a distance of two thousand leagues, and he overlooks the dagger which is at his own heart. In short, all the heights and the depths which belong to man as aspirers, all the contrasts of glory and meanness, the extremities of what is his highest and lowest in human possibility, - all met in the situation of the Roman Cæsars, and have combined to make them the most interesting studies which history has furnished.

This, as a general proposition, will be readily admitted. But meantime, it is remarkable that no field has been less trodden than the private memorials of those very Cæsars; whilst at the same time it is equally remarkable, in concurrence with that subject for wonder, that precisely with the first of the Cæsars commences the first page of what in modern times we understand by anecdotes. Suetonius is the earliest writer in that department of biography; so far as we know, he may be held first to have devised it as a mode of history. The six writers, whose sketches are collected under the general title of the *Augustan History*, followed in the same track. Though full of entertainment, and of the most curious researches, they are all of them entirely unknown, except to a few elaborate scholars. We purpose to collect from these obscure, but most interesting memorialists, a few sketches and biographical portraits of these great princes, whose public life is sometimes known, but

Thomas de Quincey

very rarely any part of their private and personal history. We must of course commence with the mighty founder of the Cæsars. In his case we cannot expect so much of absolute novelty as in that of those who succeed. But if, in this first instance, we are forced to touch a little upon old things, we shall confine ourselves as much as possible to those which are susceptible of new aspects. For the whole gallery of those who follow, we can undertake that the memorials which we shall bring forward, may be looked upon as belonging pretty much to what has hitherto been a sealed book.

CHAPTER I.

The character of the first Cæsar has perhaps never been worse appreciated than by him who in one sense described it best - that is, with most force and eloquence wherever he really *did* comprehend it. This was Lucan, who has nowhere exhibited more brilliant rhetoric, nor wandered more from the truth, than in the contrasted portraits of Cæsar and Pompey. The famous line, "*Nil actum reputans si quid superesset agendum,*" is a fine feature of the real character, finely expressed. But if it had been Lucan's purpose (as possibly, with a view to Pompey's benefit, in some respects it was) utterly and extravagantly to falsify the character of the great Dictator, by no single trait could he more effectually have fulfilled that purpose, nor in fewer words, than by this expressive passage, "*Gaudensque viam fecisse ruina.*" Such a trait would be almost extravagant applied even to Marius, who (though in many respects a perfect model of Roman grandeur, massy, columnar, imperturbable, and more perhaps than any one man recorded in history capable of justifying the bold illustration of that character in Horace, "*Si fractus illabatur orbis, impavidum ferient ruinæ*") had, however, a ferocity in his character, and a touch of the devil in him, very rarely united with the same tranquil intrepidity. But for Cæsar, the all-accomplished statesman, the splendid orator, the man of elegant habits and polished taste, the patron of the fine arts in a degree transcending all example of his own or the previous age, and as a man of general literature so much beyond his contemporaries, except Cicero, that he looked down even upon the brilliant Sylla as an illiterate person, - to class such a man with the race of furious destroyers exulting in the desolations they spread, is to err not by an individual trait, but by the whole genus. The Attilas and the Tamerlanes, who rejoice in avowing themselves the scourges of God, and the special instruments of his wrath, have no one feature of affinity to the polished and humane Cæsar, and would as little have comprehended his character, as he could have respected theirs. Even Cato, the unworthy hero of Lucan, might have suggested to him a little more truth in this instance, by a celebrated remark which he made on the characteristic distinction of Cæsar, in comparison with other revolutionary disturbers; for, whereas others had attempted the overthrow of the state in a continued paroxysm of fury, and in a state of mind resembling the lunacy of intoxication, that Cæsar, on the contrary, among that whole class of civil disturbers, was the only one who had come to the task in a temper of sobriety and moderation, (*unum accessisse sobrium ad rempublicam delendam.*)

In reality, Lucan did not think as he wrote. He had a purpose to serve; and in an age when to act like a freeman was no longer possible, he determined at least to write in that character. It is probable, also, that he wrote with a vindictive or a malicious feeling towards Nero; and, as the single means he had for gratifying *that*, resolved upon sacrificing the grandeur of Cæsar's character wherever it should be found possible. Meantime, in spite of himself, Lucan for ever betrays his lurking consciousness of the truth. Nor are there

26

any testimonies to Cæsar's vast superiority more memorably pointed, than those which are indirectly and involuntarily extorted from this Catonic poet, by the course of his narration. Never, for example, was there within the same compass of words, a more emphatic expression of Cæsar's essential and inseparable grandeur of thought, which could not be disguised or be laid aside for an instant, than is found in the three casual words - *Indocilis privata loqui*. The very mould, it seems, by Lucan's confession, of his trivial conversation was regal; nor could he, even to serve a purpose, abjure it for so much as a casual purpose. The acts of Cæsar speak also the same language; and as these are less susceptible of a false coloring than the features of a general character, we find this poet of liberty, in the midst of one continuous effort to distort the truth, and to dress up two scenical heroes, forced by the mere necessities of history into a reluctant homage to Cæsar's supremacy of moral grandeur.

Of so great a man it must be interesting to know all the well attested opinions which bear upon topics of universal interest to human nature; as indeed no others stood much chance of preservation, unless it were from as minute and curious a collector of *anecdotage* as Suetonius. And, first, it would be gratifying to know the opinion of Cæsar, if he had any peculiar to himself, on the great theme of Religion. It has been held, indeed, that the constitution of his mind, and the general cast of his character, indisposed him to religious thoughts. Nay, it has been common to class him amongst deliberate atheists; and some well known anecdotes are current in books, which illustrate his contempt for the vulgar class of auguries. In this, however, he went no farther than Cicero, and other great contemporaries, who assuredly were no atheists. One mark perhaps of the wide interval which, in Cæsar's age, had begun to separate the Roman nobility from the hungry and venal populace who were daily put up to sale, and bought by the highest bidder, manifested itself in the increasing disdain for the tastes and ruling sympathies of the lowest vulgar. No mob could be more abjectly servile than was that of Rome to the superstition of portents, prodigies, and omens. Thus far, in common with his order, and in this sense, Julius Cæsar was naturally a despiser of superstition. Mere strength of understanding would, perhaps, have made him so in any age, and apart from the circumstances of his personal history. This natural tendency in him would doubtless receive a further bias in the same direction from the office of Pontifex Maximus, which he held at an early stage of his public career. This office, by letting him too much behind the curtain, and exposing too entirely the base machinery of ropes and pulleys, which sustained the miserable jugglery played off upon the popular credulity, impressed him perhaps even unduly with contempt for those who could be its dupes. And we may add - that Cæsar was constitutionally, as well as by accident of position, too much a man of the world, had too powerful a leaning to the virtues of active life, was governed by too partial a sympathy with the whole class of *active* forces in human nature, as contradistinguished from those which tend to contemplative purposes, under any circumstances, to have become a profound believer, or a steadfast reposer of his fears and anxieties, in religious influences. A man of the world is but another designation for a man indisposed to religious awe or contemplative enthusiasm. Still it is a doctrine which we cherish - that grandeur of mind in any one

Thomas de Quincey

department whatsoever, supposing only that it exists in excess, disposes a man to some degree of sympathy with all other grandeur, however alien in its quality or different in its form. And upon this ground we presume the great Dictator to have had an interest in religious themes by mere compulsion of his own extraordinary elevation of mind, after making the fullest allowance for the special quality of that mind, which did certainly, to the whole extent of its characteristics, tend entirely to estrange him from such themes. We find, accordingly, that though sincerely a despiser of superstition, and with a frankness which must sometimes have been hazardous in that age, Cæsar was himself also superstitious. No man could have been otherwise who lived and conversed with that generation and people. But if superstitious, he was so after a mode of his own. In his very infirmities Cæsar manifested his greatness: his very littlenesses were noble.

"Nec licuit populis parvum te, Nile, videre."

That he placed some confidence in dreams, for instance, is certain: because, had he slighted them unreservedly, he would not have dwelt upon them afterwards, or have troubled himself to recall their circumstances. Here we trace his human weakness. Yet again we are reminded that it was the weakness of Cæsar; for the dreams were noble in their imagery, and Cæsarean (so to speak) in their tone of moral feeling. Thus, for example, the night before he was assassinated, he dreamt at intervals that he was soaring above the clouds on wings, and that he placed his hand within the right hand of Jove. It would seem that perhaps some obscure and half-formed image floated in his mind, of the eagle, as the king of birds; secondly, as the tutelary emblem under which his conquering legions had so often obeyed his voice; and, thirdly, as the bird of Jove. To this triple relation of the bird his dream covertly appears to point. And a singular coincidence appears between this dream and a little anecdote brought down to us, as having actually occurred in Rome about twenty-four hours before his death. A little bird, which by some is represented as a very small kind of sparrow, but which, both to the Greeks and the Romans, was known by a name implying a regal station (probably from the ambitious courage which at times prompted it to attack the eagle), was observed to direct its flight towards the senate-house, consecrated by Pompey, whilst a crowd of other birds were seen to hang upon its flight in close pursuit. What might be the object of the chase, whether the little king himself, or a sprig of laurel which he bore in his mouth, could not be determined. The whole train, pursuers and pursued, continued their flight towards Pompey's hall. Flight and pursuit were there alike arrested; the little king was overtaken by his enemies, who fell upon him as so many conspirators, and tore him limb from limb.

If this anecdote were reported to Cæsar, which is not at all improbable, considering the earnestness with which his friends labored to dissuade him from his purpose of meeting the senate on the approaching Ides of March, it is very little to be doubted that it had a considerable effect upon his feelings, and that, in fact, his own dream grew out of the impression which it had made. This way of linking the two anecdotes, as cause and effect, would also bring a third anecdote under the same *nexus*. We are told that Calpurnia, the last wife of Cæsar, dreamed on the same night, and to the same ominous result. The circumstances of *her* dream are

Thomas de Quincey

less striking, because less figurative; but on that account its import was less open to doubt: she dreamed, in fact, that after the roof of their mansion had fallen in, her husband was stabbed in her bosom. Laying all these omens together, Cæsar would have been more or less than human had he continued utterly undepressed by them. And if so much superstition as even this implies, must be taken to argue some little weakness, on the other hand let it not be forgotten, that this very weakness does but the more illustrate the unusual force of mind, and the heroic will, which obstinately laid aside these concurring prefigurations of impending destruction; concurring, we say, amongst themselves—and concurring also with a prophecy of older date, which was totally independent of them all.

There is another and somewhat sublime story of the same class, which belongs to the most interesting moment of Cæsar's life; and those who are disposed to explain all such tales upon physiological principles, will find an easy solution of this, in particular, in the exhaustion of body, and the intense anxiety which must have debilitated even Cæsar under the whole circumstances of the case. On the ever memorable night when he had resolved to take the first step (and in such a case the first step, as regarded the power of retreating, was also the final step) which placed him in arms against the state, it happened that his headquarters were at some distance from the little river Rubicon, which formed the boundary of his province. With his usual caution, that no news of his motions might run before himself, on this night Cæsar gave an entertainment to his friends, in the midst of which he slipped away unobserved, and with a small retinue proceeded through the woods to the point of the river at which he designed to cross. The night [Footnote: It is an interesting circumstance in the habits of the ancient Romans, that their journeys were pursued very much in the night-time, and by torchlight. Cicero, in one of his letters, speaks of passing through the towns of Italy by night, as a serviceable scheme for some political purpose, either of avoiding too much to publish his motions, or of evading the necessity (else perhaps not avoidable), of drawing out the party sentiments of the magistrates in the circumstances of honor or neglect with which they might choose to receive him. His words, however, imply that the practice was by no means an uncommon one. And, indeed, from some passages in writers of the Augustan era, it would seem that this custom was not confined to people of distinction, but was familiar to a class of travellers so low in rank as to be capable of abusing their opportunities of concealment for the infliction of wanton injury upon the woods and fences which bounded the margin, of the high-road. Under the cloud of night and solitude, the mischief-loving traveller was often in the habit of applying his torch to the withered boughs of woods, or to artificial hedges; and extensive ravages by fire, such as now happen, not unfrequently in the American woods, (but generally from careless- ness in scattering the glowing embers of a fire, or even the ashes of a pipe,) were then occasionally the result of mere wantonness of mischief. Ovid accordingly notices, as one amongst the familiar images of daybreak, the half-burnt torch of the traveller; and, apparently, from the position which it holds in his description, where it is ranked with the most familiar of all circumstances in all countries, - that of the rural laborer going out to his morning tasks, - it must have been common indeed:

Thomas de Quincey

"Semiustamque facem vigilatâ nocte viator
Ponet; et ad solitum rusticus ibit opus."

This occurs in the *Fasti*; - elsewhere he notices it for
its danger:

"Ut facibus sepes ardent, cum forte viator
Vel nimis admovit, vel jam sub luce reliquit."

He, however, we see, good-naturedly ascribes the
danger to mere carelessness, in bringing the torch too
near to the hedge, or tossing it away at daybreak. But
Varro, a more matter-of-fact observer, does not
disguise the plain truth, that these disasters were often
the product of pure malicious frolic. For instance, in
recommending a certain kind of quickset fence, he
insists upon it, as one of its advantages, that it will not
readily ignite under the torch of the mischievous
wayfarer: "Naturale sepimentum," says he, "quod
obseri solet virgultis aut spinis, *prætereuntis lascivi
non metuet facem.*" It is not easy to see the origin or
advantage of this practice of nocturnal travelling
(which must have considerably increased the hazards
of a journey), excepting only in the heats of summer. It
is probable, however, that men of high rank and public
station may have introduced the practice by way of
releasing corporate bodies in large towns from the
burdensome ceremonies of public receptions; thus
making a compromise between their own dignity and
the convenience of the provincial public. Once
introduced, and the arrangements upon the road for
meeting the wants of travellers once adapted to such a
practice, it would easily become universal. It is,
however, very possible that mere horror of the heats of
day-time may have been the original ground for it. The
ancients appear to have shrunk from no hardship so

trying and insufferable as that of heat. And in relation to that subject, it is interesting to observe the way in which the ordinary use of language has accommodated itself to that feeling. Our northern way of expressing effeminacy is derived chiefly from the hardships of cold. He that shrinks from the trials and rough experience of real life in any department, is described by the contemptuous prefix of *chimney-corner*, as if shrinking from the cold which he would meet on coming out into the open air amongst his fellow-men. Thus, a *chimney-corner* politician, for a mere speculator or unpractical dreamer. But the very same indolent habit of aerial speculation, which courts no test of real life and practice, is described by the ancients under the term *umbraticus*, or seeking the cool shade, and shrinking from the heat. Thus, an *umbraticus doctor* is one who has no practical solidity in his teaching. The fatigue and hardship of real life, in short, is represented by the ancients under the uniform image of heat, and by the moderns under that of cold.] was stormy, and by the violence of the wind all the torches of his escort were blown out, so that the whole party lost their road, having probably at first intentionally deviated from the main route, and wandered about through the whole night, until the early dawn enabled them to recover their true course. The light was still gray and uncertain, as Cæsar and his retinue rode down upon the banks of the fatal river - to cross which with arms in his hands, since the further bank lay within the territory of the Republic, *ipso facto* proclaimed any Roman a rebel and a traitor. No man, the firmest or the most obtuse, could be otherwise than deeply agitated, when looking down upon this little brook - so insignificant in itself, but invested by law with a sanctity so awful, and so dire a consecration. The whole course of future history, and the fate of

Thomas de Quincey

every nation, would necessarily be determined by the irretrievable act of the next half hour.

In these moments, and with this spectacle before him, and contemplating these immeasurable consequences consciously for the last time that could allow him a retreat, - impressed also by the solemnity and deep tranquillity of the silent dawn, whilst the exhaustion of his night wanderings predisposed him to nervous irritation, - Cæsar, we may be sure, was profoundly agitated. The whole elements of the scene were almost scenically disposed; the law of antagonism having perhaps never been employed with so much effect: the little quiet brook presenting a direct, antithesis to its grand political character; and the innocent dawn, with its pure, untroubled repose, contrasting potently, to a man of any intellectual sensibility, with the long chaos of bloodshed, darkness, and anarchy, which was to take its rise from the apparently trifling acts of this one morning. So prepared, we need not much wonder at what followed. Cæsar was yet lingering on the hither bank, when suddenly, at a point not far distant from himself, an apparition was descried in a sitting posture, and holding in its hand what seemed a flute. This phantom was of unusual size, and of beauty more than human, so far as its lineaments could be traced in the early dawn. What is singular, however, in the story, on any hypothesis which would explain it out of Cæsar's individual condition, is, that others saw it as well as he; both pastoral laborers, (who were present, probably, in the character of guides,) and some of the sentinels stationed at the passage of the river. These men fancied even that a strain of music issued from this aerial flute. And some, both of the shepherds and the Roman soldiers, who were bolder than the rest, advanced towards the figure. Amongst this party, it happened that there were a few Roman trumpeters. From one of these, the phantom, rising as they advanced nearer, suddenly caught a trumpet, and blowing through it a blast of superhuman strength, plunged into the Rubicon, passed to the other bank, and disappeared in the dusky twilight of the dawn. Upon which Cæsar exclaimed: - "It is finished - the die is cast - let us follow whither the guiding portents from Heaven, and the malice of our enemy, alike summon us to go." So saying, he crossed the river with impetuosity; and, in a sudden rapture of passionate and vindictive ambition, placed himself and his retinue upon the Italian soil; and, as if by inspiration from Heaven, in one moment involved himself and his followers in treason, raised the standard of revolt, put his foot upon the neck of the invincible republic which had humbled all the kings of the earth, and founded an empire which was to last for a thousand and half a thousand years. In what manner this spectral appearance was managed - whether Cæsar were its author, or its dupe - will remain unknown for ever. But undoubtedly this was the first time that the advanced guard of a victorious army was headed by an apparition; and we may conjecture that it will be the last. [Footnote: According to Suetonius, the circumstances of this memorable night were as follows: - As soon as the decisive intelligence was received, that the intrigues of his enemies had prevailed at Rome, and that the interposition of the popular magistrates (the tribunes) was set aside, Cæsar sent forward the troops, who were then at his head-quarters, but in as private a manner as possible. He himself, by way of masque, (*per dissimulationem,*) attended a public spectacle, gave an audience to an architect who wished to lay before him a plan for a school of gladiators which Cæsar designed to build, and finally presented himself at a banquet, which was

Thomas de Quincey

very numerously attended. From this, about sunset, he set forward in a carriage, drawn by mules, and with a small escort (*modico comitatu.*) Losing his road, which was the most private he could find (*occultissimum*), he quitted his carriage and proceeded on foot. At dawn he met with a guide; after which followed the above incidents.]

In the mingled yarn of human life, tragedy is never far asunder from farce; and it is amusing to retrace in immediate succession to this incident of epic dignity, which has its only parallel by the way in the case of Vasco de Gama, (according to the narrative of Camoens,) when met and confronted by a sea phantom, whilst attempting to double the Cape of Storms, (Cape of Good Hope,) a ludicrous passage, in which one felicitous blunder did Cæsar a better service than all the truths which Greece and Rome could have furnished. In our own experience, we once witnessed a blunder about as gross. The present Chancellor, in his first electioneering contest with the Lowthers, upon some occasion where he was recriminating upon the other party, and complaining that stratagems, which *they* might practise with impunity, were denied to him and his, happened to point the moral of his complaint, by alleging the old adage, that one man might steal a horse with more hope of indulgence than another could look over the hedge. Whereupon, by benefit of the universal mishearing in the outermost ring of the audience, it became generally reported that Lord Lowther had once been engaged in an affair of horse stealing; and that he, Henry Brougham, could (had he pleased) have lodged an information against him, seeing that he was then looking over the hedge. And this charge naturally won the more credit, because it was notorious and past denying that his lordship was a capital horseman, fond of horses, and much connected with the turf. To this hour, therefore, amongst some worthy shepherds and others, it is a received article of their creed, and (as they justly observe in northern pronunciation,) a *sham* ful thing to be told, that Lord Lowther was once a horse stealer, and that he escaped *lagging* by reason of Harry Brougham's pity for his tender years and hopeful looks. Not less was the blunder which, on the banks of the Rubicon, befriended Cæsar. Immediately after crossing, he harangued the troops whom he had sent forward, and others who there met him from the neighboring garrison of Ariminium. The tribunes of the people, those great officers of the democracy, corresponding by some of their functions to our House of Commons, men personally, and by their position in the state, entirely in his interest, and who, for his sake, had fled from home, there and then he produced to the soldiery; thus identified his cause, and that of the soldiers, with the cause of the people of Rome and of Roman liberty; and perhaps with needless rhetoric attempted to conciliate those who were by a thousand ties and by claims innumerable, his own already; for never yet has it been found, that with the soldier, who, from youth upwards, passes his life in camps, could the duties or the interests of citizens survive those stronger and more personal relations connecting him with his military superior. In the course of this harangue, Cæsar often raised his left hand with Demosthenic action, and once or twice he drew off the ring, which every Roman gentleman - simply *as* such - wore as the inseparable adjunct and symbol of his rank. By this action he wished to give emphasis to the accompanying words, in which he protested, that, sooner than fail in satisfying and doing justice to any the least of those who heard him and followed his fortunes, he would be content to part with his own birthright, and to forego his dearest claims. This was what he really said; but the outermost circle of his auditors, who rather saw his gestures than distinctly heard his words, carried off the notion, (which they were careful every where to disperse amongst the legions afterwards associated with them in the same camps,) that Cæsar had vowed never to lay down his arms until he had obtained for every man, the very meanest of those who heard him, the rank, privileges and appointments of a Roman knight. Here was a piece of sovereign good luck. Had he really made such a promise, Cæsar might have found that he had laid himself under very embarrassing obligations; but, as the case stood, he had, through all his following campaigns, the total benefit of such a promise, and yet could always absolve himself from the penalties of responsibility which it imposed, by appealing to the evidence of those who happened to stand in the first ranks of his audience. The blunder was gross and palpable; and yet, with the unreflecting and dull-witted soldier, it did him service greater than all the subtilties of all the schools could have accomplished, and a service which subsisted to the end of the war.

Great as Cæsar was by the benefit of his original nature, there can - be no doubt that he, like others, owed something to circumstances; and perhaps, amongst these which were most favorable to the premature development of great self-dependence, we must reckon the early death of his father. It is, or it is not, according to the nature of men, an advantage to be orphaned at an early age. Perhaps utter orphanage is rarely or never such: but to lose a father betimes profits a strong mind greatly. To Cæsar it was a prodigious benefit that he lost his father when not much more than fifteen. Perhaps it was an advantage also to his father that he died thus early. Had he stayed a year longer, he would have seen himself despised, baffled, and made ridiculous. For where, let us ask, in any age, was the father capable of adequately sustaining that relation to the unique Caius Julius - to him, in the appropriate language of Shakspeare,

"The foremost man of all this world?"

And, in this fine and Cæsarean line, "this world" is to be understood not of the order of co-existences merely, but also of the order of successions; he was the foremost man not only of his contemporaries, but also of men generally - of all that ever should come after him, or should sit on thrones under the denominations of Czars, Kesars, or Cæsars of the Bosphorus and the Danube; of all in every age that should inherit his supremacy of mind, or should subject to themselves the generations of ordinary men by qualities analogous to his. Of this infinite superiority some part must be ascribed to his early emancipation from paternal control. There are very many cases in which, simply from considerations of sex, a female cannot stand forward as the head of a family, or as its suitable representative. If they are even ladies paramount, and in situations of command, they are also women. The staff of authority does not annihilate their sex; and scruples of female delicacy interfere for ever to unnerve and emasculate in their hands the sceptre however otherwise potent. Hence we see, in noble families, the merest boys put forward to represent the family dignity, as fitter supporters of that burden than their mature mothers. And of Cæsar's mother, though little is recorded, and that little incidentally, this much at least, we learn - that, if she looked down upon him

Thomas de Quincey

with maternal pride and delight, she looked up to him with female ambition as the re-edifier of her husband's honors, with reverence as to a column of the Roman grandeur, and with fear and feminine anxieties as to one whose aspiring spirit carried him but too prematurely into the fields of adventurous honor. One slight and evanescent sketch of the relations which subsisted between Cæsar and his mother, caught from the wrecks of time, is preserved both by Plutarch and Suetonius. We see in the early dawn the young patrician standing upon the steps of his paternal portico, his mother with her arms wreathed about his neck, looking up to his noble countenance, sometimes drawing auguries of hope from features so fitted for command, sometimes boding an early blight to promises so prematurely magnificent. That she had something of her son's aspiring character, or that he presumed so much in a mother of his, we learn from the few words which survive of their conversation. He addressed to her no language that could tranquillize her fears. On the contrary, to any but a Roman mother his valedictory words, taken in connection with the known determination of his character, were of a nature to consummate her depression, as they tended to confirm the very worst of her fears. He was then going to stand his chance in a popular election for an office of dignity, and to launch himself upon the storms of the Campus Martius. At that period, besides other and more ordinary dangers, the bands of gladiators, kept in the pay of the more ambitious amongst the Roman nobles, gave a popular tone of ferocity and of personal risk to the course of such contests; and either to forestall the victory of an antagonist, or to avenge their own defeat, it was not at all impossible that a body of incensed competitors might intercept his final triumph by assassination. For this danger, however, he had no leisure in his thoughts of consolation; the sole danger which *he* contemplated, or supposed his mother to contemplate, was the danger of defeat, and for that he reserved his consolations. He bade her fear nothing; for that without doubt he would return with victory, and with the ensigns of the dignity he sought, or would return a corpse.

Early indeed did Cæsar's trials commence; and it is probable, that, had not the death of his father, by throwing him prematurely upon his own resources, prematurely developed the masculine features of his character, forcing him whilst yet a boy under the discipline of civil conflict and the yoke of practical life, even *his* energies would have been insufficient to sustain them. His age is not exactly ascertained, but it is past a doubt that he had not reached his twentieth year when he had the hardihood to engage in a struggle with Sylla, then Dictator, and exercising the immoderate powers of that office with the license and the severity which history has made so memorable. He had neither any distinct grounds of hope, nor any eminent example at that time, to countenance him in this struggle - which yet he pushed on in the most uncompromising style, and to the utmost verge of defiance. The subject of the contrast gives it a further interest. It was the youthful wife of the youthful Cæsar who stood under the shadow of the great Dictator's displeasure; not personally, but politically, on account of her connections: and her it was, Cornelia, the daughter of a man who had been four times consul, that Cæsar was required to divorce: but he spurned the haughty mandate, and carried his determination to a triumphant issue, notwithstanding his life was at stake, and at one time saved only by shifting his place of concealment every night; and this young lady it was

Thomas de Quincey

who afterwards became the mother of his only daughter. Both mother and daughter, it is remarkable, perished prematurely, and at critical periods of Cæsar's life; for it is probable enough that these irreparable wounds to Cæsar's domestic affections threw him with more exclusiveness of devotion upon the fascinations of glory and ambition than might have happened under a happier condition of his private life. That Cæsar should have escaped destruction in this unequal contest with an enemy then wielding the whole thunders of the state, is somewhat surprising; and historians have sought their solution of the mystery in the powerful intercessions of the vestal virgins, and several others of high rank amongst the connections of his great house. These may have done something; but it is due to Sylla, who had a sympathy with every thing truly noble, to suppose him struck with powerful admiration for the audacity of the young patrician, standing out in such severe solitude among so many examples of timid concession; and that to this magnanimous feeling in the Dictator, much of his indulgence was due. In fact, according to some accounts, it was not Sylla, but the creatures of Sylla (*adjutores*), who pursued Cæsar. We know, at all events, that Sylla formed a right estimate of Cæsar's character, and that, from the complexion of his conduct in this one instance, he drew his famous prophecy of his future destiny; bidding his friends beware of that slipshod boy, "for that in him lay couchant many a Marius." A grander testimony to the awe which Cæsar inspired, or from one who knew better the qualities of that man by whom he measured him, cannot be imagined.

It is not our intention, or consistent with our plan, to pursue this great man through the whole circumstances of his romantic career; though it is certain that many parts of his life require investigation much keener than has ever been applied to them, and that many might easily be placed in a new light. Indeed, the whole of this most momentous section of ancient history ought to be recomposed with the critical scepticism of a Niebuhr, and the same comprehensive collation of authorities. In reality it is the hinge upon which turned the future destiny of the whole earth, and having therefore a common relation to all modern nations whatsoever, should naturally have been cultivated with the zeal which belongs to a personal concern. In general, the anecdotes which express most vividly the splendid character of the first Cæsar, are those which illustrate his defiance of danger in extremity, - the prodigious energy and rapidity of his decisions and motions in the field; the skill with which he penetrated the designs of his enemies, and the exemplary speed with which he provided a remedy for disasters; the extraordinary presence of mind which he showed in turning adverse omens to his own advantage, as when, upon stumbling in coming on shore, (which was esteemed a capital omen of evil,) he transfigured as it were in one instant its whole meaning by exclaiming, "Thus do I take possession of thee, oh Africa!" in that way giving to an accident the semblance of a symbolic purpose; the grandeur of fortitude with which he faced the whole extent of a calamity when palliation could do no good, "non negando, minuendove, sed insuper amplificando, *ementiendoque*;" as when, upon finding his soldiery alarmed at the approach of Juba, with forces really great, but exaggerated by their terrors, he addressed them in a military harangue to the following effect: "Know that within a few days the king will come up with us, bringing with him sixty thousand legionaries, thirty thousand cavalry, one hundred thousand light troops, besides three hundred elephants.

Thomas de Quincey

Such being the case, let me hear no more of conjectures and opinions, for you have now my warrant for the fact, whose information is past doubting. Therefore, be satisfied; otherwise, I will put every man of you on board some crazy old fleet, and whistle you down the tide - no matter under what winds, no matter towards what shore." Finally, we might seek for the *characteristic* anecdotes of Cæsar in his unexampled liberalities and contempt of money. [Footnote: Middleton's Life of Cicero, which still continues to be the most readable digest of these affairs, is feeble and contradictory. He discovers that Cæsar was no general! And the single merit which his work was supposed to possess, viz. the better and more critical arrangement of Cicero's Letters, in respect to their chronology, has of late years been detected as a robbery from the celebrated Bellenden, of James the First's time.]

Upon this last topic it is the just remark of Casaubon, that some instances of Cæsar's munificence have been thought apocryphal, or to rest upon false readings, simply from ignorance of the heroic scale upon which the Roman splendors of that age proceeded. A forum which Cæsar built out of the products of his last campaign, by way of a present to the Roman people, cost him - for the ground merely on which it stood - nearly eight hundred thousand pounds. To the *citizens* of Rome (perhaps 300,000 persons) he presented, in one *congiary*, about two guineas and a half a head. To his army, in one *donation*, upon the termination of the civil war, he gave a sum which allowed about two hundred pounds a man to the infantry, and four hundred to the cavalry. It is true that the legionary troops were then much reduced by the sword of the enemy, and by the tremendous hardships of their last campaigns. In this, however, he did perhaps no more than repay a debt. For it is an instance of military attachment, beyond all that Wallenstein or any commander, the most beloved amongst his troops, has ever experienced, that, on the breaking out of the civil war, not only did the centurions of every legion severally maintain a horse soldier, but even the privates volunteered to serve without pay - and (what might seem impossible) without their daily rations. This was accomplished by subscriptions amongst themselves, the more opulent undertaking for the maintenance of the needy. Their disinterested love for Cæsar appeared in another and more difficult illustration: it was a traditionary anecdote in Rome, that the majority of those amongst Cæsar's troops, who had the misfortune to fall into the enemy's hands, refused to accept their lives under the condition of serving against *him*.

In connection with this subject of his extraordinary munificence, there is one aspect of Cæsar's life which has suffered much from the misrepresentations of historians, and that is - the vast pecuniary embarrassments under which he labored, until the profits of war had turned the scale even more prodigiously in his favor. At one time of his life, when appointed to a foreign office, so numerous and so clamorous were his creditors, that he could not have left Rome on his public duties, had not Crassus come forward with assistance in money, or by promises, to the amount of nearly two hundred thousand pounds. And at another, he was accustomed to amuse himself with computing how much money it would require to make him worth exactly nothing (*i. e.* simply to clear him of debts); this, by one account, amounted to upwards of two millions sterling. Now the error of

Thomas de Quincey

historians has been - to represent these debts as the original ground of his ambition and his revolutionary projects, as though the desperate condition of his private affairs had suggested a civil war to his calculations as the best or only mode of redressing it. But, on the contrary, his debts were the product of his ambition, and contracted from first to last in the service of his political intrigues, for raising and maintaining a powerful body of partisans, both in Rome and elsewhere. Whosoever indeed will take the trouble to investigate the progress of Cæsar's ambition, from such materials as even yet remain, may satisfy himself that the scheme of revolutionizing the Republic, and placing himself at its head, was no growth of accident or circumstances; above all, that it did not arise upon any so petty and indirect an occasion as that of his debts; but that his debts were in their very first origin purely ministerial to his ambition; and that his revolutionary plans were at all periods of his life a direct and foremost object. In this there was in reality no want of patriotism; it had become evident to every body that Rome, under its present constitution, must fall; and the sole question was - by whom? Even Pompey, not by nature of an aspiring turn, and prompted to his ambitious course undoubtedly by circumstances and the friends who besieged him, was in the habit of saying, "Sylla potuit, ego non potero?" And the fact was, that if, from the death of Sylla, Rome recovered some transient show of constitutional integrity, that happened not by any lingering virtue that remained in her republican forms, but entirely through the equilibrium and mechanical counterpoise of rival factions.

In a case, therefore, where no benefit of choice was allowed to Rome as to the thing, but only as to the person - where a revolution was certain, and the point left open to doubt simply by whom that revolution should be accomplished - Cæsar had (to say the least) the same right to enter the arena in the character of candidate as could belong to any one of his rivals. And that he *did* enter that arena constructively, and by secret design, from his very earliest manhood, may be gathered from this - that he suffered no openings towards a revolution, provided they had any hope in them, to escape his participation. It is familiarly known that he was engaged pretty deeply in the conspiracy of Catiline, [Footnote: Suetonius, speaking of this conspiracy, says, that Cæsar was *nominatos inter socios Catilinæ*, which has been erroneously understood to mean that he was *talked of* as an accomplice; but in fact, as Casaubon first pointed out, *nominatus* is a technical term of the Roman jurisprudence, and means that he was formally denounced.] and that he incurred considerable risk on that occasion; but it is less known, and has indeed escaped the notice of historians generally, that he was a party to at least two other conspiracies. There was even a fourth, meditated by Crassus, which Cæsar so far encouraged as to undertake a journey to Rome from a very distant quarter, merely with a view to such chances as it might offer to him; but as it did not, upon examination, seem to him a very promising scheme, he judged it best to look coldly upon it, or not to embark in it by any personal co-operation. Upon these and other facts we build our inference - that the scheme of a revolution was the one great purpose of Cæsar, from his first entrance upon public life. Nor does it appear that he cared much by whom it was undertaken, provided only there seemed to be any sufficient resources for carrying it through, and for sustaining the first collision with the regular forces of the existing

Thomas de Quincey

government. He relied, it seems, on his own personal superiority for raising him to the head of affairs eventually, let who would take the nominal lead at first. To the same result, it will be found, tended the vast stream of Cæsar's liberalities. From the senator downwards to the lowest *fœx Romuli*, he had a hired body of dependents, both in and out of Rome, equal in numbers to a nation. In the provinces, and in distant kingdoms, he pursued the same schemes. Every where he had a body of mercenary partisans; kings are known to have taken his pay. And it is remarkable that even in his character of commander in chief, where the number of legions allowed to him for the accomplishment of his mission raised him for a number of years above all fear of coercion or control, he persevered steadily in the same plan of providing for the day when he might need assistance, not from the state, but *against* the state. For amongst the private anecdotes which came to light under the researches made into his history after his death, was this - that, soon after his first entrance upon his government in Gaul, he had raised, equipped, disciplined, and maintained, from his own private funds, a legion amounting, perhaps, to six or seven thousand men, who were bound by no sacrament of military obedience to the state, nor owed fealty to any auspices except those of Cæsar. This legion, from the fashion of their crested helmets, which resembled the crested heads of a small bird of the lark species, received the popular name of the *Alauda* (or Lark) legion. And very singular it was that Cato, or Marcellus, or some amongst those enemies of Cæsar, who watched his conduct during the period of his Gaulish command with the vigilance of rancorous malice, should not have come to the knowledge of this fact; in which case we may be sure that it would have been denounced to the senate.

Such, then, for its purpose and its uniform motive, was the sagacious munificence of Cæsar. Apart from this motive, and considered in and for itself, and simply with a reference to the splendid forms which it often assumed, this munificence would furnish the materials for a volume. The public entertainments of Cæsar, his spectacles and shows, his naumachiæ, and the pomps of his unrivalled triumphs, (the closing triumphs of the Republic,) were severally the finest of their kind which had then been brought forward. Sea-fights were exhibited upon the grandest scale, according to every known variety of nautical equipment and mode of conflict, upon a vast lake formed artificially for that express purpose. Mimic land-fights were conducted, in which all the circumstances of real war were so faithfully rehearsed, that even elephants "indorsed with towers," twenty on each side, took part in the combat. Dramas were represented in every known language, (*per omnium linguarum histriones.*) And hence [that is, from the conciliatory feeling thus expressed towards the various tribes of foreigners resident in Rome] some have derived an explanation of what is else a mysterious circumstance amongst the ceremonial observances at Cæsar's funeral - that all people of foreign nations then residing at Rome, distinguished themselves by the conspicuous share which they took in the public mourning; and that, beyond all other foreigners, the Jews for night after night kept watch and ward about the emperor's grave. Never before, according to traditions which lasted through several generations in Rome, had there been so vast a conflux of the human race congregated to any one centre, on any one attraction of business or of pleasure, as to Rome, on occasion of these spectacles exhibited by Cæsar.

Thomas de Quincey

In our days, the greatest occasional gatherings of the human race are in India, especially at the great fair of the *Hurdwar*, in the northern part of Hindostan; a confluence of many millions is sometimes seen at that spot, brought together under the mixed influences of devotion and commercial business, and dispersed as rapidly as they had been convoked. Some such spectacle of nations crowding upon nations, and some such Babylonian confusion of dresses, complexions, languages, and jargons, was then witnessed at Rome. Accommodations within doors, and under roofs of houses, or of temples, was altogether impossible. Myriads encamped along the streets, and along the high-roads in the vicinity of Rome. Myriads of myriads lay stretched on the ground, without even the slight protection of tents, in a vast circuit about the city. Multitudes of men, even senators, and others of the highest rank, were trampled to death in the crowds. And the whole family of man seemed at that time gathered together at the bidding of the great Dictator. But these, or any other themes connected with the public life of Cæsar, we notice only in those circumstances which have been overlooked, or partially represented by historians. Let us now, in conclusion, bring forward, from the obscurity in which they have hitherto lurked, the anecdotes which describe the habits of his private life, his tastes, and personal peculiarities.

In person, he was tall, fair, and of limbs distinguished for their elegant proportions and gracility. His eyes were black and piercing. These circumstances continued to be long remembered, and no doubt were constantly recalled to the eyes of all persons in the imperial palaces, by pictures, busts, and statues; for we find the same description of his personal appearance three centuries afterwards, in a work of the Emperor Julian's. He was a most accomplished horseman, and a master (*peritissimus*) in the use of arms. But, notwithstanding his skill in horsemanship, it seems that, when he accompanied his army on marches, he walked oftener than he rode; no doubt, with a view to the benefit of his example, and to express that sympathy with his soldiers which gained him their hearts so entirely. On other occasions, when travelling apart from his army, he seems more frequently to have rode in a carriage than on horseback. His purpose, in making this preference, must have been with a view to the transport of luggage. The carriage which he generally used was a *rheda*, a sort of gig, or rather curricle, for it was a four-wheeled carriage, and adapted (as we find from the imperial regulations for the public carriages, &c.) to the conveyance of about half a ton. The mere personal baggage which Cæsar carried with him, was probably considerable, for he was a man of the most elegant habits, and in all parts of his life sedulously attentive to elegance of personal appearance. The length of journeys which he accomplished within a given time, appears even to us at this day, and might well therefore appear to his contemporaries, truly astonishing. A distance of one hundred miles was no extraordinary day's journey for him in a *rheda*, such as we have described it. So elegant were his habits, and so constant his demand for the luxurious accommodations of polished life, as it then existed in Rome, that he is said to have carried with him, as indispensable parts of his personal baggage, the little lozenges and squares of ivory, and other costly materials, which were wanted for the tessellated flooring of his tent. Habits such as these will easily account for his travelling in a carriage rather than on horseback.

Thomas de Quincey

The courtesy and obliging disposition of Cæsar were notorious, and both were illustrated in some anecdotes which survived for generations in Rome. Dining on one occasion at a table, where the servants had inadvertently, for salad-oil, furnished some sort of coarse lamp-oil, Cæsar would not allow the rest of the company to point out the mistake to their host, for fear of shocking him too much by exposing the mistake. At another time, whilst halting at a little *cabaret*, when one of his retinue was suddenly taken ill, Cæsar resigned to his use the sole bed which the house afforded. Incidents, as trifling as these, express the urbanity of Cæsar's nature; and, hence, one is the more surprised to find the alienation of the senate charged, in no trifling degree, upon a failure in point of courtesy. Cæsar neglected to rise from his seat, on their approaching him in a body with an address of congratulation. It is said, and we can believe it, that he gave deeper offence by this one defect in a matter of ceremonial observance, than by all his substantial attacks upon their privileges. What we find it difficult to believe, however, is not that result from the offence, but the possibility of the offence itself, from one so little arrogant as Cæsar, and so entirely a man of the world. He was told of the disgust which he had given, and we are bound to believe his apology, in which he charged it upon sickness, which would not at the moment allow him to maintain a standing attitude. Certainly the whole tenor of his life was not courteous only, but kind; and, to his enemies, merciful in a degree which implied so much more magnanimity than men in general could understand, that by many it was put down to the account of weakness.

Weakness, however, there was none in Caius Cæsar; and, that there might be none, it was fortunate that conspiracy should have cut him off in the full vigor of his faculties, in the very meridian of his glory, and on the brink of completing a series of gigantic achievements. Amongst these are numbered - a digest of the entire body of laws, even then become unwieldy and oppressive; the establishment of vast and comprehensive public libraries, Greek as well as Latin; the chastisement of Dacia; the conquest of Parthia; and the cutting a ship canal through the Isthmus of Corinth. The reformation of the calendar he had already accomplished. And of all his projects it may be said, that they were equally patriotic in their purpose, and colossal in their proportions.

As an orator, Cæsar's merit was so eminent, that, according to the general belief, had he found time to cultivate this department of civil exertion, the precise supremacy of Cicero would have been made questionable, or the honors would have been divided. Cicero himself was of that opinion; and on different occasions applied the epithet *Splendidus* to Cæsar, as though in some exclusive sense, or with a peculiar emphasis, due to him. His taste was much simpler, chaster, and disinclined to the *florid* and ornamental, than that of Cicero. So far he would, in that condition of the Roman culture and feeling, have been less acceptable to the public; but, on the other hand, he would have compensated this disadvantage by much more of natural and Demosthenic fervor.

In literature, the merits of Cæsar are familiar to most readers. Under the modest title of *Commentaries*, he meant to offer the records of his Gallic and British campaigns, simply as notes, or memoranda, afterwards to be worked up by regular historians; but, as Cicero observes, their merit was such in the eyes of the

Thomas de Quincey

discerning, that all judicious writers shrank from the attempt to alter them. In another instance of his literary labors, he showed a very just sense of true dignity. Rightly conceiving that every thing patriotic was dignified, and that to illustrate or polish his native language, was a service of real patriotism, he composed a work on the grammar and orthoepy of the Latin language. Cicero and himself were the only Romans of distinction in that age, who applied themselves with true patriotism to the task of purifying and ennobling their mother tongue. Both were aware of the transcendent quality of the Grecian literature; but that splendor did not depress their hopes of raising their own to something of the same level. As respected the natural wealth of the two languages, it was the private opinion of Cicero, that the Latin had the advantage; and if Cæsar did not accompany him to that length, he yet felt that it was but the more necessary to draw forth any single advantage which it really had. [Footnote: Cæsar had the merit of being the first person to propose the daily publication of the acts and votes of the senate. In the form of public and official dispatches, he made also some useful innovations; and it may be mentioned, for the curiosity of the incident, that the cipher which he used in his correspondence, was the following very simple one: - For every letter of the alphabet he substituted that which stood fourth removed from it in the order of succession. Thus, for A, he used D; for D, G, and so on.]

Was Cæsar, upon the whole, the greatest of men? Dr. Beattie once observed, that if that question were left to be collected from the suffrages already expressed in books, and scattered throughout the literature of all nations, the scale would be found to have turned prodigiously in Cæsar's favor, as against any single competitor; and there is no doubt whatsoever, that even amongst his own countrymen, and his own contemporaries, the same verdict would have been returned, had it been collected upon the famous principle of Themistocles, that *he* should be reputed the first, whom the greatest number of rival voices had pronounced the second.

Thomas de Quincey

CHAPTER II.

The situation of the Second Cæsar, at the crisis of the great Dictator's assassination, was so hazardous and delicate, as to confer interest upon a character not otherwise attractive. To many, we know it was positively repulsive, and in the very highest degree. In particular, it is recorded of Sir William Jones, that he regarded this emperor with feelings of abhorrence so *personal* and deadly, as to refuse him his customary titular honors whenever he had occasion to mention him by name. Yet it was the whole Roman people that conferred upon him his title of *Augustus*. But Sir William, ascribing no force to the acts of a people who had sunk so low as to exult in their chains, and to decorate with honors the very instruments of their own vassalage, would not recognise this popular creation, and spoke of him always by his family name of Octavius. The flattery of the populace, by the way, must, in this instance, have been doubly acceptable to the emperor, first, for what it gave, and secondly, for what it concealed. Of his grand-uncle, the first Cæsar, a tradition survives - that of all the distinctions created in his favor, either by the senate or the people, he put most value upon the laurel crown which was voted to him after his last campaigns - a beautiful and conspicuous memorial to every eye of his great public acts, and at the same time an overshadowing veil of his one sole personal defect. This laurel diadem at once proclaimed his civic grandeur, and concealed his baldness, a defect which was more mortifying to a Roman than it would be to ourselves, from the peculiar theory which then prevailed as to its probable origin. A gratitude of the same mixed quality must naturally have been felt by the Second Cæsar for his title of *Augustus*, which, whilst it illustrated his public character by the highest expression of majesty, set apart and sequestrated to public functions, had also the agreeable effect of withdrawing from the general remembrance his obscure descent. For the Octavian house [*gens*] had in neither of its branches risen to any great splendor of civic distinction, and in his own, to little or none. The same titular decoration, therefore, so offensive to the celebrated Whig, was, in the eyes of Augustus, at once a trophy of public merit, a monument of public gratitude, and an effectual obliteration of his own natal obscurity.

But, if merely odious to men of Sir William's principles, to others the character of Augustus, in relation to the circumstances which surrounded him, was not without its appropriate interest. He was summoned in early youth, and without warning, to face a crisis of tremendous hazard, being at the same time himself a man of no very great constitutional courage; perhaps he was even a coward. And this we say without meaning to adopt as gospel truths all the party reproaches of Anthony. Certainly he was utterly unfurnished by nature with those endowments which seemed to be indispensable in a successor to the power of the great Dictator. But exactly in these deficiencies, and in certain accidents unfavorable to his ambition, lay his security. He had been adopted by his grand-uncle, Julius. That adoption made him, to all intents and purposes of law, the son of his great patron; and

Thomas de Quincey

doubtless, in a short time, this adoption would have been applied to more extensive uses, and as a station of vantage for introducing him to the public favor. From the inheritance of the Julian estates and family honors, he would have been trained to mount, as from a stepping-stone, to the inheritance of the Julian power and political station; and the Roman people would have been familiarized to regard him in that character. But, luckily for himself, the finishing, or ceremonial acts, were yet wanting in this process - the political heirship was inchoate and imperfect. Tacitly understood, indeed, it was; but, had it been formally proposed and ratified, there cannot be a doubt that the young Octavius would have been pointed out to the vengeance of the patriots, and included in the scheme of the conspirators, as a fellow-victim with his nominal father; and would have been cut off too suddenly to benefit by that reaction of popular feeling which saved the partisans of the Dictator, by separating the conspirators, and obliging them, without loss of time, to look to their own safety. It was by this fortunate accident that the young heir and adopted son of the first Cæsar not only escaped assassination, but was enabled to postpone indefinitely the final and military struggle for the vacant seat of empire, and in the mean time to maintain a coequal rank with the leaders in the state, by those arts and resources in which he was superior to his competitors. His place in the favor of Caius Julius was of power sufficient to give him a share in any triumvirate which could be formed; but, wanting the formality of a regular introduction to the people, and the ratification of their acceptance, that place was not sufficient to raise him permanently into the perilous and invidious station of absolute supremacy which he afterwards occupied. The *felicity* of Augustus was often vaunted by antiquity, (with whom success was not so much a test of merit as itself a merit of the highest quality,) and in no instance was this felicity more conspicuous than in the first act of his entrance upon the political scene. No doubt his friends and enemies alike thought of him, at the moment of Cæsar's assassination, as we now think of a young man heir-elect to some person of immense wealth, cut off by a sudden death before he has had time to ratify a will in execution of his purposes. Yet in fact the case was far otherwise. Brought forward distinctly as the successor of Cæsar's power, had he even, by some favorable accident of absence from Rome, or otherwise, escaped being involved in that great man's fate, he would at all events have been thrown upon the instant necessity of defending his supreme station by arms. To have left it unasserted, when once solemnly created in his favor by a reversionary title, would have been deliberately to resign it. This would have been a confession of weakness liable to no disguise, and ruinous to any subsequent pretensions. Yet, without preparation of means, with no development of resources nor growth of circumstances, an appeal to arms would, in his case, have been of very doubtful issue. His true weapons, for a long period, were the arts of vigilance and dissimulation. Cultivating these, he was enabled to prepare for a contest which, undertaken prematurely, must have ruined him, and to raise himself to a station of even military pre-eminence to those who naturally, and by circumstances, were originally every way superior to himself.

The qualities in which he really excelled, the gifts of intrigue, patience, long-suffering, dissimulation, and tortuous fraud, were thus brought into play, and allowed their full value. Such qualities had every

Thomas de Quincey

chance of prevailing in the long run, against the noble carelessness and the impetuosity of the passionate Anthony - and they *did* prevail. Always on the watch to lay hold of those opportunities which the generous negligence of his rival was but too frequently throwing in his way - unless by the sudden reverses of war and the accidents of battle, which as much as possible, and as long as possible, he declined - there could be little question in any man's mind, that eventually he would win his way to a solitary throne, by a policy so full of caution and subtlety. He was sure to risk nothing which could be had on easier terms; and nothing, unless for a great overbalance of gain in prospect; to lose nothing which he had once gained; and in no case to miss an advantage, or sacrifice an opportunity, by any consideration of generosity. No modern insurance office but would have guaranteed an event depending upon the final success of Augustus, on terms far below those which they must in prudence have exacted from the fiery and adventurous Anthony. Each was an ideal in his own class. But Augustus, having finally triumphed, has met with more than justice from succeeding ages. Even Lord Bacon says, that, by comparison with Julius Cæsar, he was "*non tam impar quam dispar*," surely a most extravagant encomium, applied to whomsoever. On the other hand, Anthony, amongst the most signal misfortunes of his life, might number it, that Cicero, the great dispenser of immortality, in whose hands (more perhaps than in any one man's of any age) were the vials of good and evil fame, should happen to have been his bitter and persevering enemy. It is, however, some balance to this, that Shakspeare had a just conception of the original grandeur which lay beneath that wild tempestuous nature presented by Anthony to the eye of the undiscriminating world. It is to the honor of

Shakspeare, that he should have been able to discern the true coloring of this most original character, under the smoke and tarnish of antiquity. It is no less to the honor of the great triumvir, that a strength of coloring should survive in his character, capable of baffling the wrongs and ravages of time. Neither is it to be thought strange that a character should have been misunderstood and falsely appreciated for nearly two thousand years. It happens not uncommonly, especially amongst an unimaginative people like the Romans, that the characters of men are ciphers and enigmas to their own age, and are first read and interpreted by a far distant posterity. Stars are supposed to exist, whose light has been travelling for many thousands of years without having yet reached our system; and the eyes are yet unborn upon which their earliest rays will fall. Men like Mark Anthony , with minds of chaotic composition - light conflicting with darkness, proportions of colossal grandeur disfigured by unsymmetrical arrangement, the angelic in close neighborhood with the brutal - are first read in their true meaning by an age learned in the philosophy of the human heart. Of this philosophy the Romans had, by the necessities of education and domestic discipline not less than by original constitution of mind, the very narrowest visual range. In no literature whatsoever are so few tolerable notices to be found of any great truths in Psychology. Nor could this have been otherwise amongst a people who tried every thing by the standard of *social* value; never seeking for a canon of excellence, in man considered abstractedly in and for himself, and as having an independent value - but always and exclusively in man as a gregarious being, and designed for social uses and functions. Not man in his own peculiar nature, but man in his relations to other men, was the station from which the Roman speculators

Thomas de Quincey

took up their philosophy of human nature. Tried by such standard, Mark Anthony would be found wanting. As a citizen, he was irretrievably licentious, and therefore there needed not the bitter personal feud, which circumstances had generated between them, to account for the *acharnement* with which Cicero pursued him. Had Anthony been his friend even, or his near kinsman, Cicero must still have been his public enemy. And not merely for his vices; for even the grander features of his character, his towering ambition, his magnanimity, and the fascinations of his popular qualities, - were all, in the circumstances of those times, and in *his* position, of a tendency dangerously uncivic.

So remarkable was the opposition, at all points, between the second Cæsar and his rival, that whereas Anthony even in his virtues seemed dangerous to the state, Octavius gave a civic coloring to his most indifferent actions, and, with a Machiavelian policy, observed a scrupulous regard to the forms of the Republic, after every fragment of the republican institutions, the privileges of the republican magistrates, and the functions of the great popular officers, had been absorbed into his own autocracy. Even in the most prosperous days of the Roman State, when the democratic forces balanced, and were balanced by, those of the aristocracy, it was far from being a general or common praise, that a man was of a civic turn of mind, *animo civili*. Yet this praise did Augustus affect, and in reality attain, at a time when the very object of all civic feeling was absolutely extinct; so much are men governed by words. Suetonius assures us, that many evidences were current even to his times of this popular disposition (*civilitas*) in the emperor; and that it survived every experience of servile adulation in the Roman populace, and all the effects of long familiarity with irresponsible power in himself. Such a moderation of feeling, we are almost obliged to consider as a genuine and unaffected expression of his real nature; for, as an artifice of policy, it had soon lost its uses. And it is worthy of notice, that with the army he laid aside those popular manners as soon as possible, addressing them as *milites*, not (*according* to his earlier practice) as *commilitones*. It concerned his own security, to be jealous of encroachments on his power. But of his rank, and the honors which accompanied it, he seems to have been uniformly careless. Thus, he would never leave a town or enter it by daylight, unless some higher rule of policy obliged him to do so; by which means he evaded a ceremonial of public honor which was burdensome to all the parties concerned in it. Sometimes, however, we find that men, careless of honors in their own persons, are glad to see them settling upon their family and immediate connections. But here again Augustus showed the sincerity of his moderation. For upon one occasion, when the whole audience in the Roman theatre had risen upon the entrance of his two adopted sons, at that time not seventeen years old, he was highly displeased, and even thought it necessary to publish his displeasure in a separate edict. It is another, and a striking illustration of his humility, that he willingly accepted of public appointments, and sedulously discharged the duties attached to them, in conjunction with colleagues who had been chosen with little regard to his personal partialities. In the debates of the senate, he showed the same equanimity; suffering himself patiently to be contradicted, and even with circumstances of studied incivility. In the public elections, he gave his vote like any private citizen; and, when he happened to be a

Thomas de Quincey

candidate himself, he canvassed the electors with the same earnestness of personal application, as any other candidate with the least possible title to public favor from present power or past services. But, perhaps by no expressions of his civic spirit did Augustus so much conciliate men's minds, as by the readiness with which he participated in their social pleasures, and by the uniform severity with which he refused to apply his influence in any way which could disturb the pure administration of justice. The Roman juries (*judices* they were called), were very corrupt; and easily swayed to an unconscientious verdict, by the appearance in court of any great man on behalf of one of the parties interested: nor was such an interference with the course of private justice any ways injurious to the great man's character. The wrong which he promoted did but the more forcibly proclaim the warmth and fidelity of his friendships. So much the more generally was the uprightness of the emperor appreciated, who would neither tamper with justice himself, nor countenance any motion in that direction, though it were to serve his very dearest friend, either by his personal presence, or by the use of his name. And, as if it had been a trifle merely to forbear, and to show his regard to justice in this negative way, he even allowed himself to be summoned as a witness on trials, and showed no anger when his own evidence was overborne by stronger on the other side. This disinterested love of justice, and an integrity, so rare in the great men of Rome, could not but command the reverence of the people. But their affection, doubtless, was more conciliated by the freedom with which the emperor accepted invitations from all quarters, and shared continually in the festal pleasures of his subjects. This practice, however, he discontinued, or narrowed, as he advanced in years. Suetonius, who, as a true anecdote-monger, would solve every thing, and account for every change by some definite incident, charges this alteration in the emperor's condescensions upon one particular party at a wedding feast, where the crowd incommoded him much by their pressure and heat. But, doubtless, it happened to Augustus as to other men; his spirits failed, and his powers of supporting fatigue or bustle, as years stole upon him. Changes, coming by insensible steps, and not willingly acknowledged, for some time escape notice; until some sudden shock reminds a man forcibly to do that which he has long meditated in an irresolute way. The marriage banquet may have been the particular occasion from which Augustus stepped into the habits of old age, but certainly not the cause of so entire a revolution in his mode of living.

It might seem to throw some doubt, if not upon the fact, yet at least upon the sincerity, of his *civism*, that undoubtedly Augustus cultivated his kingly connections with considerable anxiety. It may have been upon motives merely political that he kept at Rome the children of nearly all the kings then known as allies or vassals of the Roman power: a curious fact, and not generally known. In his own palace were reared a number of youthful princes; and they were educated jointly with his own children. It is also upon record, that in many instances the fathers of these princes spontaneously repaired to Rome, and there assuming the Roman dress - as an expression of reverence to the majesty of the omnipotent State - did personal 'suit and service' (*more clientum*) to Augustus. It is an anecdote of not less curiosity, that a whole 'college' of kings subscribed money for a temple at Athens, to be dedicated in the name of Augustus. Throughout his life, indeed, this emperor paid a

Thomas de Quincey

marked attention to all the royal houses then known to Rome, as occupying the thrones upon the vast margin of the empire. It is true that in part this attention might be interpreted as given politically to so many lieutenants, wielding a remote or inaccessible power for the benefit of Rome. And the children of these kings might be regarded as hostages, ostensibly entertained for the sake of education, but really as pledges for their parents' fidelity, and also with a view to the large reversionary advantages which might be expected to arise upon the basis of so early and affectionate a connection. But it is not the less true, that, at one period of his life, Augustus did certainly meditate some closer personal connection with the royal families of the earth. He speculated, undoubtedly, on a marriage for himself with some barbarous princess, and at one time designed his daughter Julia as a wife for Cotiso, the king of the Getæ. Superstition perhaps disturbed the one scheme, and policy the other. He married, as is well known, for his final wife, and the partner of his life through its whole triumphant stage, Livia Drusilla; compelling her husband, Tiberius Nero, to divorce her, notwithstanding she was then six months advanced in pregnancy. With this lady, who was distinguished for her beauty, it is certain that he was deeply in love; and that might be sufficient to account for the marriage. It is equally certain, however, upon the concurring evidence of independent writers, that this connection had an oracular sanction - not to say, suggestion; a circumstance *which was long remembered*, and was afterwards noticed by the Christian poet Prudentius:

"Idque Deûm sortes et Apollinis antra dederunt
Consilium: nunquam meliùs nam cædere tædas
Responsum est, quàm cum prægnans

nova nupta jugatur."

His daughter Julia had been promised by turns, and always upon reasons of state, to a whole muster-roll of suitors; first of all, to a son of Mark Anthony; secondly, to the barbarous king; thirdly, to her first cousin - that Marcellus, the son of Octavia, only sister to Augustus, whose early death, in the midst of great expectations, Virgil has so beautifully introduced into the vision of Roman grandeurs as yet unborn, which Æneas beholds in the shades; fourthly, she was promised (and this time the promise was kept) to the fortunate soldier, Agrippa, whose low birth was not permitted to obscure his military merits. By him she had a family of children, upon whom, if upon any in this world, the wrath of Providence seems to have rested; for, excepting one, and in spite of all the favors that earth and heaven could unite to shower upon them, all came to an early, a violent, and an infamous end. Fifthly, upon the death of Agrippa, and again upon motives of policy, and in atrocious contempt of all the ties that nature and the human heart and human laws have hallowed, she was promised, (if that word may be applied to the violent obtrusion upon a man's bed of one who was doubly a curse - first, for what she brought, and, secondly, for what she took away,) and given to Tiberius, the future emperor. Upon the whole, as far as we can at this day make out the connection of a man's acts and purposes, which, even to his own age, were never entirely cleared up, it is probable that, so long as the triumvirate survived, and so long as the condition of Roman power or intrigues, and the distribution of Roman influence, were such as to leave a possibility that any new triumvirate should arise - so long Augustus was secretly meditating a retreat for himself at some barbarous court, against any sudden

Thomas de Quincey

reverse of fortune, by means of a domestic connection, which should give him the claim of a kinsman. Such a court, however unable to make head against the collective power of Rome, might yet present a front of resistance to any single partisan who should happen to acquire a brief ascendancy; or, at the worst, as a merely defensive power, might offer a retreat, secure in distance, and difficult access; or might be available as a means of delay for recovering from some else fatal defeat. It is certain that Augustus viewed Egypt with jealousy as a province, which might be turned to account in some such way by any aspiring insurgent. And it must have often struck him as a remarkable circumstance, which by good luck had turned out entirely to the advantage of his own family, but which might as readily have had an opposite result, that the three decisive battles of Pharsalia, of Thapsus, and of Munda, in which the empire of the world was three times over staked as the prize, had severally brought upon the defeated leaders a ruin which was total, absolute, and final. One hour had seen the whole fabric of their aspiring fortunes demolished; and no resource was left to them but either in suicide, (which, accordingly, even Cæsar had meditated at one stage of the battle of Munda, when it seemed to be going against him,) or in the mercy of the victor.

That a victor in a hundred fights should in his hundred-and-first, [Footnote:
     "The painful warrior, famoused for fight,
       After a thousand victories once foil'd,
       Is from the book of honor razed quite,
     And all the rest forgot for which he toil'd."
               Shakespeare's Sonnets.]
as in his first, risk the loss of that particular battle, is inseparable from the condition of man, and the

uncertainty of human means; but that the loss of this one battle should be equally fatal and irrecoverable with the loss of his first, that it should leave him with means no more cemented, and resources no better matured for retarding his fall, and throwing a long succession of hindrances in the way of his conqueror, argues some essential defect of system. Under our modern policy, military power - though it may be the growth of one man's life - soon takes root; a succession of campaigns is required for its extirpation; and it revolves backwards to its final extinction through all the stages by which originally it grew. On the Roman system this was mainly impossible from the solitariness of the Roman power; co-rival nations who might balance the victorious party, there were absolutely none; and all the underlings hastened to make their peace, whilst peace was yet open to them, on the known terms of absolute treachery to their former master, and instant surrender to the victor of the hour. For this capital defect in the tenure of Roman power, no matter in whose hands deposited, there was no absolute remedy. Many a sleepless night, during the perilous game which he played with Anthony, must have familiarized Octavius with that view of the risk, which to some extent was inseparable from his position as the leader in such a struggle carried on in such an empire. In this dilemma, struck with the extreme necessity of applying some palliation to the case, we have no doubt that Augustus would devise the scheme of laying some distant king under such obligations to fidelity as would suffice to stand the first shock of misfortune. Such a person would have power enough, of a direct military kind, to face the storm at its outbreak. He would have power of another kind in his distance. He would be sustained by the courage of hope, as a kinsman having a contingent interest in a

Thomas de Quincey

kinsman's prosperity. And, finally, he would be sustained by the courage of despair, as one who never could expect to be trusted by the opposite party. In the worst case, such a prince would always offer a breathing time and a respite to his friends, were it only by his remoteness, and if not the *means* of rallying, yet at least the *time* for rallying, more especially as the escape to his frontier would be easy to one who had long forecast it. We can hardly doubt that Augustus meditated such schemes; that he laid them aside only as his power began to cement and to knit together after the battle of Actium; and that the memory and the prudential tradition of this plan survived in the imperial family so long as itself survived. Amongst other anecdotes of the same tendency, two are recorded of Nero, the emperor in whom expired the line of the original Cæsars, which strengthen us in a belief of what is otherwise in itself so probable. Nero, in his first distractions, upon receiving the fatal tidings of the revolt in Gaul, when reviewing all possible plans of escape from the impending danger, thought at intervals of throwing himself on the protection of the barbarous King Vologesus. And twenty years afterwards, when the Pseudo-Nero appeared, he found a strenuous champion and protector in the king of the Parthians. Possibly, had an opportunity offered for searching the Parthian chancery, some treaty would have been found binding the kings of Parthia, from the age of Augustus through some generations downwards, in requital of services there specified, or of treasures lodged, to secure a perpetual asylum to the prosperity of the Julian family.

The cruelties of Augustus were perhaps equal in atrocity to any which are recorded; and the equivocal apology for those acts (one which might as well be used to aggravate as to palliate the case) is, that they were not prompted by a ferocious nature, but by calculating policy. He once actually slaughtered upon an altar, a large body of his prisoners; and such was the contempt with which he was regarded by some of that number, that, when led out to death, they saluted their other proscriber, Anthony, with military honors, acknowledging merit even in an enemy, but Augustus they passed with scornful silence, or with loud reproaches. Too certainly no man has ever contended for empire with unsullied conscience, or laid pure hands upon the ark of so magnificent a prize. Every friend to Augustus must have wished that the twelve years of his struggle might for ever be blotted out from human remembrance. During the forty-two years of his prosperity and his triumph, being above fear, he showed the natural lenity of his temper.

That prosperity, in a public sense, has been rarely equalled; but far different was his fate, and memorable was the contrast, within the circuit of his own family. This lord of the universe groaned as often as the ladies of his house, his daughter and grand-daughter, were mentioned. The shame which he felt on their account, led him even to unnatural designs, and to wishes not less so; for at one time he entertained a plan for putting the elder Julia to death - and at another, upon hearing that Phoebe (one of the female slaves in his household) had hanged herself, he exclaimed audibly, - "Would that I had been the father of Phoebe!" It must, however, be granted, that in this miserable affair he behaved with very little of his usual discretion. In the first paroxysms of his rage, on discovering his daughter's criminal conduct, he made a communication of the whole to the senate. That body could do nothing in such a matter, either by act or by suggestion; and in

Thomas de Quincey

a short time, as every body could have foreseen, he himself repented of his own want of self-command. Upon the whole, it cannot be denied, that, according to the remark of Jeremy Taylor, of all the men signally decorated by history, Augustus Cæsar is that one who exemplifies, in the most emphatic terms, the mixed tenor of human life, and the equitable distribution, even on this earth, of good and evil fortune. He made himself master of the world, and against the most formidable competitors; his power was absolute, from the rising to the setting sun; and yet in his own house, where the peasant who does the humblest chares, claims an undisputed authority, he was baffled, dishonored, and made ridiculous. He was loved by nobody; and if, at the moment of his death, he desired his friends to dismiss him from this world by the common expression of scenical applause, (*vos plaudite!*) in that valedictory injunction he expressed inadvertently the true value of his own long life, which, in strict candor, may be pronounced one continued series of histrionic efforts, and of excellent acting, adapted to selfish ends.

CHAPTER III.

The three next emperors, Caligula, Claudius, and Nero, were the last princes who had any connection by blood [Footnote: And this was entirely by the female side. The family descent of the first six Cæsars is so intricate, that it is rarely understood accurately; so that it may be well to state it briefly. Augustus was grand nephew to Julius Cæsar, being the son of his sister's daughter. He was also, by adoption, the *son* of Julius. He himself had one child only, viz. the infamous Julia, who was brought him by his second wife Scribonia; and through this Julia it was that the three princes, who succeeded to Tiberius, claimed relationship to Augustus. On that emperor's last marriage with Livia, he adopted the two sons whom she had borne to her divorced husband. These two noblemen, who stood in no degree of consanguinity whatever to Augustus, were Tiberius and Drusus. Tiberius left no children; but Drusus, the younger of the two brothers, by his marriage with the younger Antonia, (daughter of Mark Anthony,) had the celebrated Germanicus, and Claudius, (afterwards emperor.) Germanicus, though adopted by his uncle Tiberius, and destined to the empire, died prematurely. But, like Banquo, though he wore no crown, he left descendants who did. For, by his marriage with Agrippina, a daughter of Julia's by Agrippa, (and therefore grand-daughter of Augustus,) he had a large family, of whom one son became the

Thomas de Quincey

Emperor Caligula; and one of the daughters, Agrippina the younger, by her marriage with a Roman nobleman, became the mother of the Emperor Nero. Hence it appears that Tiberius was uncle to Claudius, Claudius was uncle to Caligula, Caligula was uncle to Nero. But it is observable, that Nero and Caligula stood in another degree of consanguinity to each other through their grandmothers, who were both daughters of Mark Anthony the triumvir; for the elder Antonia married the grandfather of Nero; the younger Antonia (as we have stated, above) married Drusus, the grandfather of Caligula; and again, by these two ladies, they were connected not only with each other, but also with the Julian house, for the two Antonias were daughters of Mark Anthony by Octavia, sister to Augustus.] with the Julian house. In Nero, the sixth emperor, expired the last of the Cæsars, who was such in reality. These three were also the first in that long line of monsters, who, at different times, under the title of Cæsars, dishonored humanity more memorably, than was possible, except in the cases of those (if any such can be named) who have abused the same enormous powers in times of the same civility, and in defiance of the same general illumination. But for them it is a fact, than some crimes, which now stain the page of history, would have been accounted fabulous dreams of impure romancers, taxing their extravagant imaginations to create combinations of wickedness more hideous than civilized men would tolerate, and more unnatural than the human heart could conceive. Let us, by way of example, take a short chapter from the diabolic life of Caligula: In what way did he treat his nearest and tenderest female connections? His mother had been tortured and murdered by another tyrant almost as fiendish as himself. She was happily removed from his cruelty. Disdaining, however, to acknowledge any connection with the blood of so obscure a man as Agrippa, he publicly gave out that his mother was indeed the daughter of Julia, but by an incestuous commerce with her father Augustus. His three sisters he debauched. One died, and her he canonized; the other two he prostituted to the basest of his own attendants. Of his wives, it would be hard to say whether they were first sought and won with more circumstances of injury and outrage, or dismissed with more insult and levity. The one whom he treated best, and with most profession of love, and who commonly rode by his side, equipped with spear and shield, to his military inspections and reviews of the soldiery, though not particularly beautiful, was exhibited to his friends at banquets in a state of absolute nudity. His motive for treating her with so much kindness, was probably that she brought him a daughter; and her he acknowledged as his own child, from the early brutality with which she attacked the eyes and cheeks of other infants who were presented to her as play-fellows. Hence it would appear that he was aware of his own ferocity, and treated it as a jest. The levity, indeed, which he mingled with his worst and most inhuman acts, and the slightness of the occasions upon which he delighted to hang his most memorable atrocities, aggravated their impression at the time, and must have contributed greatly to sharpen the sword of vengeance. His palace happened to be contiguous to the circus. Some seats, it seems, were open indiscriminately to the public; consequently, the only way in which they could be appropriated, was by taking possession of them as early as the midnight preceding any great exhibitions. Once, when it happened that his sleep was disturbed by such an occasion, he sent in soldiers to eject them; and with orders so rigorous, as it appeared by the event, that in

Thomas de Quincey

this singular tumult, twenty Roman knights, and as many mothers of families, were cudgelled to death upon the spot, to say nothing of what the reporter calls "innumeram turbam ceteram."

But this is a trifle to another anecdote reported by the same authority: - On some occasion it happened that a dearth prevailed, either generally of cattle, or of such cattle as were used for feeding the wild beasts reserved for the bloody exhibitions of the amphitheatre. Food could be had, and perhaps at no very exorbitant price, but on terms somewhat higher than the ordinary market price. A slight excuse served with Caligula for acts the most monstrous. Instantly repairing to the public jails, and causing all the prisoners to pass in review before him (*custodiarum seriem recognoscens*), he pointed to two bald-headed men, and ordered that the whole file of intermediate persons should be marched off to the dens of the wild beasts: "Tell them off," said he, "from the bald man to the bald man." Yet these were prisoners committed, not for punishment, but trial. Nor, had it been otherwise, were the charges against them equal, but running through every gradation of guilt. But the *elogia* or records of their commitment, he would not so much as look at. With such inordinate capacities for cruelty, we cannot wonder that he should in his common conversation have deplored the tameness and insipidity of his own times and reign, as likely to be marked by no wide-spreading calamity." Augustus," said he, "was happy; for in his reign occurred the slaughter of Varus and his legions. Tiberius was happy; for in his occurred that glorious fall of the great amphitheatre at Fidenæ. But for me - alas! alas!" And then he would pray earnestly for fire or slaughter - pestilence or famine. Famine indeed was to some extent in his own power; and accordingly, as far as his courage would carry him, he did occasionally try that mode of tragedy upon the people of Rome, by shutting up the public granaries against them. As he blended his mirth and a truculent sense of the humorous with his cruelties, we cannot wonder that he should soon blend his cruelties with his ordinary festivities, and that his daily banquets would soon become insipid without them. Hence he required a daily supply of executions in his own halls and banqueting rooms; nor was a dinner held to be complete without such a dessert. Artists were sought out who had dexterity and strength enough to do what Lucan somewhere calls *ensem rotare*, that is, to cut off a human head with one whirl of the sword. Even this became insipid, as wanting one main element of misery to the sufferer, and an indispensable condiment to the jaded palate of the connoisseur, viz., a lingering duration. As a pleasant variety, therefore, the tormentors were introduced with their various instruments of torture; and many a dismal tragedy in that mode of human suffering was conducted in the sacred presence during the emperor's hours of amiable relaxation.

The result of these horrid indulgences was exactly what we might suppose, that even such scenes ceased to irritate the languid appetite, and yet that without them life was not endurable. Jaded and exhausted as the sense of pleasure had become in Caligula, still it could be roused into any activity by nothing short of these murderous luxuries. Hence, it seems, that he was continually tampering and dallying with the thought of murder; and like the old Parisian jeweller Cardillac, in Louis XIV.'s time, who was stung with a perpetual lust for murdering the possessors of fine diamonds - not so much for the value of the prize (of which he never

Thomas de Quincey

hoped to make any use), as from an unconquerable desire of precipitating himself into the difficulties and hazards of the murder, - Caligula never failed to experience (and sometimes even to acknowledge) a secret temptation to any murder which seemed either more than usually abominable, or more than usually difficult. Thus, when the two consuls were seated at his table, he burst out into sudden and profuse laughter; and, upon their courteously requesting to know what witty and admirable conceit might be the occasion of the imperial mirth, he frankly owned to them, and doubtless he did not improve their appetites by this confession, that in fact he was laughing, and that he could not but laugh, (and then the monster laughed immoderately again,) at the pleasant thought of seeing them both headless, and that with so little trouble to himself, (*uno suo nutu,*) he could have both their throats cut. No doubt he was continually balancing the arguments for and against such little escapades; nor had any person a reason for security in the extraordinary obligations, whether of hospitality or of religious vows, which seemed to lay him under some peculiar restraints in that case above all others; for such circumstances of peculiarity, by which the murder would be stamped with unusual atrocity, were but the more likely to make its fascinations irresistible. Hence he dallied with the thoughts of murdering her whom he loved best, and indeed exclusively - his wife Cæsonia; and whilst fondling her, and toying playfully with her polished throat, he was distracted (as he half insinuated to her) between the desire of caressing it, which might be often repeated, and that of cutting it, which could be gratified but once.

Nero (for as to Claudius, he came too late to the throne to indulge any propensities of this nature with so little discretion) was but a variety of the same species. He also was an amateur, and an enthusiastic amateur of murder. But as this taste, in the most ingenious hands, is limited and monotonous in its modes of manifestation, it would be tedious to run through the long Suetonian roll-call of his peccadilloes in this way. One only we shall cite, to illustrate the amorous delight with which he pursued any murder which happened to be seasoned highly to his taste by enormous atrocity, and by almost unconquerable difficulty. It would really be pleasant, were it not for the revolting consideration of the persons concerned, and their relation to each other, to watch the tortuous pursuit of the hunter, and the doubles of the game, in this obstinate chase. For certain reasons of state, as Nero attempted to persuade himself, but in reality because no other crime had the same attractions of unnatural horror about it, he resolved to murder his mother Agrippina. This being settled, the next thing was to arrange the mode and the tools. Naturally enough, according to the custom then prevalent in Rome, he first attempted the thing by poison. The poison failed: for Agrippina, anticipating tricks of this kind, had armed her constitution against them, like Mithridates; and daily took potent antidotes and prophylactics. Or else (which is more probable) the emperor's agent in such purposes, fearing his sudden repentance and remorse on first hearing of his mother's death, or possibly even witnessing her agonies, had composed a poison of inferior strength. This had certainly occurred in the case of Britannicus, who had thrown off with ease the first dose administered to him by Nero. Upon which he had summoned to his presence the woman employed in the affair, and compelling her by threats to mingle a more powerful potion in his own presence, had tried it successively upon different animals, until he was

Thomas de Quincey

satisfied with its effects; after which, immediately inviting Britannicus to a banquet, he had finally dispatched him. On Agrippina, however, no changes in the poison, whether of kind or strength, had any effect; so that, after various trials, this mode of murder was abandoned, and the emperor addressed himself to other plans. The first of these was some curious mechanical device, by which a false ceiling was to have been suspended by bolts above her bed; and in the middle of the night, the bolt being suddenly drawn, a vast weight would have descended with a ruinous destruction to all below. This scheme, however, taking air from the indiscretion of some amongst the accomplices, reached the ears of Agrippina; upon which the old lady looked about her too sharply to leave much hope in that scheme: so *that* also was abandoned. Next, he conceived the idea of an artificial ship, which, at the touch of a few springs, might fall to pieces in deep water. Such a ship was prepared, and stationed at a suitable point. But the main difficulty remained, which was to persuade the old lady to go on board. Not that she knew in this case *who* had been the ship-builder, for that would have ruined all; but it seems that she took it ill to be hunted in this murderous spirit, and was out of humor with her son; besides, that any proposal coming from him, though previously indifferent to her, would have instantly become suspected. To meet this difficulty, a sort of reconciliation was proposed, and a very affectionate message sent, which had the effect of throwing Agrippina off her guard, and seduced her to Baiæ for the purpose of joining the emperor's party at a great banquet held in commemoration of a solemn festival. She came by water in a sort of light frigate, and was to return in the same way. Meantime Nero tampered with the commander of her vessel, and prevailed upon him to wreck it. What was to be done?

The great lady was anxious to return to Rome, and no proper conveyance was at hand. Suddenly it was suggested, as if by chance, that a ship of the emperor's, new and properly equipped, was moored at a neighboring station. This was readily accepted by Agrippina: the emperor accompanied her to the place of embarkation, took a most tender leave of her, and saw her set sail. It was necessary that the vessel should get into deep water before the experiment could be made; and with the utmost agitation this pious son awaited news of the result. Suddenly a messenger rushed breathless into his presence, and horrified him by the joyful information that his august mother had met with an alarming accident; but, by the blessing of Heaven, had escaped safe and sound, and was now on her road to mingle congratulations with her affectionate son. The ship, it seems, had done its office; the mechanism had played admirably; but who can provide for every thing? The old lady, it turned out, could swim like a duck; and the whole result had been to refresh her with a little sea-bathing. Here was worshipful intelligence. Could any man's temper be expected to stand such continued sieges? Money, and trouble, and infinite contrivance, wasted upon one old woman, who absolutely would not, upon any terms, be murdered! Provoking it certainly was; and of a man like Nero it could not be expected that he should any longer dissemble his disgust, or put up with such repeated affronts. He rushed upon his simple congratulating friend, swore that he had come to murder him, and as nobody could have suborned him but Agrippina, he ordered her off to instant execution. And, unquestionably, if people will not be murdered quietly and in a civil way, they must expect that such forbearance is not to continue for ever; and obviously have themselves only to blame for any harshness or

Thomas de Quincey

violence which they may have rendered necessary.

It is singular, and shocking at the same time, to mention, that, for this atrocity, Nero did absolutely receive solemn congratulations from all orders of men. With such evidences of base servility in the public mind, and of the utter corruption which they had sustained in their elementary feelings, it is the less astonishing that he should have made other experiments upon the public patience, which seem expressly designed to try how much it would support. Whether he were really the author of the desolating fire which consumed Rome for six [Footnote: But a memorial stone, in its inscription, makes the time longer: "Quando urbs per novem dies arsit Neronianis temporibus."] days and seven nights, and drove the mass of the people into the tombs and sepulchres for shelter, is yet a matter of some doubt. But one great presumption against it, founded on its desperate imprudence, as attacking the people in their primary comforts, is considerably weakened by the enormous servility of the Romans in the case just stated: they who could volunteer congratulations to a son for butchering his mother, (no matter on what pretended suspicions,) might reasonably be supposed incapable of any resistance which required courage even in a case of self-defence, or of just revenge. The direct reasons, however, for implicating him in this affair, seem at present insufficient. He was displeased, it seems, with the irregularity and unsightliness of the antique buildings, and also with the streets, as too narrow and winding, (*angustiis flexurisque vicorum.*) But in this he did but express what was no doubt the common judgment of all his contemporaries, who had seen the beautiful cities of Greece and Asia Minor. The Rome of that time was in many parts built of wood;

and there is much probability that it must have been a *picturesque* city, and in parts almost grotesque. But it is remarkable, and a fact which we have nowhere seen noticed, that the ancients, whether Greeks or Romans, had no eye for the picturesque; nay, that it was a sense utterly unawakened amongst them; and that the very conception of the picturesque, as of a thing distinct from the beautiful, is not once alluded to through the whole course of ancient literature, nor would it have been intelligible to any ancient critic; so that, whatever attraction for the eye might exist in the Rome of that day, there is little doubt that it was of a kind to be felt only by modern spectators. Mere dissatisfaction with its external appearance, which must have been a pretty general sentiment, argued, therefore, no necessary purpose of destroying it. Certainly it would be a weightier ground of suspicion, if it were really true, that some of his agents were detected on the premises of different senators in the act of applying combustibles to their mansions. But this story wears a very fabulous air. For why resort to the private dwellings of great men, where any intruder was sure of attracting notice, when the same effect, and with the same deadly results, might have been attained quietly and secretly in so many of the humble Roman *coenacula*?

The great loss on this memorable occasion was in the heraldic and ancestral honors of the city. Historic Rome then went to wreck for ever. Then perished the *domus priscorum ducum hostilibus adhuc spoliis adornatæ*; the "rostral" palace; the mansion of the Pompeys; the Blenheims and the Strathfieldsays of the Scipios, the Marcelli, the Paulli, and the Cæsars; then perished the aged trophies from Carthage and from Gaul; and, in short, as the historian sums up the

Thomas de Quincey

lamentable desolation, *"quidquid visendum atque memorabile ex antiquitate duraverat."* And this of itself might lead one to suspect the emperor's hand as the original agent; for by no one act was it possible so entirely and so suddenly to wean the people from their old republican recollections, and in one week to obliterate the memorials of their popular forces, and the trophies of many ages. The old people of Rome were gone; their characteristic dress even was gone; for already in the time of Augustus they had laid aside the *toga*, and assumed the cheaper and scantier *pænula*, so that the eye sought in vain for Virgil's

"Romanes rerum dominos gentemque *togatam*."

Why, then, after all the constituents of Roman grandeur had passed away, should their historical trophies survive, recalling to them the scenes of departed heroism, in which they had no personal property, and suggesting to them vain hopes, which for them were never to be other than chimeras? Even in that sense, therefore, and as a great depository of heart-stirring historical remembrances, Rome was profitably destroyed; and in any other sense, whether for health or for the conveniences of polished life, or for architectural magnificence, there never was a doubt that the Roman people gained infinitely by this conflagration. For, like London, it arose from its ashes with a splendor proportioned to its vast expansion of wealth and population; and marble took the place of wood. For the moment, however, this event must have been felt by the people as an overwhelming calamity. And it serves to illustrate the passive endurance and timidity of the popular temper, and to what extent it might be provoked with impunity, that in this state of general irritation and effervescence, Nero absolutely forbade them to meddle with the ruins of their own dwellings - taking that charge upon himself, with a view to the vast wealth which he anticipated from sifting the rubbish. And, as if that mode of plunder were not sufficient, he exacted compulsory contributions to the rebuilding of the city so indiscriminately, as to press heavily upon all men's finances; and thus, in the public account which universally imputed the fire to him, he was viewed as a twofold robber, who sought to heal one calamity by the infliction of another and a greater.

The monotony of wickedness and outrage becomes at length fatiguing to the coarsest and most callous senses; and the historian, even, who caters professedly for the taste which feeds upon the monstrous and the hyperbolical, is glad at length to escape from the long evolution of his insane atrocities, to the striking and truly scenical catastrophe of retribution which overtook them, and avenged the wrongs of an insulted world. Perhaps history contains no more impressive scenes than those in which the justice of Providence at length arrested the monstrous career of Nero.

It was at Naples, and, by a remarkable fatality, on the very anniversary of his mother's murder, that he received the first intelligence of the revolt in Gaul under the Proprætor Vindex. This news for about a week he treated with levity; and, like Henry VII. of England, who was nettled, not so much at being proclaimed a rebel, as because he was described under the slighting denomination of "one Henry Tidder or Tudor," he complained bitterly that Vindex had mentioned him by his family name of Ænobarbus, rather than his assumed one of Nero. But much more keenly he resented the insulting description of himself

Thomas de Quincey

as a "miserable harper," appealing to all about him whether they had ever known a better, and offering to stake the truth of all the other charges against himself upon the accuracy of this in particular. So little even in this instance was he alive to the true point of the insult; not thinking it any disgrace that a Roman emperor should be chiefly known to the world in the character of a harper, but only if he should happen to be a bad one. Even in those days, however, imperfect as were the means of travelling, rebellion moved somewhat too rapidly to allow any long interval of security so light-minded as this. One courier followed upon the heels of another, until he felt the necessity for leaving Naples; and he returned to Rome, as the historian says, *prætrepidus*; by which word, however, according to its genuine classical acceptation, we apprehend is not meant that he was highly alarmed, but only that he was in a great hurry. That he was not yet under any real alarm (for he trusted in certain prophecies, which, like those made to the Scottish tyrant "kept the promise to the ear, but broke it to the sense,") is pretty evident, from his conduct on reaching the capitol. For, without any appeal to the senate or the people, but sending out a few summonses to some men of rank, he held a hasty council, which he speedily dismissed, and occupied the rest of the day with experiments on certain musical instruments of recent invention, in which the keys were moved by hydraulic contrivances. He had come to Rome, it appeared, merely from a sense of decorum.

Suddenly, however, arrived news, which fell upon him with the force of a thunderbolt, that the revolt had extended to the Spanish provinces, and was headed by Galba. He fainted upon hearing this; and falling to the ground, lay for a long time lifeless, as it seemed, and speechless. Upon coming to himself again, he tore his robe, struck his forehead, and exclaimed aloud - that for him all was over. In this agony of mind, it strikes across the utter darkness of the scene with the sense of a sudden and cheering flash, recalling to us the possible goodness and fidelity of human nature - when we read that one humble creature adhered to him, and, according to her slender means, gave him consolation during these trying moments; this was the woman who had tended his infant years; and she now recalled to his remembrance such instances of former princes in adversity, as appeared fitted to sustain his drooping spirits. It seems, however, that, according to the general course of violent emotions, the rebound of high spirits was in proportion to his first despondency. He omitted nothing of his usual luxury or self-indulgence, and he even found spirits for going *incognito* to the theatre, where he took sufficient interest in the public performances, to send a message to a favorite actor. At times, even in this hopeless situation, his native ferocity returned upon him, and he was believed to have framed plans for removing all his enemies at once - the leaders of the rebellion, by appointing successors to their offices, and secretly sending assassins to dispatch their persons; the senate, by poison at a great banquet; the Gaulish provinces, by delivering them up for pillage to the army; the city, by again setting it on fire, whilst, at the same time, a vast number of wild beasts was to have been turned loose upon the unarmed populace - for the double purpose of destroying them, and of distracting their attention from the fire. But, as the mood of his frenzy changed, these sanguinary schemes were abandoned, (not, however, under any feelings of remorse, but from mere despair of effecting them,) and on the same day, but after a luxurious dinner, the imperial monster grew bland and pathetic in his ideas; he would proceed to the

Thomas de Quincey

rebellious army; he would present himself unarmed to their view; and would recall them to their duty by the mere spectacle of his tears. Upon the pathos with which he would weep he was resolved to rely entirely. And having received the guilty to his mercy without distinction, upon the following day he would unite *his* joy with *their* joy, and would chant hymns of victory (*epinicia*) - "which by the way," said he, suddenly, breaking off to his favorite pursuits, "it is necessary that I should immediately compose." This caprice vanished like the rest; and he made an effort to enlist the slaves and citizens into his service, and to raise by extortion a large military chest. But in the midst of these vascillating purposes fresh tidings surprised him - other armies had revolted, and the rebellion was spreading contagiously. This consummation of his alarms reached him at dinner; and the expressions of his angry fears took even a scenical air; he tore the dispatches, upset the table, and dashed to pieces upon the ground two crystal beakers - which had a high value as works of art, even in the *Aurea Domus*, from the sculptures which adorned them.

He now prepared for flight; and, sending forward commissioners to prepare the fleet at Ostia for his reception, he tampered with such officers of the army as were at hand, to prevail upon them to accompany his retreat. But all showed themselves indisposed to such schemes, and some flatly refused. Upon which he turned to other counsels; sometimes meditating a flight to the King of Parthia, or even to throw himself on the mercy of Galba; sometimes inclining rather to the plan of venturing into the forum in mourning apparel, begging pardon for his past offences, and, as a last resource, entreating that he might receive the appointment of Egyptian prefect. This plan, however, he hesitated to adopt, from some apprehension that he should be torn to pieces in his road to the forum; and, at all events, he concluded to postpone it to the following day. Meantime events were now hurrying to their catastrophe, which for ever anticipated that intention. His hours were numbered, and the closing scene was at hand.

In the middle of the night he was aroused from slumber with the intelligence that the military guard, who did duty at the palace, had all quited their posts. Upon this the unhappy prince leaped from his couch, never again to taste the luxury of sleep, and dispatched messengers to his friends. No answers were returned; and upon that he went personally with a small retinue to their hotels. But he found their doors every where closed; and all his importunities could not avail to extort an answer. Sadly and slowly he returned to his own bedchamber; but there again he found fresh instances of desertion, which had occurred during his short absence; the pages of his bedchamber had fled, carrying with them the coverlids of the imperial bed, which were probably inwrought with gold, and even a golden box, in which Nero had on the preceding day deposited poison prepared against the last extremity. Wounded to the heart by this general desertion, and perhaps by some special case of ingratitude, such as would probably enough be signalized in the flight of his personal favorites, he called for a gladiator of the household to come and dispatch him. But none appearing, - "What!" said he, "have I neither friend nor foe?" And so saying, he ran towards the Tiber, with the purpose of drowning himself. But that paroxysm, like all the rest, proved transient; and he expressed a wish for some hiding-place, or momentary asylum, in which he might collect his unsettled spirits, and fortify his wandering resolution. Such a retreat was offered to him by his *libertus* Phaon, in his own rural villa, about four miles distant from Rome. The offer was accepted; and the emperor, without further preparation than that of throwing over his person a short mantle of a dusky hue, and enveloping his head and face in a handkerchief, mounted his horse, and left Rome with four attendants. It was still night, but probably verging towards the early dawn; and even at that hour the imperial party met some travellers on their way to Rome (coming up, no doubt, [Footnote: At this early hour, witnesses, sureties, &c., and all concerned in the law courts, came up to Rome from villas, country towns, &c. But no ordinary call existed to summon travellers in the opposite direction; which accounts for the comment of the travellers on the errand of Nero and his attendants.] on law business) - who said, as they passed, "These men are certainly in chase of Nero." Two other incidents, of an interesting nature, are recorded of this short but memorable ride; at one point of the road, the shouts of the soldiery assailed their ears from the neighboring encampment of Galba. They were probably then getting under arms for their final march to take possession of the palace. At another point, an accident occurred of a more unfortunate kind, but so natural and so well circumstantiated, that it serves to verify the whole narrative; a dead body was lying on the road, at which the emperor's horse started so violently as nearly to dismount his rider, and under the difficulty of the moment compelled him to withdraw the hand which held up the handkerchief, and suddenly to expose his features. Precisely at this critical moment it happened that an old half-pay officer passed, recognised the emperor, and saluted him. Perhaps it was with some purpose of applying a remedy to this unfortunate rencontre, that the party dismounted at a point where several roads met, and turned their horses adrift to graze at will amongst the furze and brambles. Their own purpose was, to make their way to the back of the villa; but, to accomplish that, it was necessary that they should first cross a plantation of reeds, from the peculiar state of which they found themselves obliged to cover successively each space upon which they trode with parts of their dress, in order to gain any supportable footing. In this way, and contending with such hardships, they reached at length the postern side of the villa. Here we must suppose that there was no regular ingress; for, after waiting until an entrance was pierced, it seems that the emperor could avail himself of it in no more dignified posture, than by creeping through the hole on his hands and feet, (*quadrupes per angustias receptus.*)

Now, then, after such anxiety, alarm, and hardship, Nero had reached a quiet rural asylum. But for the unfortunate concurrence of his horse's alarm with the passing of the soldier, he might perhaps have counted on a respite of a day or two in this noiseless and obscure abode. But what a habitation for him who was yet ruler of the world in the eye of law, and even *de facto* was so, had any fatal accident befallen his aged competitor! The room in which (as the one most removed from notice and suspicion) he had secreted himself, was a cella, or little sleeping closet of a slave, furnished only with a miserable pallet and a coarse rug. Here lay the founder and possessor of the Golden House, too happy if he might hope for the peaceable possession even of this miserable crypt. But that, he knew too well, was impossible. A rival pretender to the empire was like the plague of fire - as dangerous in the shape of a single spark left unextinguished, as in that of a prosperous conflagration. But a few brief sands

Thomas de Quincey

yet remained to run in the emperor's hour-glass; much variety of degradation or suffering seemed scarcely within the possibilities of his situation, or within the compass of the time. Yet, as though Providence had decreed that his humiliation should pass through every shape, and speak by every expression which came home to his understanding, or was intelligible to his senses, even in these few moments he was attacked by hunger and thirst. No other bread could be obtained (or, perhaps, if the emperor's presence were concealed from the household, it was not safe to raise suspicion by calling for better) than that which was ordinarily given to slaves, coarse, black, and, to a palate so luxurious, doubtless disgusting. This accordingly he rejected; but a little tepid water he drank. After which, with the haste of one who fears that he may be prematurely interrupted, but otherwise, with all the reluctance which we may imagine, and which his streaming tears proclaimed, he addressed himself to the last labor in which he supposed himself to have any interest on this earth - that of digging a grave. Measuring a space adjusted to the proportions of his person, he inquired anxiously for any loose fragments of marble, such as might suffice to line it. He requested also to be furnished with wood and water, as the materials for the last sepulchral rites. And these labors were accompanied, or continually interrupted by tears and lamentations, or by passionate ejaculations on the blindness of fortune, in suffering so divine an artist to be thus violently snatched away, and on the calamitous fate of musical science, which then stood on the brink of so dire an eclipse. In these moments he was most truly in an *agony*, according to the original meaning of that word; for the conflict was great between two master principles of his nature: on the one hand, he clung with the weakness of a girl to life, even in that miserable shape to which it had now sunk; and like the poor malefactor, with whose last struggles Prior has so atrociously amused himself, "he often took leave, but was loath to depart." Yet, on the other hand, to resign his life very speedily, seemed his only chance for escaping the contumelies, perhaps the tortures, of his enemies; and, above all other considerations, for making sure of a burial, and possibly of burial rites; to want which, in the judgment of the ancients, was the last consummation of misery. Thus occupied, and thus distracted - sternly attracted to the grave by his creed, hideously repelled by infirmity of nature - he was suddenly interrupted by a courier with letters for the master of the house; letters, and from Rome! What was their import? That was soon told - briefly that Nero was adjudged to be a public enemy by the senate, and that official orders were issued for apprehending him, in order that he might be brought to condign punishment according to the method of ancient precedent. Ancient precedent! *more majorum!* And how was that? eagerly demanded the emperor. He was answered - that the state criminal in such cases was first stripped naked, then impaled as it were between the prongs of a pitchfork, and in that condition scourged to death. Horror-struck with this account, he drew forth two poniards, or short swords, tried their edges, and then, in utter imbecility of purpose, returned them to their scabbards, alleging that the destined moment had not yet arrived. Then he called upon Sporus, the infamous partner in his former excesses, to commence the funeral anthem. Others, again, he besought to lead the way in dying, and to sustain him by the spectacle of their example. But this purpose also he dismissed in the very moment of utterance; and turning away despairingly, he apostrophized himself in words reproachful or animating, now taxing his nature

Thomas de Quincey

with infirmity of purpose, now calling on himself by name, with adjurations to remember his dignity, and to act worthy of his supreme station: *ou prepei Neroni,* cried he, *ou prepeu næphein dei en tois toidætois ale, eleire seauton* - i.e. "Fie, fie, then Nero! such a season calls for perfect self-possession. Up, then, and rouse thyself to action."

Thus, and in similar efforts to master the weakness of his reluctant nature - weakness which would extort pity from the severest minds, were it not from the odious connection which in him it had with cruelty the most merciless - did this unhappy prince, *jam non salutis spem sed exitii solatium quærens,* consume the flying moments, until at length his ears caught the fatal sounds or echoes from a body of horsemen riding up to the villa. These were the officers charged with his arrest; and if he should fall into their hands alive, he knew that his last chance was over for liberating himself, by a Roman death, from the burthen of ignominious life, and from a lingering torture. He paused from his restless motions, listened attentively, then repeated a line from Homer -

Ippon m' ochupodon amphi chtupos ouata ballei

(The resounding tread of swift-footed horses reverberates upon my ears); - then under some momentary impulse of courage, gained perhaps by figuring to himself the bloody populace rioting upon his mangled body, yet even then needing the auxiliary hand and vicarious courage of his private secretary, the feeble-hearted prince stabbed himself in the throat. The wound, however, was not such as to cause instant death. He was still breathing, and not quite speechless, when the centurion who commanded the party entered the closet; and to this officer, who uttered a few hollow words of encouragement, he was still able to make a brief reply. But in the very effort of speaking he expired, and with an expression of horror impressed upon his stiffened features, which communicated a sympathetic horror to all beholders.

Such was the too memorable tragedy which closed for ever the brilliant line of the Julian family, and translated the august title of Cæsar from its original purpose as a proper name to that of an official designation. It is the most striking instance upon record of a dramatic and extreme vengeance overtaking extreme guilt; for, as Nero had exhausted the utmost possibilities of crime, so it may be affirmed that he drank off the cup of suffering to the very extremity of what his peculiar nature allowed. And in no life of so short a duration, have there ever been crowded equal extremities of gorgeous prosperity and abject infamy. It may be added, as another striking illustration of the rapid mutability and revolutionary excesses which belonged to what has been properly called the Roman *stratocracy* then disposing of the world, that within no very great succession of weeks that same victorious rebel, the Emperor Galba, at whose feet Nero had been self-immolated, was laid a murdered corpse in the same identical cell which had witnessed the lingering agonies of his unhappy victim. This was the act of an emancipated slave, anxious, by a vindictive insult to the remains of one prince, to place on record his gratitude to another. "So runs the world away!" And in this striking way is retribution sometimes dispensed.

In the sixth Cæsar terminated the Julian line. The three next princes in the succession were personally uninteresting; and, with a slight reserve in favor of

Thomas de Quincey

Otho, whose motives for committing suicide (if truly reported) argue great nobility of mind, [Footnote: We may add that the unexampled public grief which followed the death of Otho, exceeding even that which followed the death of Germanicus, and causing several officers to commit suicide, implies some remarkable goodness in this Prince, and a very unusual power of conciliating attachment.] were even brutal in the tenor of their lives and monstrous; besides that the extreme brevity of their several reigns (all three, taken conjunctly, having held the supreme power for no more than twelve months and twenty days) dismisses them from all effectual station or right to a separate notice in the line of Cæsars. Coming to the tenth in succession, Vespasian, and his two sons, Titus and Domitian, who make up the list of the twelve Cæsars, as they are usually called, we find matter for deeper political meditation and subjects of curious research. But these emperors would be more properly classed with the five who succeed them - Nerva, Trajan, Hadrian, and the two Antonines; after whom comes the young ruffian, Commodus, another Caligula or Nero, from whose short and infamous reign Gibbon takes up his tale of the decline of the empire. And this classification would probably have prevailed, had not the very curious work of Suetonius, whose own life and period of observation determined the series and cycle of his subjects, led to a different distribution. But as it is evident that, in the succession of the first twelve Cæsars, the six latter have no connection whatever by descent, collaterally, or otherwise, with the six first, it would be a more logical distribution to combine them according to the fortunes of the state itself, and the succession of its prosperity through the several stages of splendor, declension, revival, and final decay. Under this arrangement, the first seventeen would belong to the first stage; Commodus would open the second; Aurelian down to Constantine or Julian would fill the third; and Jovian to Augustulus would bring up the melancholy rear. Meantime it will be proper, after thus briefly throwing our eyes over the monstrous atrocities of the early Cæsars, to spend a few lines in examining their origin, and the circumstances which favored their growth. For a mere hunter after hidden or forgotten singularities; a lover on their own account of all strange perversities and freaks of nature, whether in action, taste, or opinion; for a collector and amateur of misgrowths and abortions; for a Suetonius, in short, it may be quite enough to state and to arrange his cabinet of specimens from the marvellous in human nature. But certainly in modern times, any historian, however little affecting the praise of a philosophic investigator, would feel himself called upon to remove a little the taint of the miraculous and preternatural which adheres to such anecdotes, by entering into the psychological grounds of their possibility; whether lying in any peculiarly vicious education, early familiarity with bad models, corrupting associations, or other plausible key to effects, which, taken separately, and out of their natural connection with their explanatory causes, are apt rather to startle and revolt the feelings of sober thinkers. Except, perhaps, in some chapters of Italian history, as, for example, among the most profligate of the Papal houses, and amongst some of the Florentine princes, we find hardly any parallel to the atrocities of Caligula and Nero; nor indeed was Tiberius much (if at all) behind them, though otherwise so wary and cautious in his conduct. The same tenor of licentious- ness beyond the needs of the individual, the same craving after the marvellous and the stupendous in guilt, is continually emerging in succeeding emperors - in Vitellius , in Domitian , in Commodus, in

Thomas de Quincey

Caracalla - every where, in short, where it was not overruled by one of two causes, either by original goodness of nature too powerful to be mastered by ordinary seductions, (and in some cases removed from their influence by an early apprenticeship to camps,) or by the terrors of an exemplary ruin immediately preceding. For such a determinate tendency to the enormous and the anomalous, sufficient causes must exist. What were they?

In the first place, we may observe that the people of Rome in that age were generally more corrupt by many degrees than has been usually supposed possible. The effect of revolutionary times, to relax all modes of moral obligation, and to unsettle the moral sense, has been well and philosophically stated by Mr. Coleridge; but that would hardly account for the utter licentiousness and depravity of Imperial Rome. Looking back to Republican Rome, and considering the state of public morals but fifty years before the emperors, we can with difficulty believe that the descendants of a people so severe in their habits could thus rapidly degenerate, and that a populace, once so hardy and masculine, should assume the manners which we might expect in the debauchees of Daphne (the infamous suburb of Antioch) or of Canopus, into which settled the very lees and dregs of the vicious Alexandria. Such extreme changes would falsify all that we know of human nature; we might *à priori* pronounce them impossible; and in fact, upon searching history, we find other modes of solving the difficulty. In reality, the citizens of Rome were at this time a new race, brought together from every quarter of the world, but especially from Asia. So vast a proportion of the ancient citizens had been cut off by the sword, and partly to conceal this waste of population, but much more by way of cheaply requiting services, or of showing favor, or of acquiring influence, slaves had been emancipated in such great multitudes, and afterwards invested with all the rights of citizens, that, in a single generation, Rome became almost transmuted into a baser metal; the progeny of those whom the last generation had purchased from the slave merchants. These people derived their stock chiefly from Cappadocia, Pontus, &c., and the other populous regions of Asia Minor; and hence the taint of Asiatic luxury and depravity, which was so conspicuous to all the Romans of the old republican severity. Juvenal is to be understood more literally than is sometimes supposed, when he complains that long before his time the Orontes (that river which washed the infamous capital of Syria) had mingled its impure waters with those of the Tiber. And a little before him, Lucan speaks with mere historic gravity when he says -

"Vivant Galatæque Syrique
Cappadoces, Gallique, extremique orbis Iberi,
Armenii, Cilices: nam post civilia bella
Hic Populus Romanus erit."

[Footnote: Blackwell, in his Court of Augustus, vol. i. p. 382, when noticing these lines upon occasion of the murder of Cicero, in the final proscription under the last triumvirate, comments thus: "Those of the greatest and truly Roman spirit had been murdered in the field by Julius Cæsar; the rest were now massacred in the city by his son and successors; in their room came Syrians, Cappadocians, Phrygians, and other enfranchised slaves from the conquered nations;" - "these in half a century had sunk so low, that Tiberius pronounced her very senators to be *homines ad sermtutem natos*, men born to be slaves."]

Thomas de Quincey

Probably in the time of Nero, not one man in six was of pure Roman descent. [Footnote: Suetonius indeed pretends that Augustus, personally at least, struggled against this ruinous practice - thinking it a matter of the highest moment, "Sincerum atque ab omni colluvione peregrini et servilis sanguinis incorruptum servare populum." And Horace is ready with his flatteries on the same topic, lib. 3, Od. 6. But the facts are against them; for the question is not what Augustus did in his own person, (which at most could not operate very widely except by the example,) but what he permitted to be done. Now there was a practice familiar to those times; that when a congiary or any other popular liberality was announced, multitudes were enfranchised by avaricious masters in order to make them capable of the bounty, (as citizens,) and yet under the condition of transferring to their emancipators whatsoever they should receive; *ina ton dæmosios d domenon siton lambanontes chata mæna - pherosi tois dedochasi tæn eleutherian* says Dionysius of Halicarnassus, in order that after receiving the corn given publicly in every month, they might carry it to those who had bestowed upon them their freedom. In a case, then, where an extensive practice of this kind was exposed to Augustus, and publicly reproved by him, how did he proceed? Did he reject the new-made citizens? No; he contented himself with diminishing the proportion originally destined for each, so that the same absolute sum being distributed among a number increased by the whole amount of the new enrolments, of necessity the relative sum for each separately was so much less. But this was a remedy applied only to the pecuniary fraud as it would have affected himself. The permanent mischief to the state went unredressed.] And the consequences were suitable. Scarcely a family has come down to our knowledge that could not in one generation enumerate a long catalogue of divorces within its own contracted circle. Every man had married a series of wives; every woman a series of husbands. Even in the palace of Augustus, who wished to be viewed as an *exemplar* or ideal model of domestic purity, every principal member of his family was tainted in that way; himself in a manner and a degree infamous even at that time. [Footnote: Part of the story is well known, but not the whole. Tiberius Nero, a promising young nobleman, had recently married a very splendid beauty. Unfortunately for him, at the marriage of Octavia (sister to Augustus) with Mark Anthony, he allowed his young wife, then about eighteen, to attend upon the bride. Augustus was deeply and suddenly fascinated by her charms, and without further scruple sent a message to Nero - intimating that he was in love with his wife, and would thank him to resign her. The other, thinking it vain, in those days of lawless proscription, to contest a point of this nature with one who commanded twelve legions, obeyed the requisition. Upon some motive, now unknown, he was persuaded even to degrade himself farther; for he actually officiated at the marriage in character of father, and gave away the young beauty to his rival, although at that time six months advanced in pregnancy by himself. These humiliating concessions were extorted from him, and yielded (probably at the instigation of friends) in order to save his life. In the sequel they had the very opposite result; for he died soon after, and it is reasonably supposed of grief and mortification. At the marriage feast, an incident occurred which threw the whole company into confusion: A little boy, roving from couch to couch among the guests, came at length to that in which Livia (the bride) was lying by the side of Augustus, on which he cried out aloud, - "Lady, what are you doing here?

Thomas de Quincey

You are mistaken - this is not your husband - he is there," (pointing to Tiberius,) "go, go - rise, lady, and recline beside *him*."] For the first 400 years of Rome, not one divorce had been granted or asked, although the statute which allowed of this indulgence had always been in force. But in the age succeeding to the civil wars men and women "married," says one author, "with a view to divorce, and divorced in order to marry. Many of these changes happened within the year, especially if the lady had a large fortune, which always went with her, and procured her choice of transient husbands." And, "can one imagine," asks the same writer, "that the fair one, who changed her husband every quarter, strictly kept her matrimonial faith all the three months?" Thus the very fountain of all the "household charities" and household virtues was polluted. And after that we need little wonder at the assassinations, poisonings, and forging of wills, which then laid waste the domestic life of the Romans.

2. A second source of the universal depravity was the growing inefficacy of the public religion; and this arose from its disproportion and inadequacy to the intellectual advances of the nation. *Religion*, in its very etymology, has been held to imply a *religatio*, that is, a reiterated or secondary obligation of morals; a sanction supplementary to that of the conscience. Now, for a rude and uncultivated people, the Pagan mythology might not be too gross to discharge the main functions of a useful religion. So long as the understanding could submit to the fables of the Pagan creed, so long it was possible that the hopes and fears built upon that creed might be practically efficient on men's lives and intentions. But when the foundation gave way, the whole superstructure of necessity fell to the ground. Those who were obliged to reject the ridiculous

legends which invested the whole of their Pantheon, together with the fabulous adjudgers of future punishments, could not but dismiss the punishments, which were, in fact, as laughable, and as obviously the fictions of human ingenuity, as their dispensers. In short, the civilized part of the world in those days lay in this dreadful condition; their intellect had far outgrown their religion; the disproportions between the two were at length become monstrous; and as yet no purer or more elevated faith was prepared for their acceptance. The case was as shocking as if, with our present intellectual needs, we should be unhappy enough to have no creed on which to rest the burden of our final hopes and fears, of our moral obligations, and of our consolations in misery, except the fairy mythology of our nurses. The condition of a people so situated, of a people under the calamity of having outgrown its religious faith, has never been sufficiently considered. It is probable that such a condition has never existed before or since that era of the world. The consequences to Rome were - that the reasoning and disputatious part of her population took refuge from the painful state of doubt in Atheism; amongst the thoughtless and irreflective the consequences were chiefly felt in their morals, which were thus sapped in their foundation.

3. A third cause, which from the first had exercised a most baleful influence upon the arts and upon literature in Rome, had by this time matured its disastrous tendencies towards the extinction of the moral sensibilities. This was the circus, and the whole machinery, form and substance, of the Circensian shows. Why had tragedy no existence as a part of the Roman literature? Because - and *that* was a reason which would have sufficed to stifle all the dramatic

Thomas de Quincey

genius of Greece and England - there was too much tragedy in the shape of gross reality, almost daily before their eyes. The amphitheatre extinguished the theatre. How was it possible that the fine and intellectual griefs of the drama should win their way to hearts seared and rendered callous by the continual exhibition of scenes the most hideous, in which human blood was poured out like water, and a human life sacrificed at any moment either to caprice in the populace, or to a strife of rivalry between the *ayes* and the *noes*, or as the penalty for any trifling instance of awkwardness in the performer himself? Even the more innocent exhibitions, in which brutes only were the sufferers, could not but be mortal to all the finer sensibilities. Five thousand wild animals, torn from their native abodes in the wilderness or forest, were often turned out to be hunted, or for mutual slaughter, in the course of a single exhibition of this nature; and it sometimes happened, (a fact which of itself proclaims the course of the public propensities,) that the person at whose expense the shows were exhibited, by way of paying special court to the people and meriting their favor, in the way most conspicuously open to him, issued orders that all, without a solitary exception, should be slaughtered. He made it known, as the very highest gratification which the case allowed, that (in the language of our modern auctioneers) the whole, "without reserve," should perish before their eyes. Even such spectacles must have hardened the heart, and blunted the more delicate sensibilities; but these would soon cease to stimulate the pampered and exhausted sense. From the combats of tigers or leopards, in which the passions could only be gathered indirectly, and by way of inference from the motions, the transition must have been almost inevitable to those of men, whose nobler and more varied passions spoke directly, and by the intelligible language of the eye, to human spectators; and from the frequent contemplation of these authorized murders, in which a whole people, women [Footnote: Augustus, indeed, strove to exclude the women from one part of the circension spectacles; and what was that? Simply from the sight of the *Athletæ*, as being naked. But that they should witness the pangs of the dying gladiators, he deemed quite allowable. The smooth barbarian considered; that a license of the first sort offended against decorum, whilst the other violated only the sanctities of the human heart, and the whole sexual character of women. It is our opinion, that to the brutalizing effect of these exhibitions we are to ascribe not only the early extinction of the Roman drama, but generally the inferiority of Rome to Greece in every department of the fine arts. The fine temper of Roman sensibility, which no culture could have brought to the level of the Grecian, was thus dulled for *every* application.] as much as men, and children intermingled with both, looked on with leisurely indifference, with anxious expectation, or with rapturous delight, whilst below them were passing the direct sufferings of humanity, and not seldom its dying pangs, it was impossible to expect a result different from that which did in fact take place, - universal hardness of heart, obdurate depravity, and a twofold degradation of human nature, which acted simulta-neously upon the two pillars of morality, (which are otherwise not often assailed together,) of natural sensibility in the first place, and, in the second, of conscientious principle.

4. But these were circumstances which applied to the whole population indiscriminately. Superadded to these, in the case of the emperor, and affecting *him*

Thomas de Quincey

exclusively, was this prodigious disadvantage - that ancient reverence for the immediate witnesses of his actions, and for the people and senate who would under other circumstances have exercised the old functions of the censor, was, as to the emperor, pretty nearly obliterated. The very title of *imperator*, from which we have derived our modern one of *emperor*, proclaims the nature of the government, and the tenure of that office. It was purely a government by the sword, or permanent *stratocracy* having a movable head. Never was there a people who inquired so impertinently as the Romans into the domestic conduct of each private citizen. No rank escaped this jealous vigilance; and private liberty, even in the most indifferent circumstances of taste or expense, was sacrificed to this inquisitorial rigor of *surveillance* exercised on behalf of the State, sometimes by erroneous patriotism, too often by malice in disguise. To this spirit the highest public officers were obliged to bow; the consuls, not less than others. And even the occasional dictator, if by law irresponsible, acted nevertheless as one who knew that any change which depressed his party, might eventually abrogate his privilege. For the first time in the person of an imperator was seen a supreme autocrat, who had virtually and effectively all the irresponsibility which the law assigned, and the origin of his office presumed. Satisfied to know that he possessed such power, Augustus, as much from natural taste as policy, was glad to dissemble it, and by every means to withdraw it from public notice. But he had passed his youth as citizen of a republic; and in the state of transition to autocracy, in his office of triumvir, had experimentally known the perils of rivalship, and the pains of foreign control, too feelingly to provoke unnecessarily any sleeping embers of the republican spirit. Tiberius, though familiar from his infancy with the servile homage of a court, was yet modified by the popular temper of Augustus; and he came late to the throne. Caligula was the first prince on whom the entire effect of his political situation was allowed to operate; and the natural results were seen - he was the first absolute monster. He must early have seen the realities of his position, and from what quarter it was that any cloud could arise to menace his security. To the senate or people any respect which he might think proper to pay, must have been imputed by all parties to the lingering superstitions of custom, to involuntary habit, to court dissimulation, or to the decencies of external form, and the prescriptive reverence of ancient names. But neither senate nor people could enforce their claims, whatever they might happen to be. Their sanction and ratifying vote might be worth having, as consecrating what was already secure, and conciliating the scruples of the weak to the absolute decision of the strong. But their resistance, as an original movement, was so wholly without hope, that they were never weak enough to threaten it.

The army was the true successor to their places, being the *ultimate* depository of power. Yet, as the army was necessarily subdivided, as the shifting circumstances upon every frontier were continually varying the strength of the several divisions as to numbers and state of discipline, one part might be balanced against the other by an imperator standing in the centre of the whole. The rigor of the military *sacramentum*, or oath of allegiance, made it dangerous to offer the first overtures to rebellion; and the money, which the soldiers were continually depositing in the bank, placed at the foot of their military standards, if sometimes turned against the emperor, was also liable

Thomas de Quincey

to be sequestrated in his favor. There were then, in fact, two great forces in the government acting in and by each other - the Stratocracy, and the Autocracy. Each needed the other; each stood in awe of each. But, as regarded all other forces in the empire, constitutional or irregular, popular or senatorial, neither had any thing to fear. Under any ordinary circumstances, therefore, considering the hazards of a rebellion, the emperor was substantially liberated from all control. Vexations or outrages upon the populace were not such to the army. It was but rarely that the soldier participated in the emotions of the citizen. And thus, being effectually without check, the most vicious of the Cæsars went on without fear, presuming upon the weakness of one part of his subjects, and the indifference of the other, until he was tempted onwards to atrocities, which armed against him the common feelings of human nature, and all mankind, as it were, rose in a body with one voice, and apparently with one heart, united by mere force of indignant sympathy, to put him down, and "abate" him as a monster. But, until he brought matters to this extremity, Cæsar had no cause to fear. Nor was it at all certain, in any one instance, where this exemplary chastisement overtook him, that the apparent unanimity of the actors went further than the *practical* conclusion of "abating" the imperial nuisance, or that their indignation had settled upon the same offences. In general the army measured the guilt by the public scandal, rather than by its moral atrocity; and Cæsar suffered perhaps in every case, not so much because he had violated his duties, as because he had dishonored his office.

It is, therefore, in the total absence of the checks which have almost universally existed to control other despots, under some indirect shape, even where none was provided by the laws, that we must seek for the main peculiarity affecting the condition of the Roman Cæsar, which peculiarity it was, superadded to the other three, that finally made those three operative in their fullest extent. It is in the perfection of the stratocracy that we must look for the key to the excesses of the autocrat. Even in the bloody despotisms of the Barbary States, there has always existed in the religious prejudices of the people, which could not be violated with safety, one check more upon the caprices of the despot than was found at Rome. Upon the whole, therefore, what affects us on the first reading as a prodigy or anomaly in the frantic outrages of the early Cæsars - falls within the natural bounds of intelligible human nature, when we state the case considerately. Surrounded by a population which had not only gone through a most vicious and corrupting discipline, and had been utterly ruined by the license of revolutionary times, and the bloodiest proscriptions, but had even been extensively changed in its very elements, and from the descendants of Romulus had been transmuted into an Asiatic mob; - starting from this point, and considering as the second feature of the case, that this transfigured people, *morally* so degenerate, were carried, however, by the progress of civilization to a certain intellectual altitude, which the popular religion had not strength to ascend - but from inherent disproportion remained at the base of the general civilization, incapable of accompanying the other elements in their advance; - thirdly, that this polished condition of society, which should naturally with the evils of a luxurious repose have counted upon its pacific benefits, had yet, by means of its circus and its gladiatorial contests, applied a constant irritation, and a system of provocations to the appetites for blood, such as in all other nations are connected with the

Thomas de Quincey

rudest stages of society, and with the most barbarous modes of warfare, nor even in such circumstances without many palliatives wanting to the spectators of the circus; - combining these considerations, we have already a key to the enormities and hideous excesses of the Roman Imperator. The hot blood which excites, and the adventurous courage which accompanies, the excesses of sanguinary warfare, presuppose a condition of the moral nature not to be compared for malignity and baleful tendency to the cool and cowardly spirit of amateurship, in which the Roman (perhaps an effeminate Asiatic) sat looking down upon the bravest of men, (Thracians, or other Europeans,) mangling each other for his recreation. When, lastly, from such a population, and thus disciplined from his nursery days, we suppose the case of one individual selected, privileged, and raised to a conscious irresponsibility, except at the bar of one extra-judicial tribunal, not easily irritated, and notoriously to be propitiated by other means than those of upright or impartial conduct, we lay together the elements of a situation too trying for poor human nature, and fitted only to the faculties of an angel or a demon; of an angel, if we suppose him to resist its full temptations; of a demon, if we suppose him to use its total opportunities. Thus interpreted and solved, Caligula and Nero become ordinary men.

But, finally, what if, after all, the worst of the Cæsars, and those in particular, were entitled to the benefit of a still shorter and more conclusive apology? What if, in a true medical sense, they were insane? It is certain that a vein of madness ran in the family; and anecdotes are recorded of the three worst, which go far to establish it as a fact, and others which would imply it as symptoms - preceding or accompanying. As belonging to the former class, take the following story:

At midnight an elderly gentleman suddenly sends round a message to a select party of noblemen, rouses them out of bed, and summons them instantly to his palace. Trembling for their lives from the suddenness of the summons, and from the unseasonable hour, and scarcely doubting that by some anonymous *delator* they have been implicated as parties to a conspiracy, they hurry to the palace - are received in portentous silence by the ushers and pages in attendance - are conducted to a saloon, where (as in every where else) the silence of night prevails, united with the silence of fear and whispering expectation. All are seated - all look at each other in ominous anxiety. Which is accuser? Which is the accused? On whom shall their suspicion settle - on whom their pity? All are silent - almost speechless - and even the current of their thoughts is frost-bound by fear. Suddenly the sound of a fiddle or a viol is caught from a distance - it swells upon the ear - steps approach - and in another moment in rushes the elderly gentleman, grave and gloomy as his audience, but capering about in a frenzy of excitement. For half an hour he continues to perform all possible evolutions of caprioles, pirouettes, and other extravagant feats of activity, accompanying himself on the fiddle; and, at length, not having once looked at his guests, the elderly gentleman whirls out of the room in the same transport of emotion with which he entered it; the panic-struck visitors are requested by a slave to consider themselves as dismissed: they retire; resume their couches: - the nocturnal pageant has "dislimned" and vanished; and on the following morning, were it not for their concurring testimonies, all would be disposed to take this interruption of their sleep for one of its most fantastic dreams. The elderly gentleman, who figured in this delirious *pas seul* - who was he? He was

Thomas de Quincey

Tiberius Cæsar, king of kings, and lord of the terraqueous globe. Would a British jury demand better evidence than this of a disturbed intellect in any formal process *de lunatico inquirendo*? For Caligula, again, the evidence of symptoms is still plainer. He knew his own defect; and purposed going through a course of hellebore. Sleeplessness, one of the commonest indications of lunacy, haunted him in an excess rarely recorded. [Footnote: No fiction of romance presents so awful a picture of the ideal tyrant as that of Caligula by Suetonius. His palace - radiant with purple and gold, but murder every where lurking beneath flowers; his smiles and echoing laughter - masking (yet hardly meant to mask) his foul treachery of heart; his hideous and tumultuous dreams - his baffled sleep - and his sleepless nights - compose the picture of an Æschylus. What a master's sketch lies in these few lines: "Incitabatur insomnio maxime; neque enim plus tribus horis nocturnis quiescebat; ac ne his placida quiete, at pavida miris rerum imaginibus: ut qui inter ceteras pelagi quondam speciem colloquentem secum videre visus sit. Ideoque magna parte noctis, vigilse cubandique tsedio, nunc toro residens, nunc per longissimas porticus vagus, invocare identidem atque exspectare lucem consueverat:" - i. e., But, above all, he was tormented with nervous irritation, by sleeplessness; for he enjoyed not more than three hours of nocturnal repose; nor these even in pure untroubled rest, but agitated by phantasmata of portentous augury; as, for example, upon one occasion he fancied that he saw the sea, under some definite impersonation, conversing with himself. Hence it was, and from this incapacity of sleeping, and from weariness of lying awake, that he had fallen into habits of ranging all the night long through the palace, sometimes throwing himself on a couch, sometimes wandering along the vast corridors, watching for the earliest dawn, and anxiously invoking its approach.] The same, or similar facts, might be brought forward on behalf of Nero. And thus these unfortunate princes, who have so long (and with so little investigation of their cases) passed for monsters or for demoniac counterfeits of men, would at length be brought back within the fold of humanity, as objects rather of pity than of abhorrence, would be reconciled to our indulgent feelings, and, at the same time, made intelligible to our understandings.

Thomas de Quincey

CHAPTER IV.

The five Cæsars who succeeded immediately to the first twelve, were, in as high a sense as their office allowed, patriots. Hadrian is perhaps the first of all whom circumstances permitted to show his patriotism without fear. It illustrates at one and the same moment a trait in this emperor's character, and in the Roman habits, that he acquired much reputation for hardiness by walking bareheaded. "Never, on any occasion," says one of his memorialists (Dio,) "neither in summer heat nor in winter's cold, did he cover his head; but, as well in the Celtic snows as in Egyptian heats, he went about bareheaded." This anecdote could not fail to win the especial admiration of Isaac Casaubon, who lived in an age when men believed a hat no less indispensable to the head, even within doors, than shoes or stockings to the feet. His astonishment on the occasion is thus expressed: "Tantum est *hæ aschæsis*:" such and so mighty is the force of habit and daily use. And then he goes on to ask - "Quis hodie nudum caput radiis solis, aut omnia perurenti frigori, ausit exponere?" Yet we ourselves, and our illustrious friend, Christopher North, have walked for twenty years amongst our British lakes and mountains hatless, and amidst both snow and rain, such as Romans did not often experience. We were naked, and yet not ashamed. Nor in this are we altogether singular. But, says Casaubon, the Romans went farther; for they walked about the streets of Rome [Footnote: And hence we may the better estimate the trial to a Roman's feelings in the personal deformity of baldness, connected with the Roman theory of its cause, for the exposure of it was perpetual.] bareheaded, and never assumed a hat or a cap, a *petasus* or a *galerus*, a Macedonian *causia*, or a *pileus*, whether Thessalian, Arcadian, or Laconic, unless when they entered upon a journey. Nay, some there were, as Masinissa and Julius Cæsar, who declined even on such an occasion to cover their heads. Perhaps in imitation of these celebrated leaders, Hadrian adopted the same practice, but not with the same result; for to him, either from age or constitution, this very custom proved the original occasion of his last illness.

Imitation, indeed, was a general principle of action with Hadrian, and the key to much of his public conduct; and allowably enough, considering the exemplary lives (in a public sense) of some who had preceded him, and the singular anxiety with which he distinguished between the lights and shadows of their examples. He imitated the great Dictator, Julius, in his vigilance of inspection into the civil, not less than the martial police of his times, shaping his new regulations to meet abuses as they arose, and strenuously maintaining the old ones in vigorous operation. As respected the army, this was matter of peculiar praise, because peculiarly disinterested; for his foreign policy was pacific; [Footnote: "Expeditiones sub eo," says Spartian, "graves nullæ fuerunt. Bella etiam silentio pene transacta." But he does not the less add, "A militibus, propter curam exercitus nimiam, multum amatus est."] he made no new conquests; and he retired from the old ones of Trajan, where they could not have been maintained without disproportionate bloodshed,

Thomas de Quincey

or a jealousy beyond the value of the stake. In this point of his administration he took Augustus for his model; as again in his care of the army, in his occasional bounties, and in his paternal solicitude for their comforts, he looked rather to the example of Julius. Him also he imitated in his affability and in his ambitious courtesies; one instance of which, as blending an artifice of political subtlety and simulation with a remarkable exertion of memory, it may be well to mention. The custom was, in canvassing the citizens of Rome, that the candidate should address every voter by his name; it was a fiction of republican etiquette, that every man participating in the political privileges of the State must be personally known to public aspirants. But, as this was supposed to be, in a literal sense, impossible to all men with the ordinary endowments of memory, in order to reconcile the pretensions of republican hauteur with the necessities of human weakness, a custom had grown up of relying upon a class of men, called *nomenclators*, whose express business and profession it was to make themselves acquainted with the person and name of every citizen. One of these people accompanied every candidate, and quietly whispered into his ear the name of each voter as he came in sight. Few, indeed, were they who could dispense with the services of such an assessor; for the office imposed a twofold memory, that of names and of persons; and to estimate the immensity of the effort, we must recollect that the number of voters often far exceeded one quarter of a million. The very same trial of memory he undertook with respect to his own army, in this instance recalling the well known feat of Mithridates. And throughout his life he did not once forget the face or name of any veteran soldier whom he ever had occasion to notice, no matter under what remote climate, or under what difference of circumstances. Wonderful is the effect upon soldiers of such enduring and separate remembrance, which operates always as the most touching kind of personal flattery, and which, in every age of the world, since the social sensibilities of men have been much developed, military commanders are found to have played upon as the most effectual chord in the great system which they modulated; some few, by a rare endowment of nature; others, as Napoleon Bonaparte, by elaborate mimicries of pantomimic art. [Footnote: In the true spirit of Parisian mummery, Bonaparte caused letters to be written from the War-office, in his own name, to particular soldiers of high military reputation in every brigade, (whose private history he had previously caused to be investigated,) alluding circumstantially to the leading facts in their personal or family career; a furlough accompanied this letter, and they were requested to repair to Paris, where the emperor anxiously desired to see them. Thus was the paternal interest expressed, which their leader took in each man's fortunes; and the effect of every such letter, it was not doubted, would diffuse itself through ten thousand other men.]

Other modes he had of winning affection from the army; in particular that, so often practised before and since, of accommodating himself to the strictest ritual of martial discipline and castrensian life. He slept in the open air, or, if he used a tent (papilio), it was open at the sides. He ate the ordinary rations of cheese, bacon, &c.; he used no other drink than that composition of vinegar and water, known by the name of *posca*, which formed the sole beverage allowed in the Roman camps. He joined personally in the periodical exercises of the army - those even which were trying to the most vigorous youth and health:

Thomas de Quincey

marching, for example, on stated occasions, twenty English miles without intermission, in full armor and completely accoutred. Luxury of every kind he not only interdicted to the soldier by severe ordinances, himself enforcing their execution, but discountenanced it (though elsewhere splendid and even gorgeous in his personal habits) by his own continual example. In dress, for instance, he sternly banished the purple and gold embroideries, the jewelled arms, and the floating draperies so little in accordance with the-severe character of "*war in procinct*" [Footnote: "*War in procinct*" - a phrase of Milton's in Paradise Regained, which strikingly illustrates his love of Latin phraseology; for unless to a scholar, previously acquainted with the Latin phrase of *in procinctu*, it is so absolutely unintelligible as to interrupt the current of the feeling.] Hardly would he allow himself an ivory hilt to his sabre. The same severe proscription he extended to every sort of furniture, or decorations of art, which sheltered even in the bosom of camps those habits of effeminate luxury - so apt in all great empires to steal by imperceptible steps from the voluptuous palace to the soldier's tent - following in the equipage of great leading officers, or of subalterns highly connected. There was at that time a practice prevailing, in the great standing camps on the several frontiers and at all the military stations, of renewing as much as possible the image of distant Rome by the erection of long colonnades and piazzas - single, double, or triple; of crypts, or subterranean [Footnote: "*Crypts*" - these, which Spartian, in his life of Hadrian, denominates simply *cryptæ*, are the same which, in the Roman jurisprudence, and in the architectural works of the Romans, yet surviving, are termed *hypogæa deambulationes, i. e.* subterranean parades. Vitruvius treats of this luxurious class of apartments in connection with the Apothecæ, and other repositories or store-rooms, which were also in many cases under ground, for the same reason as our ice-houses, wine-cellars, &c. He (and from him Pliny and Apollonaris Sidonius), calls them *crypto-porticus* (cloistral colonnades); and Ulpian calls them *refugia* (sanctuaries, or places of refuge); St. Ambrose notices them under the name of *hypogæa* and *umbrosa penetralia*, as the resorts of voluptuaries: *Luxuriosorum est*, says he, *hypogæa quærere - captantium frigus æstivum*; and again he speaks of *desidiosi qui ignava sub terris agant otia*.] saloons, (and sometimes subterranean galleries and corridors,) for evading the sultry noontides of July and August; of verdant cloisters or arcades, with roofs high over-arched, constructed entirely out of flexile shrubs, box-myrtle, and others, trained and trimmed in regular forms; besides endless other applications of the *topiary* [Footnote: "*The topiary art*" - so called, as Salmasius thinks, from *ropæion, a rope*; because the process of construction was conducted chiefly by means of cords and strings. This art was much practised in the 17th century; and Casaubon describes one, which existed in his early days somewhere in the suburbs of Paris, on so elaborate a scale, that it represented Troy besieged, with the two hosts, their several leaders, and all other objects in their full proportion.] art, which in those days (like the needlework of Miss Linwood in ours), though no more than a mechanic craft, in some measure realized the effects of a fine art by the perfect skill of its execution. All these modes of luxury, with a policy that had the more merit as it thwarted his own private inclinations, did Hadrian peremptorily abolish; perhaps, amongst other more obvious purposes, seeking to intercept the earliest buddings of those local attachments which are as injurious to the martial

Thomas de Quincey

character and the proper pursuits of men whose vocation obliges them to consider themselves eternally under marching orders, as they are propitious to all the best interests of society in connection with the feelings of civic life.

We dwell upon this prince not without reason in this particular; for, amongst the Cæsars, Hadrian stands forward in high relief as a reformer of the army. Well and truly might it be said of him - that, *post Cæsarem Octavianum labantem disciplinam, incurid superiorum principum, ipse retinuit.* Not content with the cleansings and purgations we have mentioned, he placed upon a new footing the whole tenure, duties, and pledges, of military offices. [Footnote: Very remarkable it is, and a fact which speaks volumes as to the democratic constitution of the Roman army, in the midst of that aristocracy which enveloped its parent state in a civil sense, that although there was a name for a *common soldier* (or *sentinel*, as he was termed by our ancestors) - viz. *miles gregarius*, or *miles manipularis* - there was none for an *officer*; that is to say, each several rank of officers had a name; but there was no generalization to express the idea of an officer abstracted from its several species or classes.] It cannot much surprise us that this department of the public service should gradually have gone to ruin or decay. Under the senate and people, under the auspices of those awful symbols - letters more significant and ominous than ever before had troubled the eyes of man, except upon Belshazzar's wall - S.P.Q.R., the officers of the Roman army had been kept true to their duties, and vigilant by emulation and a healthy ambition. But, when the ripeness of corruption had by dissolving the body of the State brought out of its ashes a new mode of life, and had recast the aristocratic republic, by aid of its democratic elements then suddenly victorious, into a pure autocracy - whatever might be the advantages in other respects of this great change, in one point it had certainly injured the public service, by throwing the higher military appointments, all in fact which conferred any authority, into the channels of court favor - and by consequence into a mercenary disposal. Each successive emperor had been too anxious for his own immediate security, to find leisure for the remoter interests of the empire: all looked to the army, as it were, for their own immediate security against competitors, without venturing to tamper with its constitution, to risk popularity by reforming abuses, to balance present interest against a remote one, or to cultivate the public welfare at the hazard of their own: contented with obtaining *that*, they left the internal arrangements of so formidable a body in the state to which circumstances had brought it, and to which naturally the views of all existing beneficiaries had gradually adjusted themselves. What these might be, and to what further results they might tend, was a matter of moment doubtless to the empire. But the empire was strong; if its motive energy was decaying, its *vis inertia* was for ages enormous, and could stand up against assaults repeated for many ages: whilst the emperor was in the beginning of his authority weak, and pledged by instant interest, no less than by express promises, to the support of that body whose favor had substantially supported himself. Hadrian was the first who turned his attention effectually in that direction; whether it were that he first was struck with the tendency of the abuses, or that he valued the hazard less which he incurred in correcting them, or that, having no successor of his own blood, he had a less personal and affecting interest at stake in setting this

Thomas de Quincey

hazard at defiance. Hitherto, the highest regimental rank, that of tribune, had been disposed of in two ways, either civilly upon popular favor and election, or upon the express recommendation of the soldiery. This custom had prevailed under the republic, and the force of habit had availed to propagate that practice under a new mode of government. But now were introduced new regulations: the tribune was selected for his military qualities and experience: none was appointed to this important office, "*nisi barbâ plenâ*" The centurion's truncheon, [Footnote: *Vitis*: and it deserves to be mentioned, that this staff, or cudgel, which was the official engine and cognizance of the Centurion's dignity, was meant expressly to be used in caning or cudgelling the inferior soldiers: "*propterea* vitis in manum data," says Salmasius, "*verberando scilicet militi qui deliquisset.*" We are no patrons of corporal chastisement, which, on the contrary, as the vilest of degradations, we abominate. The soldier, who does not feel himself dishonored by it, is already dishonored beyond hope or redemption. But still let this degradation not be imputed to the English army exclusively.] again, was given to no man, "*nisi robusto et bonæ famæ.*" The arms and military appointments (*supellectilis*) were revised; the register of names was duly called over; and none suffered to remain in the camps who was either above or below the military age. The same vigilance and jealousy were extended to the great stationary stores and repositories of biscuit, vinegar, and other equipments for the soldiery. All things were in constant readiness in the capital and the provinces, in the garrisons and camps, abroad and at home, to meet the outbreak of a foreign war or a domestic sedition. Whatever were the service, it could by no possibility find Hadrian unprepared. And he first, in fact, of all the Cæsars, restored to its ancient republican standard, as reformed and perfected by Marius, the old martial discipline of the Scipios and the Paulli - that discipline, to which, more than to any physical superiority of her soldiery, Rome had been indebted for her conquest of the earth; and which had inevitably decayed in the long series of wars growing out of personal ambition. From the days of Marius, every great leader had sacrificed to the necessities of courting favor from the troops, as much as was possible of the hardships incident to actual service, and as much as he dared of the once rigorous discipline. Hadrian first found himself in circumstances, or was the first who had courage enough to decline a momentary interest in favor of a greater in reversion; and a personal object which was transient, in favor of a state one continually revolving.

For a prince, with no children of his own, it is in any case a task of peculiar delicacy to select a successor. In the Roman empire the difficulties were much aggravated. The interests of the State were, in the first place, to be consulted; for a mighty burthen of responsibility rested upon the emperor in the most personal sense. Duties of every kind fell to his station, which, from the peculiar constitution of the government, and from circumstances rooted in the very origin of the imperatorial office, could not be devolved upon a council. Council there was none, nor could be recognised as such in the State machinery. The emperor, himself a sacred and sequestered creature, might be supposed to enjoy the secret tutelage of the Supreme Deity; but a council, composed of subordinate and responsible agents, could *not*. Again, the auspices of the emperor, and his edicts, apart even from any celestial or supernatural inspiration, simply as emanations of his own divine character, had a value

Thomas de Quincey

and a consecration which could never belong to those of a council - or to those even which had been sullied by the breath of any less august reviser. The emperor, therefore, or - as with a view to his solitary and unique character we ought to call him - in the original irrepresentable term, the imperator, could not delegate his duties, or execute them in any avowed form by proxies or representatives. He was himself the great fountain of law - of honor - of preferment - of civil and political regulations. He was the fountain also of good and evil fame. He was the great chancellor, or supreme dispenser of equity to all climates, nations, languages, of his mighty dominions, which connected the turbaned races of the Orient, and those who sat in the gates of the rising sun, with the islands of the West, and the unfathomed depths of the mysterious Scandinavia. He was the universal guardian of the public and private interests which composed the great edifice of the social system as then existing amongst his subjects. Above all, and out of his own private purse, he supported the heraldries of his dominions - the peerage, senatorial or prætorian, and the great gentry or chivalry of the Equites. These were classes who would have been dishonored by the censorship of a less august comptroller. And, for the classes below these, - by how much they were lower and more remote from his ocular superintendence, - by so much the more were they linked to him in a connection of absolute dependence. Cæsar it was who provided their daily food, Cæsar who provided their pleasures and relaxations. He chartered the fleets which brought grain to the Tiber - he bespoke the Sardinian granaries whilst yet unformed - and the harvests of the Nile whilst yet unsown. Not the connection between a mother and her unborn infant is more intimate and vital, than that which subsisted between the mighty populace of the Roman capital and their paternal emperor. They drew their nutriment from him; they lived and were happy by sympathy with the motions of his will; to him also the arts, the knowledge, and the literature of the empire looked for support. To him the armies looked for their laurels, and the eagles in every clime turned their aspiring eyes, waiting to bend their flight according to the signal of his Jovian nod. And all these vast functions and ministrations arose partly as a natural effect, but partly also they were a cause of the emperor's own divinity. He was capable of services so exalted, because he also was held a god, and had his own altars, his own incense, his own worship and priests. And that was the cause, and that was the result of his bearing, on his own shoulders, a burthen so mighty and Atlantean.

Yet, if in this view it was needful to have a man of talent, on the other hand there was reason to dread a man of talents too adventurous, too aspiring, or too intriguing. His situation, as Cæsar, or Crown Prince, flung into his hands a power of fomenting conspiracies, and of concealing them until the very moment of explosion, which made him an object of almost exclusive terror to his principal, the Cæsar Augustus. His situation again, as an heir voluntarily adopted, made him the proper object of public affection and caresses, which became peculiarly embarrassing to one who had, perhaps, soon found reasons for suspecting, fearing, and hating him beyond all other men.

The young nobleman, whom Hadrian adopted by his earliest choice, was Lucius Aurelius Verus, the son of Cejonius Commodus. These names were borne also by the son; but, after his adoption into the Ælian family,

Thomas de Quincey

he was generally known by the appellation of Ælius Verus. The scandal of those times imputed his adoption to the worst motives. "*Adriano*," says one author, ("*ut malevoli loquuntur*) *acceptior formâ quam moribus*" And thus much undoubtedly there is to countenance so shocking an insinuation, that very little is recorded of the young prince but such anecdotes as illustrate his excessive luxury and effeminate dedication to pleasure. Still it is our private opinion, that Hadrian's real motives have been misrepresented; that he sought in the young man's extraordinary beauty - [for he was, says Spartian, *pulchritudinis regiæ*] - a plausible pretext that should he sufficient to explain and to countenance his preference, whilst under this provisional adoption he was enabled to postpone the definitive choice of an imperator elect, until his own more advanced age might diminish the motives for intriguing against himself. It was, therefore, a mere *ad interim* adoption; for it is certain, however we may choose to explain that fact, that Hadrian foresaw and calculated on the early death of Ælius. This prophetic knowledge may have been grounded on a private familiarity with some constitutional infirmity affecting his daily health, or with some habits of life incompatible with longevity, or with both combined. It is pretended that this distinguished mark of favor was conferred in fulfilment of a direct contract on the emperor's part, as the price of favors such as the Latin reader will easily understand from the strong expression of Spartian above cited. But it is far more probable that Hadrian relied on this admirable beauty, and allowed it so much weight, as the readiest and most intelligible justification to the multitude, of a choice which thus offered to their homage a public favorite - and to the nobility, of so invidious a preference, which placed one of their own number far above the level of his natural rivals. The necessities of the moment were thus satisfied without present or future danger; - as respected the future, he knew or believed that Verus was marked out for early death; and would often say, in a strain of compliment somewhat disproportionate, applying to him the Virgilian lines on the hopeful and lamented Marcellus,

"Ostendent terris hunc tantum fata, neque ultra
Esse sinent."

And, at the same time, to countenance the belief that he had been disappointed, he would affect to sigh, exclaiming - "Ah! that I should thus fruitlessly have squandered a sum of three [Footnote: In the original *ter millies*, which is not much above two millions and 150 thousand pounds sterling; but it must be remembered that one third as much, in addition to this popular largess, had been given to the army.] millions sterling!" for so much had been distributed in largesses to the people and the army on the occasion of his inauguration. Meantime, as respected the present, the qualities of the young man were amply fitted to sustain a Roman popularity; for, in addition to his extreme and statuesque beauty of person, he was (in the report of one who did not wish to color his character advantageously) "*memor families suce, comptus, decorus, oris venerandi, eloquentice, celsioris, versufacilis, in republicâ etiam non inutilis.*" Even as a military officer, he had a respectable [Footnote: - "nam bene gesti rebus, vel potius feliciter, etsi nori summi - medii tamen obtinuit ducis famam."] character; as an orator he was more than respectable; and in other qualifications less interesting to the populace, he had that happy mediocrity of merit which was best fitted

Thomas de Quincey

for his delicate and difficult situation - sufficient to do credit to the emperor's preference - sufficient to sustain the popular regard, but not brilliant enough to throw his patron into the shade. For the rest, his vices were of a nature not greatly or necessarily to interfere with his public duties, and emphatically such as met with the readiest indulgence from the Roman laxity of morals. Some few instances, indeed, are noticed of cruelty; but there is reason to think that it was merely by accident, and as an indirect result of other purposes, that he ever allowed himself in such manifestations of irresponsible power - not as gratifying any harsh impulses of his native character. The most remarkable neglect of humanity with which he has been taxed, occurred in the treatment of his couriers; these were the bearers of news and official dispatches, at that time fulfilling the functions of the modern post; and it must be remembered that as yet they were not slaves, (as afterwards by the reformation of Alexander Severus,) but free citizens. They had been already dressed in a particular livery or uniform, and possibly they might wear some symbolical badges of their profession; but the new Cæsar chose to dress them altogether in character as winged Cupids, affixing literal wings to their shoulders, and facetiously distinguishing them by the names of the four cardinal winds, (Boreas, Aquilo, Notus, &c.) and others as levanters or hurricanes, (Circius, &c.) Thus far he did no more than indulge a blameless fancy; but in his anxiety that his runners should emulate their patron winds, and do credit to the names which he had assigned them, he is said to have exacted a degree of speed inconsistent with any merciful regard for their bodily powers.[Footnote: This, however, is a point in which royal personages claim an old prescriptive right to be unreasonable in their exactions and some, even amongst the most humane of Christian princes, have erred as flagrantly as Ælius Verus. George IV., we have understood, was generally escorted from Balkeith to Holyrood at a rate of twenty-two miles an hour. And of his father, the truly kind and paternal king, it is recorded by Miss Hawkins, (daughter of Sir J. Hawkins, the biographer of Johnson, &c.) that families who happened to have a son, brother, lover, &c. in the particular regiment of cavalry which furnished the escort for the day, used to suffer as much anxiety for the result as on the eve of a great battle.] But these were, after all, perhaps, mere improvements of malice upon some solitary incident. The true stain upon his memory, and one which is open to no doubt whatever, is excessive and extravagant luxury - excessive in degree, extravagant and even ludicrous in its forms. For example, he constructed a sort of bed or sofa - protected from insects by an awning of network composed of lilies, delicately fabricated into the proper meshes, &c., and the couches composed wholly of rose-leaves; and even of these, not without an exquisite preparation; for the white parts of the leaves, as coarser and harsher to the touch, (possibly, also, as less odorous,) were scrupulously rejected. Here he lay indolently stretched amongst favorite ladies,

"And like a naked Indian slept himself away."

He had also tables composed of the same delicate material - prepared and purified in the same elaborate way - and to these were adapted seats in the fashion of sofas (*accubationes*,) corresponding in their materials, and in their mode of preparation. He was also an expert performer, and even an original inventor, in the art of cookery; and one dish of his discovery, which, from its four component parts, obtained the name of

Thomas de Quincey

tetrapharmacum, was so far from owing its celebrity to its royal birth, that it maintained its place on Hadrian's table to the time of his death. These, however, were mere fopperies or pardonable extravagancies in one so young and so exalted; "quæ, etsi non decora," as the historian observes, "non tamen ad perniciem publicam prompta sunt." A graver mode of licentiousness appeared in his connections with women. He made no secret of his lawless amours; and to his own wife, on her expostulating with him on his aberrations in this respect, he replied - that "*wife*" was a designation of rank and official dignity, not of tenderness and affection, or implying any claim of love on either side; upon which distinction he begged that she would mind her own affairs, and leave him to pursue such as he might himself be involved in by his sensibility to female charms.

However, he and all his errors, his "regal beauty," his princely pomps, and his authorized hopes, were suddenly swallowed up by the inexorable grave; and he would have passed away like an exhalation, and leaving no remembrance of himself more durable than his own beds of rose-leaves, and his reticulated canopies of lilies, had it not been that Hadrian filled the world with images of his perfect fawn-like beauty in the shape of colossal statues, and raised temples even to his memory in various cities. This Cæsar, therefore, dying thus prematurely, never tasted of empire; and his name would have had but a doubtful title to a place in the imperatorial roll, had it not been recalled to a second chance for the sacred honors in the person of his son - whom it was the pleasure of Hadrian, by way of testifying his affection for the father, to associate in the order of succession with the philosophic Marcus Aurelius Antoninus. This fact, and the certainty that to the second Julius Verus he gave his own daughter in marriage, rather than to his associate Cæsar Marcus Aurelius, make it evident that his regret for the elder Verus was unaffected and deep; and they overthrow effectually the common report of historians - that he repented of his earliest choice, as of one that had been disappointed not by the decrees of fate, but by the violent defect of merits in its object. On the contrary, he prefaced his inauguration of this junior Cæsar by the following tender words - Let us confound the rapine of the grave, and let the empire possess amongst her rulers a second Ælius Verus.

"*Diis aliter visum est:*" the blood of the Ælian family was not privileged to ascend or aspire: it gravitated violently to extinction; and this junior Verus is supposed to have been as much indebted to his assessor on the throne for shielding his obscure vices, and drawing over his defects the ample draperies of the imperatorial robe, as he was to Hadrian, his grandfather by fiction of law, for his adoption into the reigning family, and his consecration as one of the Cæsars. He, says one historian, shed no ray of light or illustration upon the imperial house, except by one solitary quality. This bears a harsh sound; but it has the effect of a sudden redemption for his memory, when we learn - that this solitary quality, in virtue of which he claimed a natural affinity to the sacred house, and challenged a natural interest in the purple, was the very princely one of - a merciful disposition.

The two Antonines fix an era in the imperial history; for they were both eminent models of wise and good rulers; and some would say, that they fixed a crisis; for with their successor commenced, in the popular belief, the decline of the empire. That at least is the doctrine

Thomas de Quincey

of Gibbon; but perhaps it would not be found altogether able to sustain itself against a closer and philosophic examination of the true elements involved in the idea of declension as applied to political bodies. Be that as it may, however, and waiving any interest which might happen to invest the Antonines as the last princes who kept up the empire to its original level, both of them had enough of merit to challenge a separate notice in their personal characters, and apart from the accidents of their position.

The elder of the two, who is usually distinguished by the title of *Pius*, is thus described by one of his biographers: - "He was externally of remarkable beauty; eminent for his moral character, full of benign dispositions, noble, with a countenance of a most gentle expression, intellectually of singular endowments, possessing an elegant style of eloquence, distinguished for his literature, generally temperate, an earnest lover of agricultural pursuits, mild in his deportment, bountiful in the use of his own, but a stern respecter of the rights of others; and, finally, he was all this without ostentation, and with a constant regard to the proportions of cases, and to the demands of time and place." His bounty displayed itself in a way, which may be worth mentioning, as at once illustrating the age, and the prudence with which he controlled the most generous of his impulses: - "*Finus trientarium,*" says the historian, "*hoc est minimis usuris exercuit, ut patrimonio suo plurimos adjuvaret.*" The meaning of which is this: - in Rome, the customary interest for money was what was called *centesimæ usuræ*; that is, the hundredth part, or one per cent. But, as this expressed not the annual, but the *monthly* interest, the true rate was, in fact, twelve per cent.; and that is the meaning of *centesimæ usuræ*. Nor could money be obtained any where on better terms than these; and, moreover, this one per cent, was exacted rigorously as the monthly day came round, no arrears being suffered to lie over. Under these circumstances, it was a prodigious service to lend money at a diminished rate, and one which furnished many men with the means of saving themselves from ruin. Pius then, by way of extending his aid as far as possible, reduced the monthly rate of his loans to one-third per cent., which made the annual interest the very moderate one of four per cent. The channels, which public spirit had as yet opened to the beneficence of the opulent, were few indeed: charity and munificence languished, or they were abused, or they were inefficiently directed, simply through defects in the structure of society. Social organization, for its large development, demanded the agency of newspapers, (together with many other forms of assistance from the press,) of banks, of public carriages on an extensive scale, besides infinite other inventions or establishments not yet created - which support and powerfully react upon that same progress of society which originally gave birth to themselves. All things considered, in the Rome of that day, where all munificence confined itself to the direct largesses of a few leading necessaries of life, - a great step was taken, and the best step, in this lending of money at a low interest, towards a more refined and beneficial mode of charity.

In his public character, he was perhaps the most patriotic of Roman emperors, and the purest from all taint of corrupt or indirect ends. Peculation, embezzlement, or misapplication of the public funds, were universally corrected: provincial oppressors were exposed and defeated: the taxes and tributes were diminished; and the public expenses were thrown as

Thomas de Quincey

much as possible upon the public estates, and in some instances upon his own private estates. So far, indeed, did Pius stretch his sympathy with the poorer classes of his subjects, that on this account chiefly he resided permanently in the capital - alleging in excuse, partly that he thus stationed himself in the very centre of his mighty empire, to which all couriers could come by the shortest radii, but chiefly that he thus spared the provincialists those burthens which must else have alighted upon them; "for," said he, "even the slenderest retinue of a Roman emperor is burthensome to the whole line of its progress." His tenderness and consideration, indeed, were extended to all classes, and all relations, of his subjects; even to those who stood in the shadow of his public displeasure as State delinquents, or as the most atrocious criminals. To the children of great treasury defaulters, he returned the confiscated estates of their fathers, deducting only what might repair the public loss. And so resolutely did he refuse to shed the blood of any in the senatorial order, to whom he conceived himself more especially bound in paternal ties, that even a parricide, whom the laws would not suffer to live, was simply exposed upon a desert island.

Little indeed did Pius want of being a perfect Christian, in heart and in practice. Yet all this display of goodness and merciful indulgence, nay, all his munificence, would have availed him little with the people at large, had he neglected to furnish shows and exhibitions in the arena of suitable magnificence. Luckily for his reputation, he exceeded the general standard of imperial splendor not less as the patron of the amphitheatre than in his more important functions. It is recorded of him - that in one *missio* he sent forward on the arena a hundred lions. Nor was he less distinguished by the rarity of the wild animals which he exhibited than by their number. There were elephants, there were crocodiles, there were hippopotami at one time upon the stage: there was also the rhinoceros, and the still rarer *crocuta* or *corocotta*, with a few *strepsikerotes*. Some of these were matched in duels, some in general battles with tigers; in fact, there was no species of wild animal throughout the deserts and sandy Zaarras of Africa, the infinite *steppes* of Asia, or the lawny recesses and dim forests of then sylvan Europe, [Footnote: And not impossibly of America; for it must be remembered that, when we speak of this quarter of the earth as yet undiscovered, we mean - to ourselves of the western climates; since as respects the eastern quarters of Asia, doubtless America was known there familiarly enough; and the high bounties of imperial Rome on rare animals, would sometimes perhaps propagate their influence even to those regions.] no species known to natural history, (and some even of which naturalists have lost sight,) which the Emperor Pius did not produce to his Roman subjects on his ceremonious pomps. And in another point he carried his splendors to a point which set the seal to his liberality. In the phrase of modern auctioneers, he gave up the wild beasts to slaughter "without reserve." It was the custom, in ordinary cases, so far to consider the enormous cost of these far-fetched rarities as to preserve for future occasions those which escaped the arrows of the populace, or survived the bloody combats in which they were engaged. Thus, out of the overflowings of one great exhibition, would be found materials for another. But Pius would not allow of these reservations. All were given up unreservedly to the savage purposes of the spectators; land and sea were ransacked; the sanctuaries of the torrid zone were violated; columns

Thomas de Quincey

of the army were put in motion - and all for the
transient effect of crowning an extra hour with
hecatombs of forest blood, each separate minute of
which had cost a king's ransom.

Yet these displays were alien to the nature of Pius; and,
even through the tyranny of custom, he had been so
little changed, that to the last he continued to turn
aside, as often as the public ritual of his duty allowed
him, from these fierce spectacles to the gentler
amusements of fishing and hunting. His taste and his
affections naturally carried him to all domestic
pleasures of a quiet nature. A walk in a shrubbery or
along a piazza, enlivened with the conversation of a
friend or two, pleased him better than all the court
festivals; and among festivals, or anniversary
celebrations, he preferred those which, like the harvest-
home or feast of the vintagers, whilst they sanctioned a
total carelessness and dismissal of public anxieties,
were at the same time colored by the innocent gaiety
which belongs to rural and to primitive manners. In
person this emperor was tall and dignified (*staturâ
elevatâ decorus;*) but latterly he stooped; to remedy
which defect, that he might discharge his public part
with the more decorum, he wore stays. [Footnote: In
default of whalebone, one is curious to know of what
they were made: - thin tablets of the linden-tree, it
appears, were the best materials which the Augustus of
that day could command.] Of his other personal habits
little is recorded, except that, early in the morning, and
just before receiving the compliments of his friends
and dependents, (*salutatores,*) or what in modern
phrase would be called his *levee*, he took a little plain
bread, (*panem siccum comedit,*) that is, bread without
condiments or accompaniments of any kind, by way of
breakfast. In no meal has luxury advanced more upon

the model of the ancients than in this: the dinners (*cœnæ*) of the Romans were even more luxurious, and a thousand times more costly, than our own; but their breakfasts were scandalously meagre; and, with many men, breakfast was no professed meal at all. Galen tells us that a little bread, and at most a little seasoning of oil, honey, or dried fruits, was the utmost breakfast which men generally allowed themselves: some indeed drank wine after it, but this was far from being a common practice. [Footnote: There is, however, a good deal of delusion prevalent on such subjects. In some English cavalry regiments, the custom is for the privates to take only one meal a day, which of course is dinner; and by some curious experiments it has appeared that such a mode of life is the healthiest. But at the same time, we have ascertained that the quantity of porter or substantial ale drunk in these regiments does virtually allow many meals, by comparison with the washy tea breakfasts of most Englishmen.]

The Emperor Pius died in his seventieth year. The immediate occasion of his death was - not breakfast nor *cæna*, but something of the kind. He had received a present of Alpine cheese, and he ordered some for supper. The trap for his life was baited with toasted cheese. There is no reason to think that he ate immoderately; but that night he was seized with indigestion. Delirium followed; during which it is singular that his mind teemed with a class of imagery and of passions the most remote (as it might have been thought) from the voluntary occupations of his thoughts. He raved about the State, and about those kings with whom he was displeased; nor were his thoughts one moment removed from the public service. Yet he was the least ambitious of princes, and his reign was emphatically said to be bloodless. Finding his

Thomas de Quincey

fever increase, he became sensible that he was dying; and he ordered the golden statue of Prosperity, a household symbol of empire, to be transferred from his own bedroom to that of his successor. Once again, however, for the last time, he gave the word to the officer of the guard; and, soon after, turning away his face to the wall against which his bed was placed, he passed out of life in the very gentlest sleep, "*quasi dormiret, spiritum reddidit;*" or, as a Greek author expresses it, *kat iso hypno to malakotato.* He was one of those few Roman emperors whom posterity truly honored with the title of *anaimatos* (or bloodless;) *solusque omnium prope principum prorsus sine civili sanguine et hostili vixit.* In the whole tenor of his life and character he was thought to resemble Numa. And Pausanias, after remarking on his title of *Eusebæs* (or Pius), upon the meaning and origin of which there are several different hypotheses, closes with this memorable tribute to his paternal qualities - *doxæ de emae, kai to onoma to te Kyros pheroito an tos presbyteros, Pater anthropon kalemenos*: *but, in my opinion, he should also bear the name of Cyrus the elder - being hailed as Father of the Human Race.*

A thoughtful Roman would have been apt to exclaim, *This is too good to last*, upon finding so admirable a ruler succeeded by one still more admirable in the person of Marcus Aurelius. From the first dawn of his infancy this prince indicated, by his grave deportment, the philosophic character of his mind; and at eleven years of age he professed himself a formal devotee of philosophy in its strictest form, - assuming the garb, and submitting to its most ascetic ordinances. In particular, he slept upon the ground, and in other respects he practised a style of living the most simple and remote from the habits of rich men [or, in his own words, *tho lithon chatha tæn diaitan, chai porro tæs pleousiachæs hagogæs*]; though it is true that he himself ascribes this simplicity of life to the influence of his mother, and not to the premature assumption of the stoical character. He pushed his austerities indeed to excess; for Dio mentions that in his boyish days he was reduced to great weakness by exercises too severe, and a diet of too little nutriment. In fact, his whole heart was set upon philosophic attainments, and perhaps upon philosophic glory. All the great philosophers of his own time, whether Stoic or Peripatetic, and amongst them Sextus of Cheronæa, a nephew of Plutarch, were retained as his instructors. There was none whom he did not enrich; and as many as were fitted by birth and manners to fill important situations, he raised to the highest offices in the State. Philosophy, however, did not so much absorb his affections, but that he found time to cultivate the fine arts, (painting he both studied and practised,) and such gymnastic exercises as he held consistent with his public dignity. Wrestling, hunting, fowling, playing at cricket (*pila*), he admired and patronized by personal participation. He tried his powers even as a runner. But with these tasks, and entering so critically, both as a connoisseur and as a practising amateur, into such trials of skill, so little did he relish the very same spectacles, when connected with the cruel exhibitions of the circus and amphitheatre, that it was not without some friendly violence on the part of those who could venture on such a liberty, nor even thus, perhaps, without the necessities of his official station, that he would be persuaded to visit either one or the other. [Footnote: So much improvement had Christianity already accomplished in the feelings of men since the time of Augustus. That prince, in whose reign the founder of this ennobling religion was born, had

Thomas de Quincey

delighted so much and indulged so freely in the spectacles of the amphitheatre, that Mæcenas summoned him reproachfully to leave them, saying, "Surge tandem, carnifex."

It is the remark of Capitoline, that "gladiatoria spectacula omnifariam temperavit; temperavit etiam scenicas donationes;" - he controlled in every possible way the gladiatorial spectacles; he controlled also the rates of allowance to the stage performers. In these latter reforms, which simply restrained the exorbitant salaries of a class dedicated to the public pleasures, and unprofitable to the state, Marcus may have had no farther view than that which is usually connected with sumptuary laws. But in the restraints upon the gladiators, it is impossible to believe that his highest purpose was not that of elevating human nature, and preparing the way for still higher regulations. As little can it be believed that this lofty conception, and the sense of a degradation entailed upon human nature itself, in the spectacle of human beings matched against each other like brute beasts, and pouring out their blood upon the arena as a libation to the caprices of a mob, could have been derived from any other source than the contagion of Christian standards and Christian sentiments, then beginning to pervade and ventilate the atmosphere of society in its higher and philosophic regions. Christianity, without expressly affirming, every where indirectly supposes and presumes the infinite value and dignity of man as a creature, exclusively concerned in a vast and mysterious economy of restoration to a state of moral beauty and power in some former age mysteriously forfeited. Equally interested in its benefits, joint heirs of its promises, all men, of every color, language, and rank, Gentile or Jew, were here first represented as in one sense (and that the most important) equal; in the eye of this religion, they were, by necessity of logic, equal, as equal participators in the ruin and the restoration. Here first, in any available sense, was communicated to the standard of human nature a vast and sudden elevation; and reasonable enough it is to suppose, that some obscure sense of this, some sympathy with the great changes for man then beginning to operate, would first of all reach the inquisitive students of philosophy, and chiefly those in high stations, who cultivated an intercourse with all the men of original genius throughout the civilized world. The Emperor Hadrian had already taken a solitary step in the improvement of human nature; and not, we may believe, without some sub-conscious influence received directly or indirectly from Christianity. So again, with respect to Marcus, it is hardly conceivable that he, a prince so indulgent and popular, could have thwarted, and violently gainsaid, a primary impulse of the Roman populace, without some adequate motive; and none *could* be adequate which was not built upon some new and exalted views of human nature, with which these gladiatorial sacrifices were altogether at war. The reforms which Marcus introduced into these "crudelissima spectacula," all having the common purpose of limiting their extent, were three. First, he set bounds to the extreme cost of these exhibitions; and this restriction of the cost covertly operated as a restriction of the practice. Secondly, - and this ordinance took effect whenever he was personally present, if not oftener, - he commanded, on great occasions, that these displays should be bloodless. Dion Cassius notices this fact in the following words: - "The Emperor Marcus was so far from taking delight in spectacles of bloodshed, that even the gladiators in Rome could not obtain his inspection of their contests,

Thomas de Quincey

unless, like the wrestlers, they contended without imminent risk; for he never allowed them the use of sharpened weapons, but universally they fought before him with weapons previously blunted." Thirdly, he repealed the old and uniform regulation, which secured to the gladiators a perpetual immunity from military service. This necessarily diminished their available amount. Being now liable to serve their country usefully in the field of battle, whilst the concurrent limitation of the expenses in this direction prevented any proportionate increase of their numbers, they were so much the less disposable in aid of the public luxury. His fatherly care of all classes, and the universal benignity with which he attempted to raise the abject estimate and condition of even the lowest *Pariars* in his vast empire, appears in another little anecdote, relating to a class of men equally with the gladiators given up to the service of luxury in a haughty and cruel populace. Attending one day at an exhibition of rope-dancing, one of the performers (a boy) fell and hurt himself; from which time the paternal emperor would never allow the rope-dancers to perform without mattrasses or feather-beds spread below, to mitigate the violence of their falls.] In this he meditated no reflection upon his father by adoption, the Emperor Pius, (who also, for aught we know, might secretly revolt from a species of amusement which, as the prescriptive test of munificence in the popular estimate, it was necessary to support;) on the contrary, he obeyed him with the punctiliousness of a Roman obedience; he watched the very motions of his countenance; and he waited so continually upon his pleasure, that for three-and-twenty years which they lived together, he is recorded to have slept out of his father's palace only for two nights. This rigor of filial duty illustrates a feature of Roman life; for such was the sanctity of law, that a father created by legal fiction was in all respects treated with the same veneration and affection, as a father who claimed upon the most unquestioned footing of natural right. Such, however, is the universal baseness of courts, that even this scrupulous and minute attention to his duties, did not protect Marcus from the injurious insinuations of whisperers. There were not wanting persons who endeavored to turn to account the general circumstances in the situation of the Cæsar, which pointed him out to the jealousy of the emperor. But these being no more than what adhere necessarily to the case of every heir *as* such, and meeting fortunately with no more proneness to suspicion in the temper of the Augustus than they did with countenance in the conduct of the Cæsar, made so little impression, that at length these malicious efforts died away, from mere defect of encouragement.

The most interesting political crisis in the reign of Marcus was the war in Germany with the Marcomanni, concurrently with pestilence in Rome. The agitation of the public mind was intense; and prophets arose, as since under corresponding circumstances in Christian countries, who announced the approaching dissolution of the world. The purse of Marcus was open, as usual, to the distresses of his subjects. But it was chiefly for the expense of funerals that his aid was claimed. In this way he alleviated the domestic calamities of his capital, or expressed his sympathy with the sufferers, where alleviation was beyond his power; whilst, by the energy of his movements and his personal presence on the Danube, he soon dissipated those anxieties of Rome which pointed in a foreign direction. The war, however, had been a dreadful one, and had excited such just fears in the most experienced heads of the

Thomas de Quincey

State, that, happening in its outbreak to coincide with a Parthian war, it was skilfully protracted until the entire thunders of Rome, and the undivided energies of her supreme captains, could be concentrated upon this single point. Both [Footnote: Marcus had been associated, as Cæsar and as emperor, with the son of the late beautiful Verus, who is usually mentioned by the same name.] emperors left Rome, and crossed the Alps; the war was thrown back upon its native seats - Austria and the modern Hungary: great battles were fought and won; and peace, with consequent relief and restoration to liberty, was reconquered for many friendly nations, who had suffered under the ravages of the Marcomanni, the Sarmatians, the Quadi, and the Vandals; whilst some of the hostile people were nearly obliterated from the map, and their names blotted out from the memory of men.

Since the days of Gaul as an independent power, no war had so much alarmed the people of Rome; and their fear was justified by the difficulties and prodigious efforts which accompanied its suppression. The public treasury was exhausted; loans were an engine of fiscal policy, not then understood or perhaps practicable; and great distress was at hand for the State. In these circumstances, Marcus adopted a wise (though it was then esteemed a violent or desperate) remedy. Time and excessive luxury had accumulated in the imperial palaces and villas vast repositories of apparel, furniture, jewels, pictures, and household utensils, valuable alike for the materials and the workmanship. Many of these articles were consecrated, by color or otherwise, to the use of the *sacred* household; and to have been found in possession of them, or with the materials for making them, would have entailed the penalties of treason. All these stores were now brought out to open day, and put up to public sale by auction, free license being first granted to the bidders, whoever they might be, to use, or otherwise to exercise the fullest rights of property upon all they bought. The auction lasted for two months. Every man was guaranteed in the peaceable ownership of his purchases. And afterwards, when the public distress had passed over, a still further indulgence was extended to the purchasers. Notice was given - that all who were dissatisfied with their purchases, or who for other means might wish to recover their cost, would receive back the purchase-money, upon returning the articles. Dinner-services of gold and crystal, murrhine vases, and even his wife's wardrobe of silken robes interwoven with gold, all these, and countless other articles were accordingly returned, and the full auction prices paid back; or were *not* returned, and no displeasure shown to those who publicly displayed them as their own. Having gone so far, overruled by the necessities of the public service, in breaking down those legal barriers by which a peculiar dress, furniture, equipage, &c., were appropriated to the imperial house, as distinguished from the very highest of the noble houses, Marcus had a sufficient pretext for extending indefinitely the effect of the dispensation then granted. Articles purchased at the auction bore no characteristic marks to distinguish them from others of the same form and texture: so that a license to use any one article of the *sacred* pattern, became necessarily a general license for all others which resembled them. And thus, without abrogating the prejudices which protected the imperial precedency, a body of sumptuary laws - the most ruinous to the progress of manufacturing skill, [Footnote: Because the most effectual extinguishers of all ambition applied in that direction; since the very

Thomas de Quincey

excellence of any particular fabric was the surest pledge of its virtual suppression by means of its legal restriction (which followed inevitably) to the use of the imperial house.] which has ever been devised - were silently suspended. One or two aspiring families might be offended by these innovations, which meantime gave the pleasures of enjoyment to thousands, and of hope to millions.

But these, though very noticeable relaxations of the existing prerogative, were, as respected the temper which dictated them, no more than everyday manifestations of the emperor's perpetual benignity. Fortunately for Marcus, the indestructible privilege of the *divina domus* exalted it so unapproachably beyond all competition, that no possible remissions of aulic rigor could ever be misinterpreted; fear there could be none, lest such paternal indulgences should lose their effect and acceptation as pure condescensions. They could neither injure their author, who was otherwise charmed and consecrated, from disrespect; nor could they suffer injury themselves by misconstruction, or seem other than sincere, coming from a prince whose entire life was one long series of acts expressing the same affable spirit. Such, indeed, was the effect of this uninterrupted benevolence in the emperor, that at length all men, according to their several ages, hailed him as their father, son, or brother. And when he died, in the sixty-first year of his life (the 18th of his reign), he was lamented with a corresponding peculiarity in the public ceremonial, such, for instance, as the studied interfusion of the senatorial body with the populace, expressive of the levelling power of a true and comprehensive grief; a peculiarity for which no precedent was found, and which never afterwards became a precedent for similar honors to the best of his successors.

But malice has the divine privilege of ubiquity; and therefore it was that even this great model of private and public virtue did not escape the foulest libels: he was twice accused of murder; once on the person of a gladiator, with whom the empress is said to have fallen in love; and again, upon his associate in the empire, who died in reality of an apoplectic seizure, on his return from the German campaign. Neither of these atrocious fictions ever gained the least hold of the public attention, so entirely were they put down by the *prima facie* evidence of facts, and of the emperor's notorious character. In fact his faults, if he had any in his public life, were entirely those of too much indulgence. In a few cases of enormous guilt, it is recorded that he showed himself inexorable. But, generally speaking, he was far otherwise; and, in particular, he carried his indulgence to his wife's vices to an excess which drew upon him the satirical notice of the stage.

The gladiators, and still more the sailors of that age, were constantly to be seen playing naked, and Faustina was shameless enough to take her station in places which gave her the advantages of a leisurely review; and she actually selected favorites from both classes on the ground of a personal inspection. With others of greater rank she is said even to have been surprised by her husband; in particular with one called Tertullus, at dinner. [Footnote: Upon which some *mimographus* built an occasional notice of the scandal then floating on the public breath in the following terms: One of the actors having asked "*Who was the adulterous paramour?*" receives for answer, *Tullus*. Who? he asks again; and again for three times running he is

Thomas de Quincey

answered, *Tullus*. But asking a fourth time, the rejoinder is, Jam dixi *ter Tullus*.] But to all remonstrances on this subject, Marcus is reported to have replied, "*Si uxorem dimittimus, reddamus et dotem;*" meaning that, having received his right of succession to the empire simply by his adoption into the family of Pius, his wife's father, gratitude and filial duty obliged him to view any dishonors emanating from his wife's conduct as joint legacies with the splendors inherited from their common father; in short, that he was not at liberty to separate the rose from its thorns. However, the facts are not sufficiently known to warrant us in criticising very severely his behavior on so trying an occasion.

It would be too much for human frailty, that absolutely no stain should remain upon his memory. Possibly the best use which can be made of such a fact is, in the way of consolation to any unhappy man, whom his wife may too liberally have endowed with honors of this kind, by reminding him that he shares this distinction with the great philosophic emperor. The reflection upon this story by one of his biographers is this - "Such is the force of daily life in a good ruler, so great the power of his sanctity, gentleness, and piety, that no breath of slander or invidious suggestion from an acquaintance can avail to sully his memory. In short, to Antonine, immutable as the heavens in the tenor of his own life, and in the manifestations of his own moral temper, and who was not by possibility liable to any impulse or 'shadow of turning' from another man's suggestion, it was not eventually an injury that he was dishonored by some of his connections; on him, invulnerable in his own character, neither a harlot for his wife, nor a gladiator for his son, could inflict a wound. Then as now, oh sacred lord

Diocletian, he was reputed a god; not as others are reputed, but specially and in a peculiar sense, and with a privilege to such worship from all men as you yourself addressed to him - who often breathe a wish to Heaven, that you were or could be such in life and merciful disposition as was Marcus Aurelius."

What this encomiast says in a rhetorical tone was literally true. Marcus was raised to divine honors, or canonized [Footnote: In reality, if by *divus* and *divine honors* we understand a saint or spiritualized being having a right of intercession with the Supreme Deity, and by his temple, &c., if we understand a shrine attended by a priest to direct the prayers of his devotees, there is no such wide chasm between this pagan superstition and the adoration of saints in the Romish church, as at first sight appears. The fault is purely in the names: *divus* and *templum* are words too undistinguishing and generic.] (as in Christian phrase we might express it.) That was a matter of course; and, considering with whom he shared such honors, they are of little account in expressing the grief and veneration which followed him. A circumstance more characteristic, in the record of those observances which attested the public feeling, is this - that he who at that time had no bust, picture, or statue of Marcus in his house, was looked upon as a profane and irreligious man. Finally, to do him honor not by testimonies of men's opinions in his favor, but by facts of his own life and conduct, one memorable trophy there is amongst the moral distinctions of the philosophic Cæsar, utterly unnoticed hitherto by historians, but which will hereafter obtain a conspicuous place in any perfect record of the steps by which civilization has advanced, and human nature has been exalted. It is this: Marcus Aurelius was the first great military leader (and his

Thomas de Quincey

civil office as supreme interpreter and creator of law consecrated his example) who allowed rights indefeasible - rights uncancelled by his misfortune in the field, to the prisoner of war. Others had been merciful and variously indulgent, upon their own discretion, and upon a random impulse to some, or possibly to all of their prisoners; but this was either in submission to the usage of that particular war, or to special self-interest, or at most to individual good feeling. None had allowed a prisoner to challenge any forbearance as of right. But Marcus Aurelius first resolutely maintained that certain indestructible rights adhered to every soldier, simply as a man, which rights, capture by the sword, or any other accident of war, could do nothing to shake or to diminish. We have noticed other instances in which Marcus Aurelius labored, at the risk of his popularity, to elevate the condition of human nature. But those, though equally expressing the goodness and loftiness of his nature, were by accident directed to a perishable institution, which time has swept away, and along with it therefore his reformations. Here, however, is an immortal act of goodness built upon an immortal basis; for so long as armies congregate, and the sword is the arbiter of international quarrels, so long it will deserve to be had in remembrance, that the first man who set limits to the empire of wrong, and first translated within the jurisdiction of man's moral nature that state of war which had heretofore been consigned, by principle no less than by practice, to anarchy, animal violence, and brute force, was also the first philosopher who sat upon a throne.

In this, and in his universal spirit of forgiveness, we cannot but acknowledge a Christian by anticipation; nor can we hesitate to believe, that through one or other of his many philosophic friends, [Footnote: Not long after this, Alexander Severus meditated a temple to Christ; upon which design Lampridius observes, - *Quod et Hadrianus cogitâsse fertur;* and, as Lampridius was himself a pagan, we believe him to have been right in his report, in spite of all which has been written by Casaubon and others, who maintain that these imperfect temples of Hadrian were left void of all images or idols, - not in respect to the Christian practice, but because he designed them eventually to be dedicated to himself. However, be this as it may, thus much appears on the face of the story, - that Christ and Christianity had by that time begun to challenge the imperial attention; and of this there is an indirect indication, as it has been interpreted, even in the memoir of Marcus himself. The passage is this: "Fama fuit sane quod sub philosophorum specie quidam rempublicam vexarent et privates." The *philosophi*, here mentioned by Capitoline, are by some supposed to be the Christians; and for many reasons we believe it; and we understand the molestations of the public services and of private individuals, here charged upon them, as a very natural reference to the Christian doctrines falsely understood. There is, by the way, a fine remark upon Christianity, made by an infidel philosopher of Germany, which suggests a remarkable feature in the merits of Marcus Aurelius. There were, as this German philosopher used to observe, two schemes of thinking amongst the ancients, which severally fulfilled the two functions of a sound philosophy, as respected the moral nature of man. One of these schemes presented us with a just ideal of moral excellence, a standard sufficiently exalted: this was the Stoic philosophy; and thus far its pretensions were unexceptionable and perfect. But unfortunately, whilst contemplating this pure ideal of man as he ought

Thomas de Quincey

to be, the Stoic totally forgot the frail nature of man as he is; and by refusing all compromises and all condescensions to human infirmity, this philosophy of the Porch presented to us a brilliant prize and object for our efforts, but placed on an inaccessible height.

On the other hand, there was a very different philosophy at the very antagonist pole, - not blinding itself by abstractions too elevated, submitting to what it finds, bending to the absolute facts and realities of man's nature, and affably adapting itself to human imperfections. This was the philosophy of Epicurus; and undoubtedly, as a beginning, and for the elementary purpose of conciliating the affections of the pupil, it was well devised; but here the misfortune was, that the ideal, or *maximum perfectionis*, attainable by human nature, was pitched so low, that the humility of its condescensions and the excellence of its means were all to no purpose, as leading to nothing further. One mode presented a splendid end, but insulated, and with no means fitted to a human aspirant for communicating with its splendors; the other, an excellent road, but leading to no worthy or proportionate end. Yet these, as regarded morals, were the best and ultimate achievements of the pagan world. Now Christianity, said he, is the synthesis of whatever is separately excellent in either. It will abate as little as the haughtiest Stoicism of the ideal which it contemplates as the first postulate of true morality; the absolute holiness and purity which it demands are as much raised above the poor performances of actual man, as the absolute wisdom and impeccability of the Stoic. Yet, unlike the Stoic scheme, Christianity is aware of the necessity, and provides for it, that the means of appropriating this ideal perfection should be such as are consistent with the nature of a most erring and imperfect creature. Its motion is *towards* the divine, but *by* and *through* the human. In fact, it offers the Stoic humanized in his scheme of means, and the Epicurean exalted in his final objects. Nor is it possible to conceive a practicable scheme of morals which should not rest upon such a synthesis of the two elements as the Christian scheme presents; nor any other mode of fulfilling that demand than, such a one as is there first brought forward, viz., a double or Janus nature, which stands in an equivocal relation, - to the divine nature by his actual perfections, to the human nature by his participation in the same animal frailties and capacities of fleshly temptation. No other vinculum could bind the two postulates together, of an absolute perfection in the end proposed, and yet of utter imperfection in the means for attaining it.

Such was the outline of this famous tribute by an unbelieving philosopher to the merits of Christianity as a scheme of moral discipline. Now, it must be remembered that Marcus Aurelius was by profession a Stoic; and that generally, as a theoretical philosopher, but still more as a Stoic philosopher, he might be supposed incapable of descending from these airy altitudes of speculation to the true needs, infirmities, and capacities of human nature. Yet strange it is, that he, of all the good emperors, was the most thoroughly human and practical. In evidence of which, one body of records is amply sufficient, which is, the very extensive and wise reforms which he, beyond all the Cæsars, executed in the existing laws. To all the exigencies of the times, and to all the new necessities developed by the progress of society, he adjusted the old laws, or supplied new ones. The same praise, therefore, belongs to him, which the German philosopher conceded to Christianity, of reconciling

Thomas de Quincey

the austerest ideal with the practical; and hence another argument for presuming him half baptized into the new faith.] whose attention Christianity was by that time powerful to attract, some reflex images of Christian doctrines - some half-conscious perception of its perfect beauty - had flashed upon his mind. And when we view him from this distant age, as heading that shining array, the Howards and the Wilberforces, who have since then in a practical sense hearkened to the sighs of "all prisoners and captives" - we are ready to suppose him addressed by the great Founder of Christianity, in the words of Scripture, "*Verily, I say unto thee, Thou art not far from the kingdom of heaven.*"

As a supplement to the reign of Marcus Aurelius, we ought to notice the rise of one great rebel, the sole civil disturber of his time, in Syria. This was Avidius Cassius, whose descent from Cassius (the noted conspirator against the great Dictator, Julius) seems to have suggested to him a wandering idea, and at length a formal purpose of restoring the ancient republic. Avidius was the commander-in-chief of the Oriental army, whose head-quarters were then fixed at Antioch. His native disposition, which inclined him to cruelty, and his political views, made him, from his first entrance upon office, a severe disciplinarian. The well known enormities of the neighboring Daphne gave him ample opportunities for the exercise of his harsh propensities in reforming the dissolute soldiery. He amputated heads, arms, feet, and hams: he turned out his mutilated victims, as walking spectacles of warning; he burned them; he smoked them to death; and, in one instance, he crucified a detachment of his army, together with their centurions, for having, unauthorized, gained a splendid victory, and captured a large booty on the Danube. Upon this the soldiers mutinied against him, in mere indignation at his tyranny. However, he prosecuted his purpose, and prevailed, by his bold contempt of the danger which menaced him. From the abuses in the army, he proceeded to attack the abuses of the civil administration. But as these were protected by the example of the great proconsular lieutenants and provincial governors, policy obliged him to confine himself to verbal expressions of anger; until at length, sensible that this impotent railing did but expose him to contempt, he resolved to arm himself with the powers of radical reform, by open rebellion. His ultimate purpose was the restoration of the ancient republic, or, (as he himself expresses it in an interesting letter, which yet survives,) "*ut in antiquum statum publica forma reddatur*;" *i.e.* that the constitution should be restored to its original condition. And this must be effected by military violence and the aid of the executioner - or, in his own words, *multis gladiis, multis elogiis*, (by innumerable sabres, by innumerable records of condemnation.) Against this man Marcus was warned by his imperial colleague Lucius Verus, in a very remarkable letter. After expressing his suspicions of him generally, the writer goes on to say - "I would you had him closely watched. For he is a general disliker of us and of our doings; he is gathering together an enormous treasure, and he makes an open jest of our literary pursuits. You, for instance, he calls a philosophizing old woman, and me a dissolute buffoon and scamp. Consider what you would have done. For my part, I bear the fellow no ill will; but again, I say, take care that he does not do a mischief to yourself, or your children."

The answer of Marcus is noble and characteristic: "I

Thomas de Quincey

have read your letter, and I will confess to you I think it more scrupulously timid than becomes an emperor, and timid in a way unsuited to the spirit of our times. Consider this - if the empire is destined to Cassius by the decrees of Providence, in that case it will not be in our power to put him to death, however much we may desire to do so. You know your great-grandfather's saying, - No prince ever killed his own heir - no man, that is, ever yet prevailed against one whom Providence had marked out as his successor. On the other hand, if Providence opposes him, then, without any cruelty on our part, he will spontaneously fall into some snare spread for him by destiny. Besides, we cannot treat a man as under impeachment whom nobody impeaches, and whom, by your own confession, the soldiers love. Then again, in cases of high treason, even those criminals who are convicted upon the clearest evidence, yet, as friendless and deserted persons contending against the powerful, and matched against those who are armed with the whole authority of the State, seem to suffer some wrong. You remember what your grandfather said - Wretched, indeed, is the fate of princes, who then first obtain credit in any charges of conspiracy which they allege - when they happen to seal the validity of their charges against the plotters, by falling martyrs to the plot. Domitian it was, in fact, who first uttered this truth; but I choose rather to place it under the authority of Hadrian, because the sayings of tyrants, even when they are true and happy, carry less weight with them than naturally they ought. For Cassius, then, let him keep his present temper and inclinations; and the more so - being (as he is) a good General - austere in his discipline, brave, and one whom the State cannot afford to lose. For as to what you insinuate - that I ought to provide for my children's interests, by putting this man judicially out of the way, very frankly I say to you - Perish my children, if Avidius shall deserve more attachment than they, and if it shall prove salutary to the State that Cassius should live rather than the children of Marcus."

This letter affords a singular illustration of fatalism, such certainly as we might expect in a Stoic, but carried even to a Turkish excess; and not theoretically professed only, but practically acted upon in a case of capital hazard. *That no prince ever killed his own successor*, i.e., that it was vain for a prince to put conspirators to death, because, by the very possibility of doing so, a demonstration is obtained that such conspirators had never been destined to prosper, is as condensed and striking an expression of fatalism as ever has been devised. The rest of the letter is truly noble, and breathes the very soul of careless magnanimity reposing upon conscious innocence. Meantime, Cassius increased in power and influence: his army had become a most formidable engine of his ambition through its restored discipline; and his own authority was sevenfold greater, because he had himself created that discipline in the face of unequalled temptations hourly renewed and rooted in the very centre of his head-quarters. "Daphne, by Orontes," a suburb of Antioch, was infamous for its seductions; and *Daphnic luxury* had become proverbial for expressing an excess of voluptuousness, such as other places could not rival by mere defect of means, and preparations elaborate enough to sustain it in all its varieties of mode, or to conceal it from public notice. In the very purlieus of this great nest, or sty of sensuality, within sight and touch of its pollutions, did he keep his army fiercely reined up, daring and defying them , as it were, to taste of the banquet whose very

Thomas de Quincey

odor they inhaled.

Thus provided with the means, and improved instruments, for executing his purposes, he broke out into open rebellion; and, though hostile to the *principatus*, or personal supremacy of one man, he did not feel his republican purism at all wounded by the style and title of *Imperator*, - that being a military term, and a mere titular honor, which had co-existed with the severest forms of republicanism. *Imperator*, then, he was saluted and proclaimed; and doubtless the writer of the warning letter from Syria would now declare that the sequel had justified the fears which Marcus had thought so unbecoming to a Roman emperor. But again Marcus would have said, "Let us wait for the sequel of the sequel," and that would have justified him. It is often found by experience that men, who have learned to reverence a person in authority chiefly by his offices of correction applied to their own aberrations, - who have known and feared him, in short, in his character of reformer, - will be more than usually inclined to desert him on his first movement in the direction of wrong. Their obedience being founded on fear, and fear being never wholly disconnected from hatred, they naturally seize with eagerness upon the first lawful pretext for disobedience; the luxury of revenge is, in such a case, too potent, - a meritorious disobedience too novel a temptation, - to have a chance of being rejected. Never, indeed, does erring human nature look more abject than in the person of a severe exactor of duty, who has immolated thousands to the wrath of offended law, suddenly himself becoming a capital offender, a glozing tempter in search of accomplices, and in that character at once standing before the meanest of his own dependents as a self-deposed officer, liable to any man's arrest, and, *ipso facto*, a suppliant for his own mercy. The stern and haughty Cassius, who had so often tightened the cords of discipline until they threatened to snap asunder, now found, experimentally, the bitterness of these obvious truths. The trembling sentinel now looked insolently in his face; the cowering legionary, with whom "to hear was to obey," now mused or even bandied words upon his orders; the great lieutenants of his office, who stood next to his own person in authority, were preparing for revolt, open or secret, as circumstances should prescribe; not the accuser only, but the very avenger, was upon his steps; Nemesis, that Nemesis who once so closely adhered to the name and fortunes of the lawful Cæsar, turning against every one of his assassins the edge of his own assassinating sword, was already at his heels; and in the midst of a sudden prosperity, and its accompanying shouts of gratulation, he heard the sullen knells of approaching death. Antioch, it was true, the great Roman capital of the Orient, bore him, for certain motives of self-interest, peculiar good-will. But there was no city of the world in which the Roman Cæsar did not reckon many liegemen and partisans. And the very hands, which dressed his altars and crowned his Prætorian pavilion, might not improbably in that same hour put an edge upon the sabre which was to avenge the injuries of the too indulgent and long-suffering Antoninus. Meantime, to give a color of patriotism to his treason, Cassius alleged public motives; in a letter, which he wrote after assuming the purple, he says: "Wretched empire, miserable state, which endures these hungry blood-suckers battening on her vitals! - A worthy man, doubtless, is Marcus; who, in his eagerness to be reputed clement, suffers those to live whose conduct he himself abhors. Where is that L. Cassius, whose name I vainly inherit? Where is that Marcus, - not Aurelius,

Thomas de Quincey

mark you, but Cato Censorius? Where the good old discipline of ancestral times, long since indeed disused, but now not so much as looked after in our aspirations? Marcus Antoninus is a scholar; he enacts the philosopher; and he tries conclusions upon the four elements, and upon the nature of the soul; and he discourses learnedly upon the *Honestum*; and concerning the *Summum Bonum* he is unanswerable. Meanwhile, is he learned in the interests of the State? Can he argue a point upon the public economy? You see what a host of sabres is required, what a host of impeachments, sentences, executions, before the commonwealth can reassume its ancient integrity! What! shall I esteem as proconsuls, as governors, those who for that end only deem themselves invested with lieutenancies or great senatorial appointments, that they may gorge themselves with the provincial luxuries and wealth? No doubt you heard in what way our friend the philosopher gave the place of prætorian prefect to one who but three days before was a bankrupt, - insolvent, by G - , and a beggar. Be not you content: that same gentleman is now as rich as a prefect should be; and has been so, I tell you, any time these three days. And how, I pray you, how - how, my good sir? How but out of the bowels of the provinces, and the marrow of their bones? But no matter, let them be rich; let them be blood-suckers; so much, God willing, shall they regorge into the treasury of the empire. Let but Heaven smile upon our party, and the Cassiani shall return to the republic its old impersonal supremacy."

But Heaven did *not* smile; nor did man. Rome heard with bitter indignation of this old traitor's ingratitude, and his false mask of republican civism. Excepting Marcus Aurelius himself, not one man but thirsted for revenge. And that was soon obtained. He and all his supporters, one after the other, rapidly fell (as Marcus had predicted) into snares laid by the officers who continued true to their allegiance. Except the family and household of Cassius, there remained in a short time none for the vengeance of the senate, or for the mercy of the emperor. In *them* centred the last arrears of hope and fear, of chastisement or pardon, depending upon this memorable revolt. And about the disposal of their persons arose the final question to which the case gave birth. The letters yet remain in which the several parties interested gave utterance to the passions which possessed them. Faustina, the Empress, urged her husband with feminine violence to adopt against his prisoners comprehensive acts of vengeance. "Noli parcere hominibus," says she, "qui tibi non pepercerunt; et nec mihi nec filiis nostris parcerent, si vicissent." And elsewhere she irritates his wrath against the army as accomplices for the time, and as a body of men "qui, nisi opprimuntur, opprimunt." We may be sure of the result. After commending her zeal for her own family, he says, "Ego vero et ejus liberis parcam, et genero, et uxori; et ad senatum scribam ne aut proscriptio gravior sit, aut poena crudelior;" adding that, had his counsels prevailed, not even Cassius himself should have perished. As to his relatives, "Why," he asks, "should I speak of pardon to them, who indeed have done no wrong, and are blameless even in purpose?" Accordingly, his letter of intercession to the senate protests, that, so far from asking for further victims to the crime of Avidius Cassius, would to God he could call back from the dead many of those who had fallen! With immense applause, and with turbulent acclamations, the senate granted all his requests "in consideration of his philosophy, of his long-suffering, of his learning and

Thomas de Quincey

accomplishments, of his nobility, of his innocence."
And until a monster arose who delighted in the blood
of the guiltless, it is recorded that the posterity of
Avidius Cassius lived in security, and were admitted to
honors and public distinctions by favor of him, whose
life and empire that memorable traitor had sought to
undermine under the favor of his guileless master's too
confiding magnanimity.

CHAPTER V.

The Roman empire, and the Roman emperors, it might naturally be supposed by one who had not as yet traversed that tremendous chapter in the history of man, would be likely to present a separate and almost equal interest. The empire, in the first place, as the most magnificent monument of human power which our planet has beheld, must for that single reason, even though its records were otherwise of little interest, fix upon itself the very keenest gaze from all succeeding ages to the end of time. To trace the fortunes and revolutions of that unrivalled monarchy over which the Roman eagle brooded, to follow the dilapidations of that aêrial arch, which silently and steadily through seven centuries ascended under the colossal architecture of the children of Romulus, to watch the unweaving of the golden arras, and step by step to see paralysis stealing over the once perfect cohesion of the republican creations, - cannot but insure a severe, though melancholy delight. On its own separate account, the decline of this throne-shattering power must and will engage the foremost place amongst all historical reviews. The "dislimning" and unmoulding of some mighty pageantry in the heavens has its own appropriate grandeurs, no less than the gathering of its cloudy pomps. The going down of the sun is contemplated with no less awe than his rising. Nor is any thing portentous in its growth, which is not also

Thomas de Quincey

portentous in the steps and "moments" of its decay. Hence, in the second place, we might presume a commensurate interest in the characters and fortunes of the successive emperors. If the empire challenged our first survey, the next would seem due to the Cæsars who guided its course; to the great ones who retarded, and to the bad ones who precipitated, its ruin.

Such might be the natural expectation of an inexperienced reader. But it is *not* so. The Cæsars, throughout their long line, are not interesting, neither personally in themselves, nor derivatively from the tragic events to which their history is attached. Their whole interest lies in their situation - in the unapproachable altitude of their thrones. But, considered with a reference to their human qualities, scarcely one in the whole series can be viewed with a human interest apart from the circumstances of his position. "Pass like shadows, so depart!" The reason for this defect of all personal variety of interest in these enormous potentates, must be sought in the constitution of their power and the very necessities of their office. Even the greatest among them, those who by way of distinction were called *the Great*, as Constantine and Theodosius, were not great, for they were not magnanimous; nor could they be so under *their* tenure of power, which made it a duty to be suspicious, and, by fastening upon all varieties of original temper one dire necessity of bloodshed, extinguished under this monotonous cloud of cruel jealousy and everlasting panic every characteristic feature of genial human nature, that would else have emerged through so long a train of princes. There is a remarkable story told of Agrippina, that, upon some occasion, when a wizard announced to her, as truths which he had read in the heavens, the two fatal necessities impending over her son, - one that he should ascend to empire, the other that he should murder herself, she replied in these stern and memorable words - *Occidat, dum imperet*. Upon which a continental writer comments thus: "Never before or since have three such words issued from the lips of woman; and in truth, one knows not which most to abominate or to admire - the aspiring princess, or the loving mother. Meantime, in these few words lies naked to the day, in its whole hideous deformity, the very essence of Romanism and the imperatorial power, and one might here consider the mother of Nero as the impersonation of that monstrous condition."

This is true: *Occidat dum imperet*, was the watchword and very cognizance of the Roman imperator. But almost equally it was his watchword - *Occidatur dum imperet*. Doing or suffering, the Cæsars were almost equally involved in bloodshed; very few that were not murderers, and nearly all were themselves murdered.

The empire, then, must be regarded as the primary object of our interest; and it is in this way only that any secondary interest arises for the emperors. Now, with respect to the empire, the first question which presents itself is, - Whence, that is, from what causes and from what era, we are to date its decline? Gibbon, as we all know, dates it from the reign of Commodus; but certainly upon no sufficient, or even plausible grounds. Our own opinion we shall state boldly: the empire itself, from the very era of its establishment, was one long decline of the Roman power. A vast monarchy had been created and consolidated by the all-conquering instincts of a republic - cradled and nursed in wars, and essentially warlike by means of all its institutions [Footnote: Amongst these institutions,

Thomas de Quincey

none appear to us so remarkable, or fitted to accomplish so prodigious a circle of purposes belonging to the highest state policy, as the Roman method of colonization. Colonies were, in effect, the great engine of Roman conquest; and the following are among a few of the great ends to which they were applied. First of all, how came it that the early armies of Rome served, and served cheerfully, without pay? Simply because all who were victorious knew that they would receive their arrears in the fullest and amplest form upon their final discharge, viz. in the shape of a colonial estate - large enough to rear a family in comfort, and seated in the midst of similar allotments, distributed to their old comrades in arms. These lands were already, perhaps, in high cultivation, being often taken from conquered tribes; but, if not, the new occupants could rely for aid of every sort, for social intercourse, and for all the offices of good neighborhood upon the surrounding proprietors - who were sure to be persons in the same circumstances as themselves, and draughted from the same legion. For be it remembered, that in the primitive ages of Rome, concerning which it is that we are now speaking, entire legions - privates and officers - were transferred in one body to the new colony. "Antiquitus," says the learned Goesius, "deducebantur integral legiones, quibus parta victoria." Neither was there much waiting for this honorary gift. In later ages, it is true, when such resources were less plentiful, and when regular pay was given to the soldiery, it was the veteran only who obtained this splendid provision; but in the earlier times, a single fortunate campaign not seldom dismissed the young recruit to a life of ease and honor. "Multis legionibus," says Hyginus, "contigit bellum feliciter transigere, et ad laboriosam agriculturæ requiem *primo tyrocinii gradu* pervenire. Nam cum signis et aquilâ et primis ordinibus et tribunis deducebantur." Tacitus also notices this organization of the early colonies, and adds the reason of it, and its happy effect, when contrasting it with the vicious arrangements of the colonizing system in his own days. "Olim," says he, "universæ legiones deducebantur cum tribunis et centurionibus, et sui cujusque ordinis militibus, *ut consensu et charitate rempublicam efficerent.*" *Secondly,* not only were the troops in this way paid at a time when the public purse was unequal to the expenditure of war - but this pay, being contingent on the successful issue of the war, added the strength of self-interest to that of patriotism in stimulating the soldier to extraordinary efforts. Thirdly, not only did the soldier in this way reap his pay, but also he reaped a reward, (and that besides a trophy and perpetual monument of his public services,) so munificent as to constitute a permanent provision for a family; and accordingly he was now encouraged, nay, enjoined, to marry. For here was an hereditary landed estate equal to the liberal maintenance of a family. And thus did a simple people, obeying its instinct of conquest, not only discover, in its earliest days, the subtle principle of Machiavel - *Let war support war*; but (which is far more than Machiavel's view) they made each present war support many future wars - by making it support a new offset from the population, bound to the mother city by indissoluble ties of privilege and civic duties; and in many other ways they made every war, by and through the colonizing system to which it gave occasion, serviceable to future aggrandizement. War, managed in this way, and with these results, became to Rome what commerce or rural industry is to other countries, viz. the only hopeful and general way for making a fortune. *Fourthly,* by means of colonies it was that Rome

Thomas de Quincey

delivered herself from her surplus population. Prosperous and well-governed, the Roman citizens of each generation outnumbered those of the generation preceding. But the colonies provided outlets for these continual accessions of people, and absorbed them faster than they could arise. [Footnote: And in this way we must explain the fact - that, in the many successive numerations of the people continually noticed by Livy and others, we do not find that sort of multiplication which we might have looked for in a state so ably governed. The truth is, that the continual surpluses had been carried off by the colonizing drain, before they could become noticeable or troublesome.] And thus the great original sin of modern states, that heel of Achilles in which they are all vulnerable, and which (generally speaking) becomes more oppressive to the public prosperity as that prosperity happens to be greater (for in poor states and under despotic governments, this evil does not exist), that flagrant infirmity of our own country, for which no statesman has devised any commensurate remedy, was to ancient Rome a perpetual foundation and well-head of public strength and enlarged resources. With us of modern times, when population greatly outruns the demand for labor, whether it be under the stimulus of upright government, and just laws, justly administered, in combination with the manufacturing system (as in England,) or (as in Ireland) under the stimulus of idle habits, cheap subsistence, and a low standard of comfort - we think it much if we can keep down insurrection by the bayonet and the sabre. *Lucro ponamus* is our cry, if we can effect even thus much; whereas Rome, in her simplest and pastoral days, converted this menacing danger and standing opprobrium of modern statesmanship to her own immense benefit. Not satisfied merely to have neutralized it, she drew from it the vital resources of her martial aggrandizement. For, *Fifthly*, these colonies were in two ways made the corner-stones of her martial policy: 1st, They were looked to as nurseries of their armies; during one generation the original colonists, already trained to military habits, were themselves disposable for this purpose on any great emergency; these men transmitted heroic traditions to their posterity; and, at all events, a more robust population was always at hand in agricultural colonies than could be had in the metropolis. Cato the elder, and all the early writers, notice the quality of such levies as being far superior to those drawn from a population of sedentary habits. 2dly, The Italian colonies, one and all, performed the functions which in our day are assigned to garrisoned towns and frontier fortresses. In the earliest times they discharged a still more critical service, by sometimes entirely displacing a hostile population, and more often by dividing it and breaking its unity. In cases of desperate resistance to the Roman arms, marked by frequent infraction of treaties, it was usual to remove the offending population to a safer situation, separated from Rome by the Tiber; sometimes entirely to disperse and scatter it. But, where these extremities were not called for by expediency or the Roman maxims of justice, it was judged sufficient to *interpolate*, as it were, the hostile people by colonizations from Rome, which were completely organized [Footnote: That is indeed involved in the technical term of *Deductio*; for unless the ceremonies, religious and political, of inauguration and organization, were duly complied with, the colony was not entitled to be considered as *deducta* - that is, solemnly and ceremonially transplanted from the metropolis.] for mutual aid, having officers of all ranks dispersed amongst them, and for overawing the growth

Thomas de Quincey

of insurrectionary movements amongst their neighbors. Acting on this system, the Roman colonies in some measure resembled the *English Pale*, as existing at one era in Ireland. This mode of service, it is true, became obsolete in process of time, concurrently with the dangers which it was shaped to meet; for the whole of Italy proper, together with that part of Italy called Cisalpine Gaul, was at length reduced to unity and obedience by the almighty republic. But in forwarding that great end, and indispensable condition towards all foreign warfare, no one military engine in the whole armory of Rome availed so much as her Italian colonies. The other use of these colonies, as frontier garrisons, or, at any rate, as interposing between a foreign enemy and the gates of Rome, they continued to perform long after their earlier uses had passed away; and Cicero himself notices their value in this view. "Colonias," says he [*Orat. in Rullum*], "sic idoneis in locis contra suspicionem periculi collocarunt, ut esse non oppida Italiæ sed *propugnacula* imperii viderentur." *Finally*, the colonies were the best means of promoting tillage, and the culture of vineyards. And though this service, as regarded the Italian colonies, was greatly defeated in succeeding times by the ruinous largesses of corn [*frumentationes*], and other vices of the Roman policy after the vast revolution effected by universal luxury, it is not the less true that, left to themselves and their natural tendency, the Roman colonies would have yielded this last benefit as certainly as any other. Large volumes exist, illustrated by the learning of Rigaltius, Salmatius, and Goesius, upon the mere technical arrangements of the Roman colonies. And whose libraries might be written on these same colonies considered as engines of exquisite state policy.] and by the habits of the people. This monarchy had been of too slow a growth - too gradual, and too much according to the regular stages of nature herself in its development, to have any chance of being other than well cemented; the cohesion of its parts was intense; seven centuries of growth demand one or two at least for palpable decay; and it is only for harlequin empires like that of Napoleon, run up with the rapidity of pantomime, to fall asunder under the instant reaction of a few false moves in politics, or a single unfortunate campaign. Hence it was, and from the prudence of Augustus acting through a very long reign, sustained at no very distant interval by the personal inspection and revisions of Hadrian, that for some time the Roman power seemed to be stationary. What else could be expected? The mere strength of the impetus derived from the republican institutions, could not but propagate itself, and cause even a motion in advance, for some time after those institutions had themselves given way. And besides the military institutions survived all others; and the army continued very much the same in its discipline and composition, long after Rome and all its civic institutions had bent before an utter revolution. It was very possible even that emperors should have arisen with martial propensities, and talents capable of masking, for many years, by specious but transitory conquests, the causes that were silently sapping the foundations of Roman supremacy; and thus by accidents of personal character and taste, an empire might even have expanded itself in appearance, which, by all its permanent and real tendencies, was even then shrinking within narrower limits, and travelling downwards to dissolution. In reality, one such emperor there was. Trajan, whether by martial inclinations, or (as is supposed by some) by dissatisfaction with his own position at Rome, when brought into more immediate connection with the

Thomas de Quincey

senate, was driven into needless war; and he achieved conquests in the direction of Dacia as well as Parthia. But that these conquests were not substantial, - that they were connected by no true cement of cohesion with the existing empire, is evident from the rapidity with which they were abandoned. In the next reign, the empire had already recoiled within its former limits; and in two reigns further on, under Marcus Antoninus, though a prince of elevated character and warlike in his policy, we find such concessions of territory made to the Marcomanni and others, as indicate too plainly the shrinking energies of a waning empire. In reality, if we consider the polar opposition, in point of interest and situation, between the great officers of the republic and the Augustus or Cæsar of the empire, we cannot fail to see the immense effect which that difference must have had upon the permanent spirit of conquest. Cæsar was either adopted or elected to a situation of infinite luxury and enjoyment. He had no interests to secure by fighting in person: and he had a powerful interest in preventing others from fighting; since in that way only he could raise up competitors to himself, and dangerous seducers of the army. A consul, on the other hand, or great lieutenant of the senate, had nothing to enjoy or to hope for, when his term of office should have expired, unless according to his success in creating military fame and influence for himself. Those Cæsars who fought whilst the empire was or seemed to be stationary, as Trajan, did so from personal taste. Those who fought in after centuries, when the decay became apparent, and dangers drew nearer, as Aurelian, did so from the necessities of fear; and under neither impulse were they likely to make durable conquests. The spirit of conquest having therefore departed at the very time when conquest would have become more difficult even to the republican energies, both from remoteness of ground and from the martial character of the chief nations which stood beyond the frontier, - it was a matter of necessity that with the republican institutions should expire the whole principle of territorial aggrandizement; and that, if the empire seemed to be stationary for some time after its establishment by Julius, and its final settlement by Augustus, this was through no strength of its own, or inherent in its own constitution, but through the continued action of that strength which it had inherited from the republic. In a philosophical sense, therefore, it may be affirmed, that the empire of the Cæsars was *always* in decline; ceasing to go forward, it could not do other than retrograde; and even the first *appearances* of decline can, with no propriety, be referred to the reign of Commodus. His vices exposed him to public contempt and assassination; but neither one nor the other had any effect upon the strength of the empire. Here, therefore, is one just subject of complaint against Gibbon, that he has dated the declension of the Roman power from a commencement arbitrarily assumed; another, and a heavier, is, that he has failed to notice the steps and separate indications of decline as they arose, - the moments (to speak in the language of dynamics) through which the decline travelled onwards to its consummation. It is also a grievous offence as regards the true purposes of history, - and one which, in a complete exposition of the imperial history, we should have a right to insist on, - that Gibbon brings forward only such facts as allow of a scenical treatment, and seems every where, by the glancing style of his allusions, to presuppose an acquaintance with that very history which he undertakes to deliver. Our immediate purpose, however, is simply to characterize the office of emperor, and to notice such events and changes as

Thomas de Quincey

operated for evil, and for a final effect of decay, upon the Cæsars or their empire. As the best means of realizing it, we shall rapidly review the history of both, promising that we confine ourselves to the true Cæsars, and the true empire, of the West.

The first overt act of weakness, - the first expression of conscious declension, as regarded the foreign enemies of Rome, occurred in the reign of Hadrian; for it is a very different thing to forbear making conquests, and to renounce them when made. It is possible, however, that the cession then made of Mesopotamia and Armenia, however sure to be interpreted into the language of fear by the enemy, did not imply any such principle in this emperor. He was of a civic and paternal spirit, and anxious for the substantial welfare of the empire rather than its ostentatious glory. The internal administration of affairs had very much gone into neglect since the times of Augustus; and Hadrian was perhaps right in supposing that he could effect more public good by an extensive progress through the empire, and by a personal correction of abuses, than by any military enterprise. It is, besides, asserted, that he received an indemnity in money for the provinces beyond the Euphratus. But still it remains true, that in his reign the God Terminus made his first retrograde motion; and this emperor became naturally an object of public obloquy at Rome, and his name fell under the superstitious ban of a fatal tradition connected with the foundation of the capitol. The two Antonines, Titus and Marcus, who came next in succession, were truly good and patriotic princes; perhaps the only princes in the whole series who combined the virtues of private and of public life. In their reigns the frontier line was maintained in its integrity, and at the expense of some severe fighting under Marcus, who was a strenuous general at the same time that he was a severe student. It is, however, true, as we observed above, that, by allowing a settlement within the Roman frontier to a barbarous people, Marcus Aurelius raised the first ominous precedent in favor of those Gothic, Vandal, and Frankish hives, who were as yet hidden behind a cloud of years. Homes had been obtained by Trans-Danubian barbarians upon the sacred territory of Rome and Cæsar: that fact remained upon tradition; whilst the terms upon which they had been obtained, how much or how little connected with fear, necessarily became liable to doubt and to oblivion. Here we pause to remark, that the first twelve Cæsars, together with Nerva, Trajan, Hadrian, and the two Antonines, making seventeen emperors, compose the first of four nearly equal groups, who occupied the throne in succession until the extinction of the Western Empire. And at this point be it observed, - that is, at the termination of the first group, - we take leave of all genuine virtue. In no one of the succeeding princes, if we except Alexander Severus, do we meet with any goodness of heart, or even amiableness of manners. The best of the future emperors, in a public sense, were harsh and repulsive in private character.

The second group, as we have classed them, terminating with Philip the Arab, commences with Commodus. This unworthy prince, although the son of the excellent Marcus Antoninus, turned out a monster of debauchery. At the moment of his father's death, he was present in person at the head-quarters of the army on the Danube, and of necessity partook in many of their hardships. This it was which furnished his evil counsellors with their sole argument for urging his departure to the capital. A council having been convened, the faction of court sycophants pressed upon

Thomas de Quincey

his attention the inclemency of the climate, contrasting it with the genial skies and sunny fields of Italy; and the season, which happened to be winter, gave strength to their representations. What! would the emperor be content for ever to hew out the frozen water with an axe before he could assuage his thirst? And, again, the total want of fruit-trees - did that recommend their present station as a fit one for the imperial court? Commodus, ashamed to found his objections to the station upon grounds so unsoldierly as these, affected to be moved by political reasons: some great senatorial house might take advantage of his distance from home, - might seize the palace, fortify it, and raise levies in Italy capable of sustaining its pretensions to the throne. These arguments were combated by Pompeianus, who, besides his personal weight as an officer, had married the eldest sister of the young emperor. Shame prevailed for the present with Commodus, and he dismissed the council with an assurance that he would think farther of it. The sequel was easy to foresee. Orders were soon issued for the departure of the court to Rome, and the task of managing the barbarians of Dacia, was delegated to lieutenants. The system upon which these officers executed their commission was a mixed one of terror and persuasion. Some they defeated in battle; and these were the majority; for Herodian says, *pleizous ton barbaron haplois echeirosanto*: Others they bribed into peace by large sums of money. And no doubt this last article in the policy of Commodus was that which led Gibbon to assign to this reign the first rudiments of the Roman declension. But it should be remembered, that, virtually, this policy was but the further prosecution of that which had already been adopted by Marcus Aurelius. Concessions and temperaments of any sort or degree showed that the Pannonian frontier was in too formidable a condition to be treated with uncompromising rigor. To *hamerimnon onoumenos*, purchasing an immunity from all further anxiety, Commodus (as the historian expresses it) *panta edidou ta aitoumena* - conceded all demands whatever. His journey to Rome was one continued festival: and the whole population of Rome turned out to welcome him. At this period he was undoubtedly the darling of the people: his personal beauty was splendid; and he was connected by blood with some of the greatest nobility. Over this flattering scene of hope and triumph clouds soon gathered: with the mob, indeed, there is reason to think that he continued a favorite to the last; but the respectable part of the citizens were speedily disgusted with his self-degradation, and came to hate him even more than ever or by any class he had been loved. The Roman pride never shows itself more conspicuously throughout all history, than in the alienation of heart which inevitably followed any great and continued outrages upon his own majesty, committed by their emperor. Cruelties the most atrocious, acts of vengeance the most bloody, fratricide, parricide, all were viewed with more toleration than oblivion of his own inviolable sanctity. Hence we imagine the wrath with which Rome would behold Commodus, under the eyes of four hundred thousand spectators, making himself a party to the contests of gladiators. In his earlier exhibitions as an archer, it is possible that his matchless dexterity, and his unerring eye, would avail to mitigate the censures: but when the Roman Imperator actually descended to the arena in the garb and equipments of a servile prize-fighter, and personally engaged in combat with such antagonists, having previously submitted to their training and discipline - the public indignation rose a to height, which spoke aloud the language of encouragement to

Thomas de Quincey

conspiracy and treason. These were not wanting: three memorable plots against his life were defeated; one of them (that of Maternus, the robber) accompanied with romantic circumstances, [Footnote: On this occasion we may notice that the final execution of the vengeance projected by Maternus, was reserved for a public festival, exactly corresponding to the modern *carnival*; and from an expression used by Herodian, it is plain that masquerading had been an ancient practice in Rome.] which we have narrated in an earlier paper of this series. Another was set on foot by his eldest sister, Lucilla; nor did her close relationship protect her from capital punishment. In that instance, the immediate agent of her purposes, Quintianus, a young man, of signal resolution and daring, who had attempted to stab the emperor at the entrance of the amphitheatre, though baffled in his purpose, uttered a word which rang continually in the ears of Commodus, and poisoned his peace of mind for ever. His vengeance, perhaps, was thus more effectually accomplished than if he had at once dismissed his victim from life. "The senate," he had said, "sends thee this through me:" and henceforward the senate was the object of unslumbering suspicions to the emperor. Yet the public suspicions settled upon a different quarter; and a very memorable scene must have pointed his own in the same direction, supposing that he had previously been blind to his danger. On a day of great solemnity, when Rome had assembled her myriads in the amphitheatre, just at the very moment when the nobles, the magistrates, the priests, all, in short, that was venerable or consecrated in the State, with the Imperator in their centre, had taken their seats, and were waiting for the opening of the shows, a stranger, in the robe of a philosopher, bearing a staff in his hand, (which also was the professional ensign [Footnote: See

Casaubon's notes upon Theophrastus.] of a philosopher,) stepped forward, and, by the waving of his hand,
challenged the attention of Commodus. Deep silence
ensued: upon which, in a few words, ominous to the
ear as the handwriting on the wall to the eye of
Belshazzar, the stranger unfolded to Commodus the
instant peril which menaced both his life and his
throne, from his great servant Perennius. What
personal purpose of benefit to himself this stranger
might have connected with his public warning, or by
whom he might have been suborned, was never
discovered; for he was instantly arrested by the agents
of the great officer whom he had denounced, dragged
away to punishment, and put to a cruel death.
Commodus dissembled his panic for the present; but
soon after, having received undeniable proofs (as is
alleged) of the treason imputed to Perennius, in the
shape of a coin which had been struck by his son, he
caused the father to be assassinated; and, on the same
day, by means of forged letters, before this news could
reach the son, who commanded the Illyrian armies, he
lured him also to destruction, under the belief that he
was obeying the summons of his father to a private
interview on the Italian frontier. So perished those
enemies, if enemies they really were. But to these
tragedies succeeded others far more comprehensive in
their mischief, and in more continuous succession than
is recorded upon any other page of universal history.
Rome was ravaged by a pestilence - by a famine - by
riots amounting to a civil war - by a dreadful massacre
of the unarmed mob - by shocks of earthquake - and,
finally, by a fire which consumed the national bank,
[Footnote: Viz. the Temple of Peace; at that time the
most magnificent edifice in Rome. Temples, it is well
known, were the places used in ancient times as banks
of deposit. For this function they were admirably fitted

Thomas de Quincey

by their inviolable sanctity.] and the most sumptuous buildings of the city. To these horrors, with a rapidity characteristic of the Roman depravity, and possible only under the most extensive demoralization of the public mind, succeeded festivals of gorgeous pomp, and amphitheatrical exhibitions, upon a scale of grandeur absolutely unparalleled by all former attempts. Then were beheld, and familiarized to the eyes of the Roman mob - to children - and to women, animals as yet known to us, says Herodian, only in pictures. Whatever strange or rare animal could be drawn from the depths of India, from Siam and Pegu, or from the unvisited nooks of Ethiopia, were now brought together as subjects for the archery of the universal lord. [Footnote: What a prodigious opportunity for the zoologist! - And considering that these shows prevailed, for 500 years, during all which period the amphitheatre gave bounties, as it were, to the hunter and the fowler of every climate, and that, by means of a stimulus so constantly applied, scarcely any animal, the shyest, rarest, fiercest, escaped the demands of the arena, - no one fact so much illustrates the inertia of the public mind in those days, and the indifference to all scientific pursuits, as that no annotator should have risen to Pliny the elder - no rival to the immortal tutor of Alexander.] Invitations (and the invitations of kings are commands) had been scattered on this occasion profusely; not, as heretofore, to individuals or to families - but, as was in proportion to the occasion where an emperor was the chief performer, to nations. People were summoned by circles of longitude and latitude to come and see *theasumenoi ha mœ proteron mœte heormkesun mœte œkaekoeisun* - things that eye had not seen nor ear heard of] the specious miracles of nature brought together from arctic and from tropic deserts, putting forth their strength, their speed, or their beauty, and glorifying by their deaths the matchless hand of the Roman king. There was beheld the lion from Bilidulgerid, and the leopard from Hindostan - the rein-deer from polar latitudes - the antelope from the Zaara - and the leigh, or gigantic stag, from Britain. Thither came the buffalo and the bison, the white bull of Northumberland and Galloway, the unicorn from the regions of Nepaul or Thibet, the rhinoceros and the river-horse from Senegal, with the elephant of Ceylon or Siam. The ostrich and the cameleopard, the wild ass and the zebra, the chamois and the ibex of Angora, - all brought their tributes of beauty or deformity to these vast aceldamas of Rome: their savage voices ascended in tumultuous uproar to the chambers of the capitol: a million of spectators sat round them: standing in the centre was a single statuesque figure - the imperial sagittary, beautiful as an Antinous, and majestic as a Jupiter, whose hand was so steady and whose eye so true, that he was never known to miss, and who, in this accomplishment at least, was so absolute in his excellence, that, as we are assured by a writer not disposed to flatter him, the very foremost of the Parthian archers and of the Mauritanian lancers [*Parthyaion oi toxichæs hachribentes, chai Mauresion oi hachontixein harizoi*] were not able to contend with him. Juvenal, in a well known passage upon the disproportionate endings of illustrious careers, drawing one of his examples from Marius, says, that he ought, for his own glory, and to make his end correspondent to his life, to have died at the moment when he descended from his triumphal chariot at the portals of the capitol. And of Commodus, in like manner, it may be affirmed, that, had he died in the exercise of his peculiar art, with a hecatomb of victims rendering homage to his miraculous skill, by the regularity of the

Thomas de Quincey

files which they presented, as they lay stretched out dying or dead upon the arena, - he would have left a splendid and a characteristic impression of himself upon that nation of spectators who had witnessed his performance. He was the noblest artist in his own profession that the world had seen - in archery he was the Robin Hood of Rome; he was in the very meridian of his youth; and he was the most beautiful man of his own times *Ton chath eauton hathropon challei euprepestatos.* He would therefore have looked the part admirably of the dying gladiator; and he would have died in his natural vocation. But it was ordered otherwise; his death was destined to private malice, and to an ignoble hand. And much obscurity still rests upon the motives of the assassins, though its circumstances are reported with unusual minuteness of detail. One thing is evident, that the public and patriotic motives assigned by the perpetrators as the remote causes of their conspiracy, cannot have been the true ones. The grave historian may sum up his character of Commodus by saying that, however richly endowed with natural gifts, he abused them all to bad purposes; that he derogated from his noble ancestors, and disavowed the obligations of his illustrious name; and, as the climax of his offences, that he dishonored the purple - *aischrois epitædeumasin* - by the baseness of his pursuits. All that is true, and more than that. But these considerations were not of a nature to affect his parasitical attendants very nearly or keenly. Yet the story runs - that Marcia, his privileged mistress, deeply affected by the anticipation of some further outrages upon his high dignity which he was then meditating, had carried the importunity of her deprecations too far; that the irritated emperor had consequently inscribed her name, in company with others, (whom he had reason to tax with the same offence, or whom he suspected of similar sentiments,) in his little black book, or pocket souvenir of death; that this book, being left under the cushion of a sofa, had been conveyed into the hands of Marcia by a little pet boy, called Philo-Commodus, who was caressed equally by the emperor and by Marcia; that she had immediately called to her aid, and to the participation of her plot, those who participated in her danger; and that the proximity of their own intended fate had prescribed to them an immediate attempt; the circumstances of which were these. At mid-day the emperor was accustomed to bathe, and at the same time to take refreshments. On this occasion, Marcia, agreeably to her custom, presented him with a goblet of wine, medicated with poison. Of this wine, having just returned from the fatigues of the chase, Commodus drank freely, and almost immediately fell into heavy slumbers; from which, however, he was soon aroused by deadly sickness. That was a case which the conspirators had not taken into their calculations; and they now began to fear that the violent vomiting which succeeded might throw off the poison. There was no time to be lost; and the barbarous Marcia, who had so often slept in the arms of the young emperor, was the person to propose that he should now be strangled. A young gladiator, named Narcissus, was therefore introduced into the room; what passed is not known circumstantially; but, as the emperor was young and athletic, though off his guard at the moment, and under the disadvantage of sickness, and as he had himself been regularly trained in the gladiatorial discipline, there can be little doubt that the vile assassin would meet with a desperate resistance. And thus, after all, there is good reason to think that the emperor resigned his life in the character of a dying gladiator. [Footnote: It is worthy of notice, that, under any suspension of the

Thomas de Quincey

imperatorial power or office, the senate was the body to whom the Roman mind even yet continued to turn. In this case, both to color their crime with a show of public motives, and to interest this great body in their own favor by associating them in their own dangers, the conspirators pretended to have found a long roll of senatorial names included in the same page of condemnation with their own. A manifest fabrication!]

So perished the eldest and sole surviving son of the great Marcus Antoninus; and the crown passed into the momentary possession of two old men, who reigned in succession each for a few weeks. The first of these was Pertinax, an upright man, a good officer, and an unseasonable reformer; unseasonable for those times, but more so for himself. Lætus, the ringleader in the assassination of Commodus, had been at that time the prætorian prefect - an office which a German writer considers as best represented to modern ideas by the Turkish post of grand vizier. Needing a protector at this moment, he naturally fixed his eyes upon Pertinax - as then holding the powerful command of city prefect (or governor of Rome.) Him therefore he recommended to the soldiery - that is, to the prætorian cohorts. The soldiery had no particular objection to the old general, if he and they could agree upon terms; his age being doubtless appreciated as a first-rate recommendation, in a case where it insured a speedy renewal of the lucrative bargain.

The only demur arose with Pertinax himself: he had been leader of the troops in Britain, then superintendent of the police in Rome, thirdly proconsul in Africa, and finally consul and governor of Rome. In these great official stations he stood near enough to the throne to observe the dangers with which it was surrounded; and it is asserted that he declined the offered dignity. But it is added, that, finding the choice allowed him lay between immediate death [Footnote: Historians have failed to remark the contradiction between this statement and the allegation that Lætus selected Pertinax for the throne on a consideration of his ability to protect the assassins of Commodus.] and acceptance, he closed with the proposals of the praetorian cohorts, at the rate of about ninety-six pounds per man; which largess he paid by bringing to sale the rich furniture of the last emperor. The danger which usually threatened a Roman Cæsar in such cases was - lest he should not be able to fulfill his contract. But in the case of Pertinax the danger began from the moment when he *had* fulfilled it. Conceiving himself to be now released from his dependency, he commenced his reforms, civil as well as military, with a zeal which alarmed all those who had an interest in maintaining the old abuses. To two great factions he thus made himself especially obnoxious - to the praetorian cohorts, and to the courtiers under the last reign. The connecting link between these two parties was Lætus, who belonged personally to the last, and still retained his influence with the first. Possibly his fears were alarmed; but, at all events, his cupidity was not satisfied. He conceived himself to have been ill rewarded; and, immediately resorting to the same weapons which he had used against Commodus, he stimulated the praetorian guards to murder the emperor. Three hundred of them pressed into the palace: Pertinax attempted to harangue them, and to vindicate himself; but not being able to obtain a hearing, he folded his robe about his head, called upon Jove the Avenger, and was immediately dispatched.

The throne was again empty after a reign of about

Thomas de Quincey

eighty days; and now came the memorable scandal of putting up the empire to auction. There were two bidders, Sulpicianus and Didius Julianus. The first, however, at that time governor of Rome, lay under a weight of suspicion, being the father-in-law of Pertinax, and likely enough to exact vengeance for his murder. He was besides outbid by Julianus. Sulpician offered about one hundred and sixty pounds a man to the guards; his rival offered two hundred, and assured them besides of immediate payment; "for," said he, "I have the money at home, without needing to raise it from the possessions of the crown." Upon this the empire was knocked down to the highest bidder. So shocking, however, was this arrangement to the Roman pride, that the guards durst not leave their new creation without military protection. The resentment of an unarmed mob, however, soon ceased to be of foremost importance; this resentment extended rapidly to all the frontiers of the empire, where the armies felt that the prætorian cohorts had no exclusive title to give away the throne, and their leaders felt, that, in a contest of this nature, their own claims were incomparably superior to those of the present occupant. Three great candidates therefore started forward - Septimius Severus, who commanded the armies in Illyria, Pescennius Niger in Syria, and Albinus in Britain. Severus, as the nearest to Rome, marched and possessed himself of that city. Vengeance followed upon all parties concerned in the late murder. Julianus, unable to complete his bargain, had already been put to death, as a deprecatory offering to the approaching army. Severus himself inflicted death upon Lætus, and dismissed the praetorian cohorts. Thence marching against his Syrian rival, Niger, who had formerly been his friend, and who was not wanting in military skill, he overthrew him in three great battles. Niger fled to

Antioch, the seat of his late government, and was there decapitated. Meantime Albinus, the British commander-in-chief, had already been won over by the title of Cæsar, or adopted heir to the new Augustus. But the hollowness of this bribe soon became apparent, and the two competitors met to decide their pretensions at Lyons. In the great battle which followed, Severus fell from his horse, and was at first supposed to be dead. But recovering, he defeated his rival, who immediately committed suicide. Severus displayed his ferocious temper sufficiently by sending the head of Albinus to Rome. Other expressions of his natural character soon followed: he suspected strongly that Albinus had been favored by the senate; forty of that body, with their wives and children, were immediately sacrificed to his wrath; but he never forgave the rest, nor endured to live upon terms of amity amongst them. Quitting Rome in disgust, he employed himself first in making war upon the Parthians, who had naturally, from situation, befriended his Syrian rival. Their capital cities he overthrew; and afterwards, by way of employing his armies, made war in Britain. At the city of York he died; and to his two sons, Geta and Caracalla, he bequeathed, as his dying advice, a maxim of policy, which sufficiently indicates the situation of the empire at that period; it was this - "To enrich the soldiery at any price, and to regard the rest of their subjects as so many ciphers." But, as a critical historian remarks, this was a shortsighted and self-destroying policy; since in no way is the subsistence of the soldier made more insecure, than by diminishing the general security of rights and property to those who are not soldiers, from whom, after all, the funds must be sought, by which the soldier himself is to be paid and nourished. The two sons of Severus, whose bitter enmity is so memorably put on record by their actions,

Thomas de Quincey

travelled simultaneously to Rome; but so mistrustful of each other, that at every stage the two princes took up their quarters at different houses. Geta has obtained the sympathy of historians, because he happened to be the victim; but there is reason to think, that each of the brothers was conspiring against the other. The weak credulity, rather than the conscious innocence, of Geta, led to the catastrophe; he presented himself at a meeting with his brother in the presence of their common mother, and was murdered by Caracalla in his mother's arms. He was, however, avenged; the horrors of that tragedy, and remorse for the twenty thousand murders which had followed, never forsook the guilty Caracalla. Quitting Rome, but pursued into every region by the bloody image of his brother, the emperor henceforward led a wandering life at the head of his legions; but never was there a better illustration of the poet's maxim, that

'Remorse is as the mind in which it grows:
If *that* be gentle,' &c.

For the remorse of Caracalla put on no shape of repentance. On the contrary, he carried anger and oppression wherever he moved; and protected himself from plots only by living in the very centre of a nomadic camp. Six years had passed away in this manner, when a mere accident led to his assassination. For the sake of security, the office of praetorian prefect had been divided between two commissioners, one for military affairs, the other for civil. The latter of these two officers was Opilius Macrinus. This man has, by some historians, been supposed to have harbored no bad intentions; but, unfortunately, an astrologer had foretold that he was destined to the throne. The prophet was laid in irons at Rome, and letters were dispatched to Caracalla, apprizing him of the case. These letters, as yet unopened, were transferred by the emperor, then occupied in witnessing a race, to Macrinus, who thus became acquainted with the whole grounds of suspicion against himself, - grounds which, to the jealousy of the emperor, he well knew would appear substantial proofs. Upon this he resolved to anticipate the emperor in the work of murder. The head-quarters were then at Edessa; and upon his instigation, a disappointed centurion, named Martialis, animated also by revenge for the death of his brother, undertook to assassinate Caracalla. An opportunity soon offered, on a visit which the prince made to the celebrated temple of the moon at Carrhæ. The attempt was successful: the emperor perished; but Martialis paid the penalty of his crime in the same hour, being shot by a Scythian archer of the body-guard.

Macrinus, after three days' interregnum, being elected emperor, began his reign by purchasing a peace from the Parthians. What the empire chiefly needed at this moment, is evident from the next step taken by this emperor. He labored to restore the ancient discipline of the armies in all its rigor. He was aware of the risk he ran in this attempt; and that he *was* so, is the best evidence of the strong necessity which existed for reform. Perhaps, however, he might have surmounted his difficulties and dangers, had he met with no competitor round whose person the military malcontents could rally. But such a competitor soon arose; and, to the astonishment of all the world, in the person of a Syrian. The Emperor Severus, on losing his first wife, had resolved to strengthen the pretensions of his family by a second marriage with some lady having a regal "genesis," that is, whose horoscope promised a regal destiny. Julia Domna, a native of Syria, offered

Thomas de Quincey

him this dowry, and she became the mother of Geta. A sister of this Julia, called Moesa, had, through two different daughters, two grandsons - Heliogabalus and Alexander Severus. The mutineers of the army rallied round the first of these; a battle was fought; and Macrinus, with his son Diadumenianus, whom he had adopted to the succession, were captured and put to death. Heliogabalus succeeded, and reigned in the monstrous manner which has rendered his name infamous in history. In what way, however, he lost the affections of the army, has never been explained. His mother, Sooemias, the eldest daughter of Moesa, had represented herself as the concubine of Caracalla; and Heliogabalus, being thus accredited as the son of that emperor, whose memory was dear to the soldiery, had enjoyed the full benefit of that descent, nor can it be readily explained how he came to lose it.

Here, in fact, we meet with an instance of that dilemma which is so constantly occurring in the history of the Cæsars. If a prince is by temperament disposed to severity of manners, and naturally seeks to impress his own spirit upon the composition and discipline of the army, we are sure to find that he was cut off in his attempts by private assassination or by public rebellion. On the other hand, if he wallows in sensuality, and is careless about all discipline, civil or military, we then find as commonly that he loses the esteem and affections of the army to some rival of severer habits. And in the midst of such oscillations, and with examples of such contradictory interpretation, we cannot wonder that the Roman princes did not oftener take warning by the misfortunes of their predecessors. In the present instance, Alexander, the cousin of Heliogabalus, without intrigues of his own, and simply (as it appears) by the purity and sobriety of his conduct, had alienated the affections of the army from the reigning prince. Either jealousy or prudence had led Heliogabalus to make an attempt upon his rival's life; and this attempt had nearly cost him his own through the mutiny which it caused. In a second uproar, produced by some fresh intrigues of the emperor against his cousin, the soldiers became unmanageable, and they refused to pause until they had massacred Heliogabalus, together with his mother, and raised his cousin Alexander to the throne.

The reforms of this prince, who reigned under the name of Alexander Severus, were extensive and searching; not only in his court, which he purged of all notorious abuses, but throughout the economy of the army. He cashiered, upon one occasion, an entire legion: he restored, as far as he was able, the ancient discipline; and, above all, he liberated the provinces from military spoliation. "Let the soldier," said he, "be contented with his pay; and whatever more he wants, let him obtain it by victory from the enemy, not by pillage from his fellow-subject." But whatever might be the value or extent of his reforms in the marching regiments, Alexander could not succeed in binding the prætorian guards to his yoke. Under the guardianship of his mother Mammæa, the conduct of state affairs had been submitted to a council of sixteen persons, at the head of which stood the celebrated Ulpian. To this minister the prætorians imputed the reforms, and perhaps the whole spirit of reform; for they pursued him with a vengeance which is else hardly to be explained. Many days was Ulpian protected by the citizens of Rome, until the whole city was threatened with conflagration; he then fled to the palace of the young emperor, who in vain attempted to save him from his pursuers under the shelter of the imperial

Thomas de Quincey

purple. Ulpian was murdered before his eyes; nor was it found possible to punish the ringleader in this foul conspiracy, until he had been removed by something like treachery to a remote government.

Meantime, a great revolution and change of dynasty had been effected in Parthia; the line of the Arsacidæ was terminated; the Parthian empire was at an end; and the sceptre of Persia was restored under the new race of the Sassanides. Artaxerxes, the first prince of this race, sent an embassy of four hundred select knights, enjoining the Roman emperor to content himself with Europe, and to leave Asia to the Persians. In the event of a refusal, the ambassadors were instructed to offer a defiance to the Roman prince. Upon such an insult, Alexander could not do less, with either safety or dignity, than prepare for war. It is probable, indeed, that, by this expedition, which drew off the minds of the soldiery from brooding upon the reforms which offended them, the life of Alexander was prolonged. But the expedition itself was mismanaged, or was unfortunate. This result, however, does not seem chargeable upon Alexander. All the preparations were admirable on the march, and up to the enemy's frontier. The invasion it was, which, in a strategic sense, seems to have been ill combined. Three armies were to have entered Persia simultaneously: one of these, which was destined to act on a flank of the general line, entangled itself in the marshy grounds near Babylon, and was cut off by the archery of an enemy whom it could not reach. The other wing, acting upon ground impracticable for the manoeuvres of the Persian cavalry, and supported by Chosroes the king of Armenia, gave great trouble to Artaxerxes, and, with adequate support from the other armies, would doubtless have been victorious. But the central army, under the conduct of Alexander in person, discouraged by the destruction of one entire wing, remained stationary in Mesopotamia throughout the summer, and, at the close of the campaign, was withdrawn to Antioch, *re infectâ*. It has been observed that great mystery hangs over the operations and issue of this short war. Thus much, however, is evident, that nothing but the previous exhaustion of the Persian king saved the Roman armies from signal discomfiture; and even thus there is no ground for claiming a victory (as most historians do) to the Roman arms. Any termination of the Persian war, however, whether glorious or not, was likely to be personally injurious to Alexander, by allowing leisure to the soldiery for recurring to their grievances. Sensible, no doubt, of this, Alexander was gratified by the occasion which then arose for repressing the hostile movements of the Germans. He led his army off upon this expedition; but their temper was gloomy and threatening; and at length, after reaching the seat of war, at Mentz, an open mutiny broke out under the guidance of Maximin, which terminated in the murder of the emperor and his mother. By Herodian the discontents of the army are referred to the ill management of the Persian campaign, and the unpromising commencement of the new war in Germany. But it seems probable that a dissolute and wicked army, like that of Alexander, had not murmured under the too little, but the too much of military service; not the buying a truce with gold seems to have offended them, but the having led them at all upon an enterprise of danger and hardship.

Maximin succeeded, whose feats of strength, when he first courted the notice of the Emperor Severus, have been described by Gibbon. He was at that period a Thracian peasant; since then he had risen gradually to

Thomas de Quincey

high offices; but, according to historians, he retained his Thracian brutality to the last. That may have been true; but one remark must be made upon this occasion: Maximin was especially opposed to the senate; and, wherever that was the case, no justice was done to an emperor. Why it was that Maximin would not ask for the confirmation of his election from the senate, has never been explained; it is said that he anticipated a rejection. But, on the other hand, it seems probable that the senate supposed its sanction to be despised. Nothing, apparently, but this reciprocal reserve in making approaches to each other, was the cause of all the bloodshed which followed. The two Gordians, who commanded in Africa, were set up by the senate against the new emperor; and the consternation of that body must have been great, when these champions were immediately overthrown and killed. They did not, however, despair: substituting the two governors of Rome, Pupienus and Balbinus, and associating to them the younger Gordian, they resolved to make a stand; for the severities of Maximin had by this time manifested that it was a contest of extermination. Meantime, Maximin had broken up from Sirmium, the capital of Pannonia, and had advanced to Aquileia, - that famous fortress, which in every invasion of Italy was the first object of attack. The senate had set a price upon his head; but there was every probability that he would have triumphed, had he not disgusted his army by immoderate severities. It was, however, but reasonable that those, who would not support the strict but equitable discipline of the mild Alexander, should suffer under the barbarous and capricious rigor of Maximin. That rigor was his ruin: sunk and degraded as the senate was, and now but the shadow of a mighty name, it was found on this occasion to have long arms when supported by the frenzy of its opponent.

Whatever might be the real weakness of this body, the rude soldiers yet felt a blind traditionary veneration for its sanction, when prompting them as patriots to an act which their own multiplied provocations had but too much recommended to their passions. A party entered the tent of Maximin, and dispatched him with the same unpitying haste which he had shown under similar circumstances to the gentle-minded Alexander. Aquileia opened her gates immediately, and thus made it evident that the war had been personal to Maximin.

A scene followed within a short time which is in the highest degree interesting. The senate, in creating two emperors at once (for the boy Gordian was probably associated to them only by way of masking their experiment), had made it evident that their purpose was to restore the republic and its two consuls. This was their meaning; and the experiment had now been twice repeated. The army saw through it: as to the double number of emperors, *that* was of little consequence, farther than as it expressed their intention, viz. by bringing back the consular government, to restore the power of the senate, and to abrogate that of the army. The prætorian troops, who were the most deeply interested in preventing this revolution, watched their opportunity, and attacked the two emperors in the palace. The deadly feud, which had already arisen between them, led each to suppose himself under assault from the other. The mistake was not of long duration. Carried into the streets of Rome, they were both put to death, and treated with monstrous indignities. The young Gordian was adopted by the soldiery. It seems odd that even thus far the guards should sanction the choice of the senate, having the purposes which they had; but perhaps Gordian had recommended himself to their favor in a degree which

Thomas de Quincey

might outweigh what they considered the original vice of his appointment, and his youth promised them an immediate impunity. This prince, however, like so many of his predecessors, soon came to an unhappy end. Under the guardianship of the upright Misitheus, for a time he prospered; and preparations were made upon a great scale for the energetic administration of a Persian war. But Misitheus died, perhaps by poison, in the course of the campaign; and to him succeeded, as prætorian prefect, an Arabian officer, called Philip. The innocent boy, left without friends, was soon removed by murder; and a monument was afterwards erected to his memory, at the junction of the Aboras and the Euphrates. Great obscurity, however, clouds this part of history; nor is it so much as known in what way the Persian war was conducted or terminated.

Philip, having made himself emperor, celebrated, upon his arrival in Rome, the secular games, in the year 247 of the Christian era - that being the completion of a thousand years from the foundation of Rome. But Nemesis was already on his steps. An insurrection had broken out amongst the legions stationed in Mœsia; and they had raised to the purple some officer of low rank. Philip, having occasion to notice this affair in the senate, received for answer from Decius, that probably the pseudo-imperator would prove a mere evanescent phantom. This conjecture was confirmed; and Philip in consequence conceived a high opinion of Decius, whom (as the insurrection still continued) he judged to be the fittest man for appeasing it. Decius accordingly went, armed with the proper authority. But on his arrival, he found himself compelled by the insurgent army to choose between empire and death. Thus constrained, he yielded to the wishes of the troops; and then hastening with a veteran army into Italy, he fought the battle of Verona, where Philip was defeated and killed, whilst the son of Philip was murdered at Rome by the prætorian guards.

With Philip ends, according to our distribution, the second series of the Cæsars, comprehending Commodus, Pertinax, Didius Julianus, Septimius Severus, Caracalla, and Geta, Macrinus, Heliogabalus, Alexander Severus, Maximin, the two Gordians, Pupienus and Balbinus, the third Gordian, and Philip the Arab.

In looking back at this series of Cæsars, we are horror-struck at the blood-stained picture. Well might a foreign writer, in reviewing the same succession, declare, that it is like passing into a new world when the transition is made from this chapter of the human history to that of modern Europe. From Commodus to Decius are sixteen names, which, spread through a space of 59 years, assign to each Cæsar a reign of less than four years. And Casaubon remarks, that, in one period of 160 years, there were 70 persons who assumed the Roman purple; which gives to each not much more than two years. On the other hand, in the history of France, we find that, through a period of 1200 years, there have been no more than 64 kings: upon an average, therefore, each king appears to have enjoyed a reign of nearly nineteen years. This vast difference in security is due to two great principles, - that of primogeniture as between son and son, and of hereditary succession as between a son and every other pretender. Well may we hail the principle of hereditary right as realizing the praise of Burke applied to chivalry, viz., that it is "the cheap defence of nations;" for the security which is thus obtained, be it recollected, does not regard a small succession of

Thomas de Quincey

princes, but the whole rights and interests of social man: since the contests for the rights of belligerent rivals do not respect themselves only, but very often spread ruin and proscription amongst all orders of men. The principle of hereditary succession, says one writer, had it been a discovery of any one individual, would deserve to be considered as the very greatest ever made; and he adds acutely, in answer to the obvious, but shallow objection to it (viz. its apparent assumption of equal ability for reigning in father and son for ever), that it is like the Copernican system of the heavenly bodies, - contradictory to our sense and first impressions, but true notwithstanding.

CHAPTER VI.

To return, however, to our sketch of the Cæsars - at the head of the third series we place Decius. He came to the throne at a moment of great public embarrassment. The Goths were now beginning to press southwards upon the empire. Dacia they had ravaged for some time; "and here," says a German writer, "observe the shortsightedness of the Emperor Trajan." Had he left the Dacians in possession of their independence, they would, under their native kings, have made head against the Goths. But, being compelled to assume the character of Roman citizens, they had lost their warlike qualities. From Dacia the Goths had descended upon Moesia; and, passing the Danube, they laid siege to Marcianopolis, a city built by Trajan in honor of his sister. The inhabitants paid a heavy ransom for their town; and the Goths were persuaded for the present to return home. But sooner than was expected, they returned to Moesia, under their king, Kniva; and they were already engaged in the siege of Nicopolis, when Decius came in sight at the head of the Roman army. The Goths retired, but it was to Thrace; and, in the conquest of Philippopolis, they found an ample indemnity for their forced retreat and disappointment. Decius pursued, but the king of the Goths turned suddenly upon him; the emperor was obliged to fly; the Roman camp was plundered; Philippopolis was taken by storm; and its whole population, reputed at more

Thomas de Quincey

than a hundred thousand souls, destroyed.

Such was the first great irruption of the barbarians into the Roman territory: and panic was diffused on the wings of the winds over the whole empire. Decius, however, was firm, and made prodigious efforts to restore the balance of power to its ancient condition. For the moment he had some partial successes. He cut off several detachments of Goths, on their road to reinforce the enemy; and he strengthened the fortresses and garrisons of the Danube. But his last success was the means of his total ruin. He came up with the Goths at Forum Terebronii, and, having surrounded their position, their destruction seemed inevitable. A great battle ensued, and a mighty victory to the Goths. Nothing is now known of the circumstances, except that the third line of the Romans was entangled inextricably in a morass (as had happened in the Persian expedition of Alexander). Decius perished on this occasion - nor was it possible to find his dead body. This great defeat naturally raised the authority of the senate, in the same proportion as it depressed that of the army; and by the will of that body, Hostilianus, a son of Decius, was raised to the empire; and ostensibly on account of his youth, but really with a view to their standing policy of restoring the consulate, and the whole machinery of the republic, Gallus, an experienced commander, was associated in the empire. But no skill or experience could avail to retrieve the sinking power of Rome upon the Illyrian, frontier. The Roman army was disorganized, panic-stricken, reduced to skeleton battalions. Without an army, what could be done? And thus it may really have been no blame to Gallus, that he made a treaty with the Goths more degrading than any previous act in the long annals of Rome. By the terms of this infamous bargain, they were allowed to carry off an immense booty, amongst which was a long roll of distinguished prisoners; and Cæsar himself it was - not any lieutenant or agent that might have been afterwards disavowed - who volunteered to purchase their future absence by an annual tribute. The very army which had brought their emperor into the necessity of submitting to such abject concessions, were the first to be offended with this natural result of their own failures. Gallus was already ruined in public opinion, when further accumulations arose to his disgrace. It was now supposed to have been discovered, that the late dreadful defeat of Forum Terebronii was due to his bad advice; and, as the young Hostilianus happened to die about this time of a contagious disorder, Gallus was charged with his murder. Even a ray of prosperity, which just now gleamed upon the Roman arms, aggravated the disgrace of Gallus, and was instantly made the handle of his ruin. Æmilianus, the governor of Moesia and Pannonia, inflicted some check or defeat upon the Goths; and in the enthusiasm of sudden pride, upon an occasion which contrasted so advantageously for himself with the military conduct of Decius and Gallus, the soldiers of his own legion raised Æmilianus to the purple. No time was to be lost. Summoned by the troops, Æmilianus marched into Italy; and no sooner had he made his appearance there, than the prætorian guards murdered the Emperor Gallus and his son Volusianus, by way of confirming the election of Æmilianus. The new emperor offered to secure the frontiers, both in the east and on the Danube, from the incursions of the barbarians. This offer may be regarded as thrown out for the conciliation of all classes in the empire. But to the senate in particular he addressed a message, which forcibly illustrates the political position of that body in those times.

Thomas de Quincey

Æmilianus proposed to resign the whole civil administration into the hands of the senate, reserving to himself only the unenviable burthen of the military interests. His hope was, that in this way making himself in part the creation of the senate, he might strengthen his title against competitors at Rome, whilst the entire military administration going on under his own eyes, exclusively directed to that one object, would give him some chance of defeating the hasty and tumultuary competitions so apt to arise amongst the legions upon the frontier. We notice the transaction chiefly as indicating the anomalous situation of the senate. Without power in a proper sense, or no more, however, than the indirect power of wealth, that ancient body retained an immense *auctoritas* - that is, an influence built upon ancient reputation, which, in their case, had the strength of a religious superstition in all Italian minds. This influence the senators exerted with effect, whenever the course of events had happened to reduce the power of the army. And never did they make a more continuous and sustained effort for retrieving their ancient power and place, together with the whole system of the republic, than during the period at which we are now arrived. From the time of Maximin, in fact, to the accession of Aurelian, the senate perpetually interposed their credit and authority, like some *Deus ex machinâ* in the dramatic art. And if this one fact were all that had survived of the public annals at this period, we might sufficiently collect the situation of the two other parties in the empire - the army and the imperator; the weakness and precarious tenure of the one, and the anarchy of the other. And hence it is that we can explain the hatred borne to the senate by vigorous emperors, such as Aurelian, succeeding to a long course of weak and troubled reigns. Such an emperor presumed in the senate, and not without reason, that same spirit of domineering interference as ready to manifest itself, upon any opportunity offered, against himself, which, in his earlier days, he had witnessed so repeatedly in successful operation upon the fates and prospects of others.

The situation indeed of the world - that is to say, of that great centre of civilization, which, running round the Mediterranean in one continuous belt of great breadth, still composed the Roman Empire, was at this time most profoundly interesting. The crisis had arrived. In the East, a new dynasty (the Sassanides) had remoulded ancient elements into a new form, and breathed a new life into an empire, which else was gradually becoming crazy from age, and which, at any rate, by losing its unity, must have lost its vigor as an offensive power. Parthia was languishing and drooping as an anti-Roman state, when the last of the Arsacidæ expired. A perfect *Palingenesis* was wrought by the restorer of the Persian empire, which pretty nearly re-occupied (and gloried in re-occupying) the very area that had once composed the empire of Cyrus. Even this *Palingenesis* might have terminated in a divided empire: vigor might have been restored, but in the shape of a polyarchy, (such as the Saxons established in England,) rather than a monarchy; and in reality, at one moment that appeared to be a probable event. Now, had this been the course of the revolution, an alliance with one of these kingdoms would have tended to balance the hostility of another (as was in fact the case when Alexander Severus saved himself from the Persian power by a momentary alliance with Armenia.) But all the elements of disorder had in that quarter re-combined themselves into severe unity: and thus was Rome, upon her eastern frontier, laid open to

Thomas de Quincey

a new power of juvenile activity and vigor, just at the period when the languor of the decaying Parthian had allowed the Roman discipline to fall into a corresponding declension. Such was the condition of Rome upon her oriental frontier. [Footnote: And it is a striking illustration of the extent to which the revolution had gone, that, previously to the Persian expedition of the last Gordian, Antioch, the Roman capital of Syria, had been occupied by the enemy.] On the northern, it was much worse. Precisely at the crisis of a great revolution in Asia, which demanded in that quarter more than the total strength of the empire, and threatened to demand it for ages to come, did the Goths, under their earliest denomination of *Getæ* with many other associate tribes, begin to push with their horns against the northern gates of the empire: the whole line of the Danube, and, pretty nearly about the same time, of the Rhine, (upon which the tribes from Swabia, Bavaria, and Franconia, were beginning to descend,) now became insecure; and these two rivers ceased in effect to be the barriers of Rome. Taking a middle point of time between the Parthian revolution and the fatal overthrow of Forum Terebronii, we may fix upon the reign of Philip the Arab, [who naturalized himself in Rome by the appellation of Marcus Julius,] as the epoch from which the Roman empire, already sapped and undermined by changes from within, began to give way, and to dilapidate from without. And this reign dates itself in the series by those ever-memorable secular or jubilee games, which celebrated the completion of the thousandth year from the foundation of Rome. [Footnote: This Arab emperor reigned about five years; and the jubilee celebration occurred in his second year. Another circumstance gives importance to the Arabian, that, according to one tradition, he was the first Christian emperor. If so, it is singular that one of the bitterest persecutors of Christianity should have been his immediate successor - Decius.]

Resuming our sketch of the Imperial history, we may remark the natural embarrassment which must have possessed the senate, when two candidates for the purple were equally earnest in appealing to them, and their deliberate choice, as the best foundation for a valid election. Scarcely had the ground been cleared for Æmilianus, by the murder of Gallus and his son, when Valerian, a Roman senator, of such eminent merit, and confessedly so much the foremost noble in all the qualities essential to the very delicate and comprehensive functions of a Censor, [Footnote: It has proved a most difficult problem, in the hands of all speculators upon the imperial history, to fathom the purposes, or throw any light upon the purposes, of the Emperor Decius, in attempting the revival of the ancient but necessarily obsolete office of a public censorship. Either it was an act of pure verbal pedantry, or a mere titular decoration of honor, (as if a modern prince should create a person Arch-Grand-Elector, with no objects assigned to his electing faculty,) or else, if it really meant to revive the old duties of the censorship, and to assign the very same field for the exercise of those duties, it must be viewed as the very grossest practical anachronism that has ever been committed. We mean by an anachronism, in common usage, that sort of blunder when a man ascribes to one age the habits, customs, or generally the characteristics of another. This, however, may be a mere lapse of memory, as to a matter of fact, and implying nothing at all discreditable to the understanding, but only that a man has shifted the boundaries of chronology a little this way or that; as if, for example, a writer should speak of printed books as

Thomas de Quincey

existing at the day of Agincourt, or of artillery as existing in the first Crusade, here would be an error, but a venial one. A far worse kind of anachronism, though rarely noticed as such, is where a writer ascribes sentiments and modes of thought incapable of co-existing with the sort or the degree of civilization then attained, or otherwise incompatible with the structure of society in the age or the country assigned. For instance, in Southey's Don Roderick there is a cast of sentiment in the Gothic king's remorse and contrition of heart, which has struck many readers as utterly unsuitable to the social and moral development of that age, and redolent of modern methodism. This, however, we mention only as an illustration, without wishing to hazard an opinion upon the justice of that criticism. But even such an anachronism is less startling and extravagant when it is confined to an ideal representation of things, than where it is practically embodied and brought into play amongst the realities of life. What would be thought of a man who should attempt, in 1833, to revive the ancient office of *Fool*, as it existed down to the reign, suppose, of our Henry VIII. in England? Yet the error of the Emperor Decius was far greater, if he did in sincerity and good faith believe that the Rome of his times was amenable to that license of unlimited correction, and of interference with private affairs, which republican freedom and simplicity had once conceded to the censor. In reality, the ancient censor, in some parts of his office, was neither more nor less than a compendious legislator. Acts of attainder, divorce bills, &c., illustrate the case in England; they are cases of law, modified to meet the case of an individual; and the censor, having a sort of equity jurisdiction, was intrusted with discretionary powers for reviewing, revising, and amending, *pro re nata*, whatever in the private life of a Roman citizen seemed, to his experienced eye, alien to the simplicity of an austere republic; whatever seemed vicious or capable of becoming vicious, according to their rude notions of political economy; and, generally, whatever touched the interests of the commonwealth, though not falling within the general province of legislation, either because it might appear undignified in its circumstances, or too narrow in its range of operation for a public anxiety, or because considerations of delicacy and prudence might render it unfit for a public scrutiny. Take one case, drawn from actual experience, as an illustration: A Roman nobleman, under one of the early emperors, had thought fit, by way of increasing his income, to retire into rural lodgings, or into some small villa, whilst his splendid mansion in Rome was let to a rich tenant. That a man, who wore the *laticlave*, (which in practical effect of splendor we may consider equal to the ribbon and star of a modern order,) should descend to such a degrading method of raising money, was felt as a scandal to the whole nobility. [Footnote: This feeling still exists in France. "One winter," says the author of *The English Army in France*, vol. ii. p. 106-7, "our commanding officer's wife formed the project of hiring the chateau during the absence of the owner; but a more profound insult could not have been offered to a Chevalier de St. Louis. Hire his house! What could these people take him for? A sordid wretch who would stoop to make money by such means? They ought to be ashamed of themselves. He could never respect an Englishman again." "And yet," adds the writer, "this gentleman (had an officer been billeted there) would have *sold* him a bottle of wine out of his cellar, or a billet of wood from his stack, or an egg from his hen-house, at a profit of fifty per cent., not only without scruple, but upon no other terms. It was as common as ordering

Thomas de Quincey

wine at a tavern, to call the servant of any man's establishment where we happened to be quartered, and demand an account of the cellar, as well as the price of the wine we selected!" This feeling existed, and perhaps to the same extent, two centuries ago, in England. Not only did the aristocracy think it a degradation to act the part of landlord with respect to their own houses, but also, except in select cases, to act that of tenant. Thus, the first Lord Brooke, (the famous Fulke Greville,) writing to inform his next neighbor, a woman of rank, that the house she occupied had been purchased by a London citizen, confesses his fears that he shall in consequence lose so valuable a neighbor; for, doubtless, he adds, your ladyship will not remain as tenant to "such a fellow." And yet the man had notoriously held the office of Lord Mayor, which made him, for the time, *Right Honorable*. The Italians of this day make no scruple to let off the whole, or even part, of their fine mansions to strangers.]

Yet what could be done? To have interfered with his conduct by an express law, would be to infringe the sacred rights of property, and to say, in effect, that a man should not do what he would with his own. This would have been a remedy far worse than the evil to which it was applied; nor could it have been possible so to shape the principle of a law, as not to make it far more comprehensive than was desired. The senator's trespass was in a matter of decorum; but the law would have trespassed on the first principles of justice. Here, then, was a case within the proper jurisdiction of the censor; he took notice, in his public report, of the senator's error; or probably, before coming to that extremity, he admonished him privately on the subject. Just as, in England, had there been such an officer, he would have reproved those men of rank who mounted the coach-box, who extended a public patronage to the "fancy," or who rode their own horses at a race. Such a reproof, however, unless it were made practically operative, and were powerfully supported by the whole body of the aristocracy, would recoil upon its author as a piece of impertinence, and would soon be resented as an unwarrantable liberty taken with private rights; the censor would be kicked, or challenged to private combat, according to the taste of the parties aggrieved. The office is clearly in this dilemma: if the censor is supported by the state, then he combines in his own person both legislative and executive functions, and possesses a power which is frightfully irresponsible; if, on the other hand, he is left to such support as he can find in the prevailing spirit of manners, and the old traditionary veneration for his sacred character, he stands very much in the situation of a priesthood, which has great power or none at all, according to the condition of a country in moral and religious feeling, coupled with the more or less primitive state of manners. How, then, with any rational prospect of success, could Decius attempt the revival of an office depending so entirely on moral supports, in an age when all those supports were withdrawn? The prevailing spirit of manners was hardly fitted to sustain even a toleration of such an office; and as to the traditionary veneration for the sacred character, from long disuse of its practical functions, that probably was altogether extinct. If these considerations are plain and intelligible even to us, by the men of that day they must have been felt with a degree of force that could leave no room for doubt or speculation on the matter. How was it, then, that the emperor only should have been blind to such general light?

In the absence of all other, even plausible, solutions of

Thomas de Quincey

this difficulty, we shall state our own theory of the matter. Decius, as is evident from his fierce persecution of the Christians, was not disposed to treat Christianity with indifference, under any form which it might assume, or however masked. Yet there were quarters in which it lurked not liable to the ordinary modes of attack. Christianity was creeping up with inaudible steps into high places, - nay, into the very highest. The immediate predecessor of Decius upon the throne, Philip the Arab, was known to be a disciple of the new faith; and amongst the nobles of Rome, through the females and the slaves, that faith had spread its roots in every direction. Some secrecy, however, attached to the profession of a religion so often proscribed. Who should presume to tear away the mask which prudence or timidity had taken up? A *delator*, or professional informer, was an infamous character. To deal with the noble and illustrious, the descendants of the Marcelli and the Gracchi, there must be nothing less than a great state officer, supported by the censor and the senate, having an unlimited privilege of scrutiny and censure, authorized to inflict the brand of infamy for offences not challenged by express law, and yet emanating from an elder institution, familiar to the days of reputed liberty. Such an officer was the censor; and such were the antichristian purposes of Decius in his revival.] that Decius had revived that office expressly in his behalf, entered Italy at the head of the army from Gaul. He had been summoned to his aid by the late emperor, Gallus; but, arriving too late for his support, he determined to avenge him. Both Æmilianus and Valerian recognised the authority of the senate, and professed to act under that sanction; but it was the soldiery who cut the knot, as usual, by the sword. Æmilianus was encamped at Spoleto; but as the enemy drew near, his soldiers, shrinking no doubt from a contest with veteran troops, made their peace by murdering the new emperor, and Valerian was elected in his stead. This prince was already an old man at the time of his election; but he lived long enough to look back upon the day of his inauguration as the blackest in his life. Memorable were the calamities which fell upon himself, and upon the empire, during his reign. He began by associating to himself his son Gallienus; partly, perhaps, for his own relief, partly to indulge the senate in their steady plan of dividing the imperial authority. The two emperors undertook the military defence of the empire, Gallienus proceeding to the German frontier, Valerian to the eastern. Under Gallienus, the Franks began first to make themselves heard of. Breaking into Gaul they passed through that country and Spain; captured Tarragona in their route; crossed over to Africa, and conquered Mauritania. At the same time, the Alemanni, who had been in motion since the time of Caracalla, broke into Lombardy, across the Rhætian Alps. The senate, left without aid from either emperor, were obliged to make preparations for the common defence against this host of barbarians. Luckily, the very magnitude of the enemy's success, by overloading him with booty, made it his interest to retire without fighting; and the degraded senate, hanging upon the traces of their retiring footsteps, without fighting, or daring to fight, claimed the honors of a victory. Even then, however, they did more than was agreeable to the jealousies of Gallienus, who, by an edict, publicly rebuked their presumption, and forbade them in future to appear amongst the legions, or to exercise any military functions. He himself, meanwhile, could devise no better way of providing for the public security, than by marrying the daughter of his chief enemy, the king of

Thomas de Quincey

the Marcomanni. On this side of Europe, the barbarians were thus quieted for the present; but the Goths of the Ukraine, in three marauding expeditions of unprecedented violence, ravaged the wealthy regions of Asia Minor, as well as the islands of the Archipelago; and at length, under the guidance of deserters, landed in the port of the Pyræus. Advancing from this point, after sacking Athens and the chief cities of Greece, they marched upon Epirus, and began to threaten Italy. But the defection at this crisis of a conspicuous chieftain, and the burden of their booty, made these wild marauders anxious to provide for a safe retreat; the imperial commanders in Moesia listened eagerly to their offers: and it set the seal to the dishonors of the state, that, after having traversed so vast a range of territory almost without resistance, these blood-stained brigands were now suffered to retire under the very guardianship of those whom they had just visited with military execution.

Such were the terms upon which the Emperor Gallienus purchased a brief respite from his haughty enemies. For the moment, however, he *did* enjoy security. Far otherwise was the destiny of his unhappy father. Sapor now ruled in Persia; the throne of Armenia had vainly striven to maintain its independency against his armies, and the daggers of his hired assassins. This revolution, which so much enfeebled the Roman means of war, exactly in that proportion increased the necessity for it. War, and that instantly, seemed to offer the only chance for maintaining the Roman name or existence in Asia, Carrhæ and Nisibis, the two potent fortresses in Mesopotamia, had fallen; and the Persian arms were now triumphant on both banks of the Euphrates. Valerian was not of a character to look with indifference upon such a scene, terminated by such a prospect; prudence and temerity, fear and confidence, all spoke a common language in this great emergency; and Valerian marched towards the Euphrates with a fixed purpose of driving the enemy beyond that river. By whose mismanagement the records of history do not enable us to say, some think of Macrianus, the prætorian prefect, some of Valerian himself, but doubtless by the treachery of guides co-operating with errors in the general, the Roman army was entangled in marshy grounds; partial actions followed, and skirmishes of cavalry, in which the Romans became direfully aware of their situation; retreat was cut off, to advance was impossible; and to fight was now found to be without hope. In these circumstances they offered to capitulate. But the haughty Sapor would hear of nothing but unconditional surrender; and to that course the unhappy emperor submitted. Various traditions [Footnote: Some of these traditions have been preserved, which represent Sapor as using his imperial captive for his stepping-stone, or *anabathrum*, in mounting his horse. Others go farther, and pretend that Sapor actually flayed his unhappy prisoner whilst yet alive. The temptation to these stories was perhaps found in the craving for the marvellous, and in the desire to make the contrast more striking between the two extremes in Valerian's life.] have been preserved by history concerning the fate of Valerian: all agree that he died in misery and captivity; but some have circumstantiated this general statement by features of excessive misery and degradation, which possibly were added afterwards by scenical romancers, in order to heighten the interest of the tale, or by ethical writers, in order to point and strengthen the moral. Gallienus now ruled alone, except as regarded the restless efforts of insurgents, thirty of whom are said to have arisen in his

Thomas de Quincey

single reign. This, however, is probably an exaggeration. Nineteen such rebels are mentioned by name; of whom the chief were Calpurnius Piso, a Roman senator; Tetricus, a man of rank who claimed a descent from Pompey, Crassus, and even from Numa Pompilius, and maintained himself some time in Gaul and Spain; Trebellianus, who founded a republic of robbers in Isauria which survived himself by centuries; and Odenathus, the Syrian. Others were mere *Terra filii,* or adventurers, who flourished and decayed in a few days or weeks, of whom the most remarkable was a working armorer named Marius. Not one of the whole number eventually prospered, except Odenathus; and he, though originally a rebel, yet, in consideration of services performed against Persia, was suffered to retain his power, and to transmit his kingdom of Palmyra to his widow Zenobia. He was even complimented with the title of Augustus. All the rest perished. Their rise, however, and local prosperity at so many different points of the empire, showed the distracted condition of the state, and its internal weakness. That again proclaimed its external peril. No other cause had called forth this diffusive spirit of insurrection than the general consciousness, so fatally warranted, of the debility which had emasculated the government, and its incompetency to deal vigorously with the public enemies. [Footnote: And this incompetency was *permanently* increased by rebellions that were brief and fugitive: for each insurgent almost necessarily maintained himself for the moment by spoliations and robberies which left lasting effects behind them; and too often he was tempted to ally himself with some foreign enemy amongst the barbarians, and perhaps to introduce him into the heart of the empire.] The very granaries of Rome, Sicily and Egypt, were the seats of continued distractions; in

Alexandria, the second city of the empire, there was even a civil war which lasted for twelve years. Weakness, dissension, and misery were spread like a cloud over the whole face of the empire.

The last of the rebels who directed his rebellion personally against Gallienus was Aureolus. Passing the Rhætian Alps, this leader sought out and defied the emperor. He was defeated, and retreated upon Milan; but Gallienus, in pursuing him, was lured into an ambuscade, and perished from the wound inflicted by an archer. With his dying breath he is said to have recommended Claudius to the favor of the senate; and at all events Claudius it was who succeeded. Scarcely was the new emperor installed, before he was summoned to a trial not only arduous in itself, but terrific by the very name of the enemy. The Goths of the Ukraine, in a new armament of six thousand vessels, had again descended by the Bosphorus into the south, and had sat down before Thessalonica, the capitol of Macedonia. Claudius marched against them with the determination to vindicate the Roman name and honor: "Know," said he, writing to the senate, "that 320,000 Goths have set foot upon the Roman soil. Should I conquer them, your gratitude will be my reward. Should I fall, do not forget who it is that I have succeeded; and that the republic is exhausted." No sooner did the Goths hear of his approach, than, with transports of ferocious joy, they gave up the siege, and hurried to annihilate the last pillar of the empire. The mighty battle which ensued, neither party seeking to evade it, took place at Naissus. At one time the legions were giving way, when suddenly, by some happy manoeuvre of the emperor, a Roman corps found its way to the rear of the enemy. The Goths gave way, and their defeat was total. According to most accounts they

Thomas de Quincey

left 50,000 dead upon the field. The campaign still lingered, however, at other points, until at last the emperor succeeded in driving back the relics of the Gothic host into the fastnesses of the Balkan; and there the greater part of them died of hunger and pestilence. These great services performed, within two years from his accession to the throne, by the rarest of fates the Emperor Claudius died in his bed at Sirmium, the capitol of Pannonia. His brother Quintilius who had a great command at Aquileia, immediately assumed the purple; but his usurpation lasted only seventeen days, for the last emperor, with a single eye to the public good, had recommended Aurelian as his successor, guided by his personal knowledge of that general's strategic qualities. The army of the Danube confirmed the appointment; and Quintilius committed suicide. Aurelian was of the same harsh and forbidding character as the Emperor Severus: he had, however, the qualities demanded by the times; energetic and not amiable princes were required by the exigences of the state. The hydra-headed Goths were again in the field on the Illyrian quarter: Italy itself was invaded by the Alemanni; and Tetricus, the rebel, still survived as a monument of the weakness of Gallienus. All these enemies were speedily repressed, or vanquished, by Aurelian. But it marks the real declension of the empire, a declension which no personal vigor in the emperor was now sufficient to disguise, that, even in the midst of victory, Aurelian found it necessary to make a formal surrender, by treaty, of that Dacia which Trajan had united with so much ostentation to the empire. Europe was now again in repose; and Aurelian found himself at liberty to apply his powers as a reorganizer and restorer to the East. In that quarter of the world a marvellous revolution had occurred. The little oasis of Palmyra, from a Roman colony, had grown into the leading province of a great empire. This island of the desert, together with Syria and Egypt, formed an independent monarchy under the sceptre of Zenobia. [Footnote: Zenobia is complimented by all historians for her magnanimity; but with no foundation in truth. Her first salutation to Aurelian was a specimen of abject flattery; and her last *public* words were evidences of the basest treachery in giving up her generals, and her chief counsellor Longinus, to the vengeance of the ungenerous enemy.] After two battles lost in Syria, Zenobia retreated to Palmyra. With great difficulty Aurelian pursued her; and with still greater difficulty he pressed the siege of Palmyra. Zenobia looked for relief from Persia; but at that moment Sapor died, and the Queen of Palmyra fled upon a dromedary, but was pursued and captured. Palmyra surrendered and was spared; but unfortunately, with a folly which marks the haughty spirit of the place unfitted to brook submission, scarcely had the conquering army retired when a tumult arose, and the Roman garrison was slaughtered. Little knowledge could those have had of Aurelian's character, who tempted him to acts but too welcome to his cruel nature by such an outrage as this. The news overtook the emperor on the Hellespont. Instantly, without pause, "like Até hot from hell," Aurelian retraced his steps - reached the guilty city - and consigned it, with all its population, to that utter destruction from which it has never since arisen. The energetic administration of Aurelian had now restored the empire - not to its lost vigor, that was impossible - but to a condition of repose. That was a condition more agreeable to the empire than to the emperor. Peace was hateful to Aurelian; and he sought for war, where it could seldom be sought in vain, upon the Persian frontier. But he was not destined to reach the Euphrates; and it is

Thomas de Quincey

worthy of notice, as a providential ordinance, that his own unmerciful nature was the ultimate cause of his fate. Anticipating the emperor's severity in punishing some errors of his own, Mucassor, a general officer in whom Aurelian placed especial confidence, assassinated him between Byzantium and Heraclea. An interregnum of eight months succeeded, during which there occurred a contest of a memorable nature. Some historians have described it as strange and surprising. To us, on the contrary, it seems that no contest could be more natural. Heretofore the great strife had been in what way to secure the reversion or possession of that great dignity; whereas now the rivalship lay in declining it. But surely such a competition had in it, under the circumstances of the empire, little that can justly surprise us. Always a post of danger, and so regularly closed by assassination, that in a course of two centuries there are hardly to be found three or four cases of exception, the imperatorial dignity had now become burdened with a public responsibility which exacted great military talents, and imposed a perpetual and personal activity. Formerly, if the emperor knew himself to be surrounded with assassins, he might at least make his throne, so long as he enjoyed it, the couch of a voluptuary. The "*ave imperator!*" was then the summons, if to the supremacy in passive danger, so also to the supremacy in power, and honor, and enjoyment. But now it was a summons to never-ending tumults and alarms; an injunction to that sort of vigilance without intermission, which, even from the poor sentinel, is exacted only when on duty. Not Rome, but the frontier; not the *aurea domus,* but a camp, was the imperial residence. Power and rank, whilst in that residence, could be had in no larger measure by Cæsar *as* Cæsar, than by the same individual as a military commander-in-chief; and, as to enjoyment, *that* for the Roman imperator was now extinct. Rest there could be none for him. Battle was the tenure by which he held his office; and beyond the range of his trumpet's blare, his sceptre was a broken reed. The office of Cæsar at this time resembled the situation (as it is sometimes described in romances) of a knight who has achieved the favor of some capricious lady, with the present possession of her castle and ample domains, but which he holds under the known and accepted condition of meeting all challenges whatsoever offered at the gate by wandering strangers, and also of jousting at any moment with each and all amongst the inmates of the castle, as often as a wish may arise to benefit by the chances in disputing his supremacy.

It is a circumstance, moreover, to be noticed in the aspect of the Roman monarchy at this period, that the pressure of the evils we are now considering, applied to this particular age of the empire beyond all others, as being an age of transition from a greater to an inferior power. Had the power been either greater or conspicuously less, in that proportion would the pressure have been easier, or none at all. Being greater, for example, the danger would have been repelled to a distance so great that mere remoteness would have disarmed its terrors, or otherwise it would have been violently overawed. Being less, on the other hand, and less in an eminent degree, it would have disposed all parties, as it did at an after period, to regular and formal compromises in the shape of fixed annual tributes. At present the policy of the barbarians along the vast line of the northern frontier, was, to tease and irritate the provinces which they were not entirely able, or prudentially unwilling, to dismember. Yet, as the almost annual irruptions were at every instant ready to

Thomas de Quincey

be converted into *coup-de-mains* upon Aquileia - upon Verona - or even upon Rome itself, unless vigorously curbed at the outset, - each emperor at this period found himself under the necessity of standing in the attitude of a champion or propugnator on the frontier line of his territory - ready for all comers - and with a pretty certain prospect of having one pitched battle at the least to fight in every successive summer. There were nations abroad at this epoch in Europe who did not migrate occasionally, or occasionally project themselves upon the civilized portion of the globe, but who made it their steady regular occupation to do so, and lived for no other purpose. For seven hundred years the Roman Republic might be styled a republic militant: for about one century further it was an empire triumphant; and now, long retrograde, it had reached that point at which again, but in a different sense, it might be styled an empire militant. Originally it had militated for glory and power; now its militancy was for mere existence. War was again the trade of Rome, as it had been once before: but in that earlier period war had been its highest glory now it was its dire necessity.

Under this analysis of the Roman condition, need we wonder, with the crowd of unreflecting historians, that the senate, at the era of Aurelian's death, should dispute amongst each other - not, as once, for the possession of the sacred purple, but for the luxury and safety of declining it? The sad pre-eminence was finally imposed upon Tacitus, a senator who traced his descent from the historian of that name, who had reached an age of seventy - five years, and who possessed a fortune of three millions sterling. Vainly did the agitated old senator open his lips to decline the perilous honor; five hundred voices insisted upon the necessity of his compliance; and thus, as a foreign writer observes, was the descendant of him, whose glory it had been to signalize himself as the hater of despotism, under the absolute necessity of becoming, in his own person, a despot.

The aged senator then was compelled to be emperor, and forced, in spite of his vehement reluctance, to quit the comforts of a palace, which he was never to revisit, for the hardships of a distant camp. His first act was strikingly illustrative of the Roman condition, as we have just described it. Aurelian had attempted to disarm one set of enemies by turning the current of their fury upon another. The Alani were in search of plunder, and strongly disposed to obtain it from Roman provinces. "But no," said Aurelian; "if you do that, I shall unchain my legions upon you. Be better advised: keep those excellent dispositions of mind, and that admirable taste for plunder, until you come whither I will conduct you. Then discharge your fury, and welcome; besides which, I will pay you wages for your immediate abstinence; and on the other side the Euphrates you shall pay yourselves." Such was the outline of the contract; and the Alans had accordingly held themselves in readiness to accompany Aurelian from Europe to his meditated Persian campaign. Meantime, that emperor had perished by treason; and the Alani were still waiting for his successor on the throne to complete his engagements with themselves, as being of necessity the successor also to his wars and to his responsibilities. It happened, from the state of the empire, as we have sketched it above, that Tacitus really *did* succeed to the military plans of Aurelian. The Persian expedition was ordained to go forward; and Tacitus began, as a preliminary step in that expedition, to look about for his good allies the

Thomas de Quincey

barbarians. Where might they be, and how employed? Naturally, they had long been weary of waiting. The Persian booty might be good after *its* kind; but it was far away; and, *en attendant*, Roman booty was doubtless good after *its* kind. And so, throughout the provinces of Cappadocia, Pontus, &c., far as the eye could stretch, nothing was to be seen but cities and villages in flames. The Roman army hungered and thirsted to be unmuzzled and slipped upon these false friends. But this, for the present, Tacitus would not allow. He began by punctually fulfilling all the terms of Aurelian's contract, - a measure which barbarians inevitably construed into the language of fear. But then came the retribution. Having satisfied public justice, the emperor now thought of vengeance: he unchained his legions: a brief space of time sufficed for a long course of vengeance: and through every outlet of Asia Minor the Alani fled from the wrath of the Roman soldier. Here, however, terminated the military labors of Tacitus: he died at Tyana in Cappadocia, as some say, from the effects of the climate of the Caucasus, co-operating with irritations from the insolence of the soldiery; but, as Zosimus and Zonaras expressly assure us, under the murderous hands of his own troops. His brother Florianus at first usurped the purple, by the aid of the Illyrian army; but the choice of other armies, afterwards confirmed by the senate, settled upon Probus, a general already celebrated under Aurelian. The two competitors drew near to each other for the usual decision by the sword, when the dastardly supporters of Florian offered up their chosen prince as a sacrifice to his antagonist. Probus, settled in his seat, addressed himself to the regular business of those times, - to the reduction of insurgent provinces, and the liberation of others from hostile molestations. Isauria and Egypt he visited in the character of a conqueror,

Gaul in the character of a deliverer. From the Gaulish provinces he chased in succession the Franks, the Burgundians, and the Lygians. He pursued the intruders far into their German thickets; and nine of the native German princes came spontaneously into his camp, subscribed such conditions as he thought fit to dictate, and complied with his requisitions of tribute in horses and provisions. This, however, is a delusive gleam of Roman energy, little corresponding with the true condition of the Roman power, and entirely due to the *personal* qualities of Probus. Probus himself showed his sense of the true state of affairs, by carrying a stone wall, of considerable height, from the Danube to the Neckar. He made various attempts also to effect a better distribution of barbarous tribes, by dislocating their settlements, and making extensive translations of their clans, according to the circumstances of those times. These arrangements, however, suggested often by short-sighted views, and carried into effect by mere violence, were sometimes defeated visibly at the time, and, doubtless, in very few cases accomplished the ends proposed. In one instance, where a party of Franks had been transported into the Asiatic province of Pontus, as a column of defence against the intrusive Alans, being determined to revisit their own country, they swam the Hellespont, landed on the coasts of Asia Minor and of Greece, plundered Syracuse, steered for the Straits of Gibraltar, sailed along the shores of Spain and Gaul, passing finally through the English Channel and the German Ocean, right onwards to the Frisic and Batavian coasts, where they exultingly rejoined their exulting friends. Meantime, all the energy and military skill of Probus could not save him from the competition of various rivals. Indeed, it must then have been felt, as by us who look back on those times it is now felt, that,

Thomas de Quincey

amidst so continued a series of brief reigns, interrupted by murders, scarcely any idea could arise answering to our modern ideas of treason and usurpation. For the ideas of fealty and allegiance, as to a sacred and anointed monarch, could have no time to take root. Candidates for the purple must have been viewed rather as military rivals than as traitors to the reigning Cæsar. And hence one reason for the slight resistance which was often experienced by the seducers of armies. Probus, however, as accident in his case ordered it, subdued all his personal opponents, - Saturninus in the East, Proculus and Bonoses in Gaul. For these victories he triumphed in the year 281. But his last hour was even then at hand. One point of his military discipline, which he brought back from elder days, was, to suffer no idleness in his camps. He it was who, by military labor, transferred to Gaul and to Hungary the Italian vine, to the great indignation of the Italian monopolist. The culture of vineyards, the laying of military roads, the draining of marshes, and similar labors, perpetually employed the hands of his stubborn and contumacious troops. On some work of this nature the army happened to be employed near Sirmium, and Probus was looking on from a tower, when a sudden frenzy of disobedience seized upon the men: a party of the mutineers ran up to the emperor, and with a hundred wounds laid him instantly dead. We are told by some writers that the army was immediately seized with remorse for its own act; which, if truly reported, rather tends to confirm the image, otherwise impressed upon us, of the relations between the army and Cæsar as pretty closely corresponding with those between some fierce wild beast and its keeper; the keeper, if not uniformly vigilant as an Argus, is continually liable to fall a sacrifice to the wild instincts of the brute, mastering at intervals the reverence and fear under which it has been habitually trained. In this case, both the murdering impulse and the remorse seem alike the effects of a brute instinct, and to have arisen under no guidance of rational purpose or reflection. The person who profited by this murder was Carus, the captain of the guard, a man of advanced years, and a soldier, both by experience and by his propensities. He was proclaimed emperor by the army; and on this occasion there was no further reference to the senate, than by a dry statement of the facts for its information. Troubling himself little about the approbation of a body not likely in any way to affect his purposes (which were purely martial, and adapted to the tumultuous state of the empire), Carus made immediate preparations for pursuing the Persian expedition, - so long promised, and so often interrupted. Having provided for the security of the Illyrian frontier by a bloody victory over the Sarmatians, of whom we now hear for the first time, Carus advanced towards the Euphrates; and from the summit of a mountain he pointed the eyes of his eager army upon the rich provinces of the Persian empire. Varanes, the successor of Artaxerxes, vainly endeavored to negotiate a peace. From some unknown cause, the Persian armies were not at this juncture disposable against Carus: it has been conjectured by some writers that they were engaged in an Indian war. Carus, it is certain, met with little resistance. He insisted on having the Roman supremacy acknowledged as a preliminary to any treaty; and, having threatened to make Persia as bare as his own skull, he is supposed to have kept his word with regard to Mesopotamia. The great cities of Ctesiphon and Seleucia he took; and vast expectations were formed at Rome of the events which stood next in succession, when, on Christmas day, 283, a sudden and mysterious end overtook Carus and his victorious advance. The

Thomas de Quincey

story transmitted to Rome was, that a great storm, and a sudden darkness, had surprised the camp of Carus; that the emperor, previously ill, and reposing in his tent, was obscured from sight; that at length a cry had arisen, - "The emperor is dead!" and that, at the same moment, the imperial tent had taken fire. The fire was traced to the confusion of his attendants; and this confusion was imputed by themselves to grief for their master's death. In all this it is easy to read pretty circumstantially a murder committed on the emperor by corrupted servants, and an attempt afterwards to conceal the indications of murder by the ravages of fire. The report propagated through the army, and at that time received with credit, was, that Carus had been struck by lightning: and that omen, according to the Roman interpretation, implied a necessity of retiring from the expedition. So that, apparently, the whole was a bloody intrigue, set on foot for the purpose of counteracting the emperor's resolution to prosecute the war. His son Numerian succeeded to the rank of emperor by the choice of the army. But the mysterious faction of murderers were still at work. After eight months' march from the Tigris to the Thracian Bosphorus, the army halted at Chalcedon. At this point of time a report arose suddenly, that the Emperor Numerian was dead. The impatience of the soldiery would brook no uncertainty: they rushed to the spot; satisfied themselves of the fact; and, loudly denouncing as the murderer Aper, the captain of the guard, committed him to custody, and assigned to Dioclesian, whom at the same time they invested with the supreme power, the duty of investigating the case. Dioclesian acquitted himself of this task in a very summary way, by passing his sword through the captain before he could say a word in his defence. It seems that Dioclesian, having been promised the empire by a prophetess as soon as he should have killed a wild boar [Aper], was anxious to realize the omen. The whole proceeding has been taxed with injustice so manifest, as not even to seek a disguise. Meantime, it should be remembered that, *first,* Aper, as the captain of the guard, was answerable for the emperor's safety; *secondly,* that his anxiety to profit by the emperor's murder was a sure sign that he had participated in that act; and, *thirdly,* that the assent of the soldiery to the open and public act of Dioclesian, implies a conviction on their part of Aper's guilt. Here let us pause, having now arrived at the fourth and last group of the Cæsars, to notice the changes which had been wrought by time, co-operating with political events, in the very nature and constitution of the imperial office.

If it should unfortunately happen, that the palace of the Vatican, with its thirteen thousand [Footnote: *"Thirteen thousand chambers."* – The number of the chambers in this prodigious palace is usually estimated at that amount. But Lady Miller, who made particular inquiries on this subject, ascertained that the total amount, including cellars and closets, capable of receiving a bed, was fifteen thousand.] chambers, were to take fire - for a considerable space of time the fire would be retarded by the mere enormity of extent which it would have to traverse. But there would come at length a critical moment, at which the maximum of the retarding effect having been attained, the bulk and volume of the flaming mass would thenceforward assist the flames in the rapidity of their progress. Such was the effect upon the declension of the Roman empire from the vast extent of its territory. For a very long period that very extent, which finally became the overwhelming cause of its ruin, served to retard and to

Thomas de Quincey

disguise it. A small encroachment, made at any one point upon the integrity of the empire, was neither much regarded at Rome, nor perhaps in and for itself much deserved to be regarded. But a very narrow belt of encroachments, made upon almost every part of so enormous a circumference, was sufficient of itself to compose something of an antagonist force. And to these external dilapidations, we must add the far more important dilapidations from within, affecting all the institutions of the State, and all the forces, whether moral or political, which had originally raised it or maintained it. Causes which had been latent in the public arrangements ever since the time of Augustus, and had been silently preying upon its vitals, had now reached a height which would no longer brook concealment. The fire which had smouldered through generations had broken out at length into an open conflagration. Uproar and disorder, and the anarchy of a superannuated empire, strong only to punish and impotent to defend, were at this time convulsing the provinces in every point of the compass. Rome herself had been menaced repeatedly. And a still more awful indication of the coming storm had been felt far to the south of Rome. One long wave of the great German deluge had stretched beyond the Pyrenees and the Pillars of Hercules, to the very soil of ancient Carthage. Victorious banners were already floating on the margin of the Great Desert, and they were not the banners of Cæsar. Some vigorous hand was demanded at this moment, or else the funeral knell of Rome was on the point of sounding. Indeed, there is every reason to believe that, had the imbecile Carinus (the brother of Numerian) succeeded to the command of the Roman armies at this time, or any other than Dioclesian, the empire of the west would have fallen to pieces within the next ten years.

Dioclesian was doubtless that man of iron whom the times demanded; and a foreign writer has gone so far as to class him amongst the greatest of men, if he were not even himself the greatest. But the position of Dioclesian was remarkable beyond all precedent, and was alone sufficient to prevent his being the greatest of men, by making it necessary that he should be the most selfish. For the case stood thus: If Rome were in danger, much more so was Cæsar. If the condition of the empire were such that hardly any energy or any foresight was adequate to its defence, for the emperor, on the other hand, there was scarcely a possibility that he should escape destruction. The chances were in an overbalance against the empire; but for the emperor there was no chance at all. He shared in all the hazards of the empire; and had others so peculiarly pointed at himself, that his assassination was now become as much a matter of certain calculation, as seed-time or harvest, summer or winter, or any other revolution of the seasons. The problem, therefore, for Dioclesian was a double one, - so to provide for the defence and maintenance of the empire, as simultaneously (and, if possible, through the very same institution) to provide for the personal security of Cæsar. This problem he solved, in some imperfect degree, by the only expedient perhaps open to him in that despotism, and in those times. But it is remarkable, that, by the revolution which he effected, the office of Roman Imperator was completely altered, and Cæsar became henceforwards an Oriental Sultan or Padishah. Augustus, when moulding for his future purposes the form and constitution of that supremacy which he had obtained by inheritance and by arms, proceeded with so much caution and prudence, that even the style and title of his office was discussed in council as a matter of the first moment. The principle of his policy was to

Thomas de Quincey

absorb into his own functions all those offices which conferred any real power to balance or to control his own. For this reason he appropriated the tribunitian power; because that was a popular and representative office, which, as occasions arose, would have given some opening to democratic influences. But the consular office he left untouched; because all its power was transferred to the imperator, by the entire command of the army, and by the new organization of the provincial governments. [Footnote: In no point of his policy was the cunning or the sagacity of Augustus so much displayed, as in his treaty of partition with the senate, which settled the distribution of the provinces, and their future administration. Seeming to take upon himself all the trouble and hazard, he did in effect appropriate all the power, and left to the senate little more than trophies of show and ornament. As a first step, all the greater provinces, as Spain and Gaul, were subdivided into many smaller ones. This done, Augustus proposed that the senate should preside over the administration of those amongst them which were peaceably settled, and which paid a regular tribute; whilst all those which were the seats of danger, - either as being exposed to hostile inroads, or to internal commotions, - all, therefore, in fact, *which could justify the keeping up of a military force,* he assigned to himself. In virtue of this arrangement, the senate possessed in Africa those provinces which had been formed out of Carthage, Cyrene, and the kingdom of Numidia; in Europe, the richest and most quiet part of Spain *(Hispania Bœtica),* with the large islands of Sicily, Sardinia, Corsica, and Crete, and some districts of Greece; in Asia, the kingdoms of Pontus and Bithynia, with that part of Asia Minor technically called Asia; whilst, for his own share, Augustus retained Gaul, Syria, the chief part of Spain, and

Egypt, the granary of Rome; finally, all the military posts on the Euphrates, on the Danube, or the Rhine.

Yet even the showy concessions here made to the senate were defeated by another political institution, settled at the same time. It had been agreed that the governors of provinces should be appointed by the emperor and the senate jointly. But within the senatorian jurisdiction, these governors, with the title of *Proconsuls,* were to have no military power whatsoever; and the appointments were good only for a single year. Whereas, in the imperatorial provinces, where the governor bore the title of *Proprætor,* there was provision made for a military establishment; and as to duration, the office was regulated entirely by the emperor's pleasure. One other ordinance, on the same head, riveted the vassalage of the senate. Hitherto, a great source of the senate's power had been found in the uncontrolled management of the provincial revenues; but at this time, Augustus so arranged that branch of the administration, that, throughout the senatorian or proconsular provinces, all taxes were immediately paid into the *ararium*, or treasury of the state; whilst the whole revenues of the proprætorian (or imperatorial) provinces, from this time forward, flowed into the *fiscus*, or private treasure of the individual emperor.] And in all the rest of his arrangements, Augustus had proceeded on the principle of leaving as many openings to civic influences, and impressing upon all his institutions as much of the old Roman character, as was compatible with the real and substantial supremacy established in the person of the emperor. Neither is it at all certain, as regarded even this aspect of the imperatorial office, that Augustus had the purpose, or so much as the wish, to annihilate all collateral power, and to invest the

Thomas de Quincey

chief magistrate with absolute irresponsibility. For himself, as called upon to restore a shattered government, and out of the anarchy of civil wars to recombine the elements of power into some shape better fitted for duration (and, by consequence, for insuring peace and protection to the world) than the extinct republic, it might be reasonable to seek such an irresponsibility. But, as regarded his successors, considering the great pains he took to discourage all manifestations of princely arrogance, and to develop, by education and example, the civic virtues of patriotism and affability in their whole bearing towards the people of Rome, there is reason to presume that he wished to remove them from popular control, without, therefore, removing them from popular influence.

Hence it was, and from this original precedent of Augustus, aided by the constitution which he had given to the office of imperator, that up to the era of Dioclesian, no prince had dared utterly to neglect the senate, or the people of Rome. He might hate the senate, like Severus, or Aurelian; he might even meditate their extermination, like the brutal Maximin. But this arose from any cause rather than from contempt. He hated them precisely because he feared them, or because he paid them an involuntary tribute of superstitious reverence, or because the malice of a tyrant interpreted into a sort of treason the rival influence of the senate over the minds of men. But, before Dioclesian, the undervaluing of the senate, or the harshest treatment of that body, had arisen from views which were *personal* to the individual Cæsar. It was now made to arise from the very constitution of the office, and the mode of the appointment. To defend the empire, it was the opinion of Dioclesian that a single emperor was not sufficient. And it struck him, at the same time, that by the very institution of a plurality of emperors, which was now destined to secure the integrity of the empire, ample provision might be made for the personal security of each emperor. He carried his plan into immediate execution, by appointing an associate to his own rank of Augustus in the person of Maximian - an experienced general; whilst each of them in effect multiplied his own office still farther by severally appointing a Cæsar, or hereditary prince. And thus the very same partition of the public authority, by means of a duality of emperors, to which the senate had often resorted of late, as the best means of restoring their own republican aristocracy, was now adopted by Dioclesian as the simplest engine for overthrowing finally the power of either senate or army to interfere with the elective privilege. This he endeavored to centre in the existing emperors; and, at the same moment, to discourage treason or usurpation generally, whether in the party choosing or the party chosen, by securing to each emperor, in the case of his own assassination, an avenger in the person of his surviving associate, as also in the persons of the two Cæsars, or adopted heirs and lieutenants. The associate emperor, Maximian, together with the two Cæsars - Galerius appointed by himself, and Constantius Chlorus by Maximian - were all bound to himself by ties of gratitude; all owing their stations ultimately to his own favor. And these ties he endeavored to strengthen by other ties of affinity; each of the Augusti having given his daughter in marriage to his own adopted Cæsar. And thus it seemed scarcely possible that a usurpation should be successful against so firm a league of friends and relations.

The direct purposes of Dioclesian were but imperfectly attained; the internal peace of the empire lasted only

Thomas de Quincey

during his own reign; and with his abdication of the empire commenced the bloodiest civil wars which had desolated the world since the contests of the great triumvirate. But the collateral blow, which he meditated against the authority of the senate, was entirely successful. Never again had the senate any real influence on the fate of the world. And with the power of the senate expired concurrently the weight and influence of Rome. Dioclesian is supposed never to have seen Rome, except on the single occasion when he entered it for the ceremonial purpose of a triumph. Even for that purpose it ceased to be a city of resort; for Dioclesian's was the final triumph. And, lastly, even as the chief city of the empire for business or for pleasure, it ceased to claim the homage of mankind; the Cæsar was already born whose destiny it was to cashier the metropolis of the world, and to appoint her successor. This also may be regarded in effect as the ordinance of Dioclesian; for he, by his long residence at Nicomedia, expressed his opinion pretty plainly, that Rome was not central enough to perform the functions of a capital to so vast an empire; that this was one cause of the declension now become so visible in the forces of the state; and that some city, not very far from the Hellespont or the Aegean Sea, would be a capital better adapted by position to the exigencies of the times.

But the revolutions effected by Dioclesian did not stop here. The simplicity of its republican origin had so far affected the external character and expression of the imperial office, that in the midst of luxury the most unbounded, and spite of all other corruptions, a majestic plainness of manners, deportment, and dress, had still continued from generation to generation, characteristic of the Roman imperator in his intercourse with his subjects. All this was now changed; and for the Roman was substituted the Persian dress, the Persian style of household, a Persian court, and Persian manners, A diadem, or tiara beset with pearls, now encircled the temples of the Roman Augustus; his sandals were studded with pearls, as in the Persian court; and the other parts of his dress were in harmony with these. The prince was instructed no longer to make himself familiar to the eyes of men. He sequestered himself from his subjects in the recesses of his palace. None, who sought him, could any longer gain easy admission to his presence. It was a point of his new duties to be difficult of access; and they who were at length admitted to an audience, found him surrounded by eunuchs, and were expected to make their approaches by genuflexions, by servile "adorations," and by real acts of worship as to a visible god.

It is strange that a ritual of court ceremonies, so elaborate and artificial as this, should first have been introduced by a soldier, and a warlike soldier like Dioclesian. This, however, is in part explained by his education and long residence in Eastern countries.

But the same eastern training fell to the lot of Constantine, who was in effect his successor; [Footnote: On the abdication of Dioclesian and of Maximian, Galerius and Constantius succeeded as the new Augusti. But Galerius, as the more immediate representative of Dioclesian, thought himself entitled to appoint both Cæsars, - the Daza (or Maximus) in Syria, Severus in Italy. Meantime, Constantine, the son of Constantius, with difficulty obtaining permission from Galerius, paid a visit to his father; upon whose death, which followed soon after, Constantine came

Thomas de Quincey

forward as a Cæsar, under the appointment of his father. Galerius submitted with a bad grace; but Maxentius, a reputed son of Maximian, was roused by emulation with Constantine to assume the purple; and being joined by his father, they jointly attacked and destroyed Severus. Galerius, to revenge the death of his own Cæsar, advanced towards Rome; but being compelled to a disastrous retreat, he resorted to the measure of associating another emperor with himself, as a balance to his new enemies. This was Licinius; and thus, at one time, there were six emperors, either as Augusti or as Cæsars. Galerius, however, dying, all the rest were in succession destroyed by Constantine.] and the Oriental tone and standard established by these two emperors, though disturbed a little by the plain and military bearing of Julian, and one or two more emperors of the same breeding, finally re-established itself with undisputed sway in the Byzantine court.

Meantime the institutions of Dioclesian, if they had destroyed Rome and the senate as influences upon the course of public affairs, and if they had destroyed the Roman features of the Cæsars, do, notwithstanding, appear to have attained one of their purposes, in limiting the extent of imperial murders. Travelling through the brief list of the remaining Cæsars, we perceive a little more security for life; and hence the successions are less rapid. Constantine, who (like Aaron's rod) had swallowed up all his competitors *seriatim,* left the empire to his three sons; and the last of these most unwillingly to Julian. That prince's Persian expedition, so much resembling in rashness and presumption the Russian campaign of Napoleon, though so much below it in the scale of its tragic results, led to the short reign of Jovian, (or Jovinian,) which lasted only seven months. Upon his death succeeded the house of Valentinian, [Footnote: Valentinian the First, who admitted his brother Valens to a partnership in the empire, had, by his first wife, an elder son, Gratian, who reigned and associated with himself Theodosius, commonly called the Great. By his second wife he had Valentinian the Second, who, upon the death of his brother Gratian, was allowed to share the empire by Theodosius. Theodosius, by his first wife, had two sons, - Arcadius, who afterwards reigned in the east, and Honorius, whose western reign was so much illustrated by Stilicho. By a second wife, daughter to Valentinian the First, Theodosius had a daughter, (half-sister, therefore, to Honorius,) whose son was Valentinian the Third.] in whose descendant, of the third generation, the empire, properly speaking, expired. For the seven shadows who succeeded, from Avitus and Majorian to Julius Nepos and Romulus Augustulus , were in no proper sense Roman emperors, - they were not even emperors of the West, - but had a limited kingdom in the Italian peninsula. Valentinian the Third was, as we have said, the last emperor of the West.

But, in a fuller and ampler sense, recurring to what we have said of Dioclesian and the tenor of his great revolutions, we may affirm that Probus and Carus were the final representatives of the majesty of Rome: for they reigned over the whole empire, not yet incapable of sustaining its own unity; and in them were still preserved, not yet obliterated by oriental effeminacy, those majestic features which reflected republican consuls, and, through them, the senate and people of Rome. That, which had offended Dioclesian in the condition of the Roman emperors, was the grandest feature of their dignity. It is true that the peril of the office had become intolerable; each Cæsar submitted

Thomas de Quincey

to his sad inauguration with a certainty, liable even to hardly any disguise from the delusions of youthful hope, that for him, within the boundless empire which he governed, there was no coast of safety, no shelter from the storm, no retreat, except the grave, from the dagger of the assassin. Gibbon has described the hopeless condition of one who should attempt to fly from the wrath of the almost omnipresent emperor. But this dire impossibility of escape was in the end dreadfully retaliated upon the emperor; persecutors and traitors were found every where: and the vindictive or the ambitious subject found himself as omnipresent as the jealous or the offended emperor. The crown of the Cæsars was therefore a crown of thorns; and it must be admitted, that never in this world have rank and power been purchased at so awful a cost in tranquillity and peace of mind. The steps of Cæsar's throne were absolutely saturated with the blood of those who had possessed it: and so inexorable was that murderous fate which overhung that gloomy eminence, that at length it demanded the spirit of martyrdom in him who ventured to ascend it. In these circumstances, some change was imperatively demanded. Human nature was no longer equal to the terrors which it was summoned to face. But the changes of Dioclesian transmuted that golden sceptre into a base oriental alloy. They left nothing behind of what had so much challenged the veneration of man: for it was in the union of republican simplicity with the irresponsibility of illimitable power, it was in the antagonism between the merely human and approachable condition of Cæsar as a man, and his divine supremacy as a potentate and king of kings - that the secret lay of his unrivalled grandeur. This perished utterly under the reforming hands of Dioclesian. Cæsar only it was that could be permitted to extinguish Cæsar: and a Roman imperator it was who, by remodelling, did in effect abolish, by exorcising from its foul terrors, did in effect disenchant of its sanctity, that imperatorial dignity, which having once perished, could have no second existence, and which was undoubtedly the sublimest incarnation of power, and a monument the mightiest of greatness built by human hands, which upon this planet has been suffered to appear.

Thomas de Quincey